PRAISE FOR THE NOVELS OF SARAH STROHMEYER

Kindred Spirits

"Strohmeyer offers a sweet, uncomplicated, and touching work of women's fiction about friendship and forgiveness." —*Booklist*

"Strohmeyer has written a compelling and compassionate story of the ties that bind female friendships. An absolutely moving, heartfelt, and warm story to fill the soul." —Fresh Fiction

"This is both a heartwarming and heartbreaking story, which shows the true power of friendships, even ones that have seemingly fallen apart, and of course, the power of a good martini."
—Chicklit Club

"Sarah Strohmeyer hits all the right notes in *Kindred Spirits*, but manages to avoid making readers feel like they've heard all of this before . . . an ideal summer read about friends, families, and the untold things that hold them together." —Shelf Awareness

The Penny Pinchers Club

"What a lively bunch of characters! The Penny Pinchers had me laughing out loud throughout this story. . . . This is a fantastic read whether you are looking for advice or just a spot of sunshine to help push the dark clouds away."
—Coffee Time Romance and More

"An excellent read. . . . While tackling a serious issue that I'm sure many face today, Ms. Strohmeyer puts her unique spin on it and never once does an issue seem to be trivialized."
—Fresh Fiction

continued . . .

"[A] bubbly farce. . . . [Strohmeyer] finds ample humor in her family-centric story." —*Publishers Weekly*

"A fast-paced and engaging read with a truly timely topic, this book is sure to be a winner with Strohmeyer's many fans and women's fiction fans who need a summer read."—*Library Journal*

Sweet Love

"The cupcake iced with roses that adorns *Sweet Love* by Sarah Strohmeyer is much too pretty to be a mixed blessing. It signals that the romance and food are inextricably connected."
—*The New York Times*

"About 'the power of love . . . and dessert,' chick-lit queen Strohmeyer's latest features a meddling but well-meaning mom, starcrossed lovers, and a baking class. What's not to like?" —*People*

"Best newcomer Sarah Strohmeyer is making a name for herself in the suburban chick-lit category, but *Sweet Love* is something special." —*New York Daily News*

"This fast-paced novel . . . features an accessible protagonist faced at turns with some of the saddest and most lighthearted situations life has to offer." —*Library Journal*

The Sleeping Beauty Proposal

"The been-around-the-block romantic insights of her thirty-something circle ring true." —*Entertainment Weekly*

"[A] sizzling summer read." —*New York Daily News*

"[A] humorous tale of romance, heartbreak, and healing."
—*Booklist*

"Genie Michaels is a fabulous protagonist, a woman who fakes her own engagement to follow her dreams in this uniquely comical yet believable novel." —*Romantic Times* (top pick)

"Sarah Strohmeyer is a comedic genius."   —Romance Junkies

The Cinderella Pact

"Outrageous fun!"
—Meg Cabot, author of *The Princess Diaries*
and *Queen of Babble*

"A big, cheery story with enough fairy tale and froth to let us escape the mundane, and with enough intelligence to make it worthwhile."   —BookPage

"[A] delightful frolic . . . featuring an authentic woman who can't help but dabble in a little bit of fantasy." —*Kirkus Reviews*

"*The Cinderella Pact* is for every one of us whose foot was too big to stuff into that glass slipper. It's engaging, funny, and as hard to put down as a bag of M&Ms."
—Harley Jane Kozak, Agatha, Anthony, and Macavity
award–winning author of *Dating Dead Men*
and *Dating Is Murder*

"Comedy abounds. . . . It's a well-told tale of friendship, tied in with everyday, relatable issues like job satisfaction, weight issues, divorce, and love."   —*Romantic Times* (4 stars)

"This contemporary fairy tale, complete with a Prince Charming, differs from the original in that, with a little help from her friends, the lady effects her own transformation. Very enjoyable."
—*Library Journal*

Also by Sarah Strohmeyer

Kindred
Spirits

Sarah Strohmeyer

NEW AMERICAN LIBRARY

NEW AMERICAN LIBRARY
Published by New American Library, a division of
Penguin Group (USA) Inc., 375 Hudson Street,
New York, New York 10014, USA
Penguin Group (Canada), 90 Eglinton Avenue East, Suite 700, Toronto,
Ontario M4P 2Y3, Canada (a division of Pearson Penguin Canada Inc.)
Penguin Books Ltd., 80 Strand, London WC2R 0RL, England
Penguin Ireland, 25 St. Stephen's Green, Dublin 2,
Ireland (a division of Penguin Books Ltd.)
Penguin Group (Australia), 250 Camberwell Road, Camberwell, Victoria 3124,
Australia (a division of Pearson Australia Group Pty. Ltd.)
Penguin Books India Pvt. Ltd., 11 Community Centre, Panchsheel Park,
New Delhi - 110 017, India
Penguin Group (NZ), 67 Apollo Drive, Rosedale, Auckland 0632,
New Zealand (a division of Pearson New Zealand Ltd.)
Penguin Books (South Africa) (Pty.) Ltd., 24 Sturdee Avenue,
Rosebank, Johannesburg 2196, South Africa

Penguin Books Ltd., Registered Offices:
80 Strand, London WC2R 0RL, England

Published by New American Library, a division of Penguin Group (USA) Inc. Previously
published in a Dutton edition.

First New American Library Printing, July 2012
10 9 8 7 6 5 4 3 2 1

Copyright © Sarah Strohmeyer, 2011

 REGISTERED TRADEMARK—MARCA REGISTRADA

New American Library Trade Paperback ISBN: 978-0-451-23504-6

THE LIBRARY OF CONGRESS HAS CATALOGED THE HARDCOVER EDITION OF THIS TITLE AS
FOLLOWS:

Strohmeyer, Sarah.
Kindred spirits/Sarah Strohmeyer.
p. cm.
ISBN 978-0-451-525-95222-0
1. Female friendship—Fiction. 2. Death—Fiction. 3. Drinking customs—Fiction.
4. Secrets—Fiction. I. Title.
PS3569.T6972K56 2011
813'.54—dc22

Set in Bembo
Designed by Alissa Amell

Printed in the United States of America

ALWAYS LEARNING   PEARSON

For Lisa,

my "kindred spirit" for forty-three years and counting

"Friendship improves happiness and abates misery, by the doubling of our joy and the dividing of our grief."

—Cicero

(An Excerpt from *Best Recipes from the Ladies Society for the Conservation of Marshfield, 1966*)

The Art of Mixing the Perfect Martini

❧

A martini is the world's most sophisticated cocktail, a classic of beauty and simplicity that derives its intoxicating allure from the melding of four strikingly different sensations.

But there is only one way to correctly mix the perfect martini, and few know the secret method—until now.

Begin with a chilled martini glass. Add half an ounce of dry vermouth for softening, swirl, and shake out every last drop. Refrigerate the glass again.

In a clean glass pitcher, combine the best possible gin at room temperature and fresh ice made from clear mountain *springwater, and stir—never shake, lest you bruise the gin's delicate charm. Pour into the chilled glass and garnish with a thin lemon peel twist.*

Strong.

Soft.

Cold.

Tart.

These are the four diverse elements that combined in correct proportions create nothing short of a divine elixir, especially when shared with good friends.

Now you know.

—Mrs. DeeDee Patterson, Chairwoman

Chapter One

Lynne Flannery took it as an encouraging sign that the day of her last martini would be the anniversary of her first.

Even the weather was identical—a postcard-perfect New England fall afternoon heralded by red, orange, gold, and green leaves fluttering against a brilliant blue sky. That morning, Canada geese had flown overhead in an ever-shifting V, squawking and vying for top position, and now the last lingering robins had disappeared seemingly overnight.

Her brazenly illegal burn pile roared full blast, tingeing the air with the sharp scent of woodsmoke—along with a sense of change. A shift from the frenetic business of living to something quieter, something that required reflection and respect for the passing. What her father used to call the "locking-down period."

Girls just want to have fun, she hummed, systematically

emptying one pill bottle after another into the flames that leaped and cracked to catch the tablets of magnesium and Emend on their hot tongues.

"Bye-bye, suckers. Thanks for nothing!"

She threw in what was left of the ginger crackers and saltines and the self-help books with their relentlessly upbeat titles—*You, Too, Can Survive Cancer; The Top Ten Rules to Beating the Odds; Mind Does Matter: Think Your Way to Health*.

Well, she'd thought and thought and thought so hard her brain hurt almost as much as the rest of her body. For eight years, she'd thought her way to health and still those cells kept replicating and replicating, building upon one another like Tetris blocks until it was Game Over.

The fire roared in gratitude and she blew it a kiss. "No," she said, "thank *you*."

Oh, Mother dear, we're not the fortunate ones. And girls they want to have fun. Cyndi Lauper, singing Lynne's life story.

She poked the smoldering burn pile and surveyed the garden into which they'd invested a lifetime of labor—the brick patio Sean had built himself after much swearing and sweat; the asparagus patch long gone to seed; the McIntosh trees, once spindly twigs from the nursery, now drooping under the weight of ripe, red fruit. At last her gaze rested on their sons' old redwood swing set, long neglected, that after much hemming and hawing they'd decided to leave for future grandchildren.

Lynne closed her eyes, imagining those grandbabies, red-headed like her, fat cheeks dotted with freckles, laughing as they crawled up the yellow slide. It was almost as good as seeing them for real, even if she'd never be able to hold them or sink her nose into their soft curls.

Anyway, it would have to do. She was trying to be grateful for what she had been given instead of bitter over what she would lose, because what she would lose had never really been hers. This was, perhaps, the most worthwhile lesson she had gleaned from this otherwise useless, rotten, lousy disease. Life is a lease and God is the landlord. We mortals could stake no claim.

She spritzed the fire with bottles of grapeseed extract and pomegranate juice, hosed it down for good measure, and nearly stubbed her toe on the hoe her husband had carelessly deposited by the garden.

Sean would let the hoe lie there all winter, rusting under the snow. So, with much difficulty, she got herself to the garage and hung it on its hook. Slipping out of her pink garden clogs, she opened the side door to the kitchen, shrugged off her zip-up jacket, and washed her hands at the sink, leaning heavily against the basin.

Only three thirty and already the sun was low in the sky. The school bus passed, stopping with a whoosh of its brakes at the Brezinskis' house. The doors opened, unleashing the cacophony of shouting children, and the two Brezinski boys ran up their driveway, tossed their backpacks onto the lawn, and tumbled in a mock fight for the entertainment of their fellow inmates. Lynne dried her hands on the red gingham dish towel and shook her head. Those Brezinski boys were going to be making news someday. One way or another.

Time to call Tiffany.

Tiffany could barely hide her relief when Lynne told her she was giving her the night off. "Go see a movie," Lynne said. "Have some fun for once. Forget about me."

Babysitting a terminally ill woman was no job for a person with Tiff's vitality. The woman might be in her twenties, but she couldn't stand still for five minutes without bubbling like a kid. She was exactly like her mother, Mary Kay, a ball of constant energy. A force majeure!

Lynne had been worried about what would happen to Tiffany after she was gone. But lately she'd been considering the flip side, that by stepping out of the picture she'd be opening the cage doors and setting this wild bird free. Tiffany could return to her beloved Boston and a much more exciting job in the Mass General ER instead of babysitting her mother's friend who mostly dozed and stared out the window.

Yes, it would be a good thing. Good for everyone.

When she was done talking to Tiff, Lynne left the phone off the hook and tackled the stairs. It took so long, what with stopping and sitting to rest at every other step, that it was almost dusk when she reached her bedroom. After a nap, a brief shower, and a change into her pj's and fluffy flannel housecoat that she *would . . . not . . . miss,* she opened the top drawer of her bureau for a pair of socks and caught sight of the orange envelope addressed to the Ladies Society for the Conservation of Martinis. No, that would never do. Sean or his snooping sister Danielle would find it and that would be the end.

She opened the envelope to check the contents once more: a note to Julia, another to her mother, a two-page explanation for the girls, and the book that started it all—*Best Recipes from the Ladies Society for the Conservation of Marshfield, 1966*—its formerly pristine white paper cover stained with grease spots and ripped in one corner.

Sitting on a small chair Sean had brought up just for her,

she flipped past hors d'oeuvres, soups and salads, main courses, side dishes, and desserts to find what mattered most: The Art of Mixing the Perfect Martini.

Of course, these days you couldn't put out a community recipe book with alcoholic drinks—not even a sparkling wine punch—without the Carrie A. Nations of this politically correct town wielding their hatchets. But back in the sixties, as Lynne vaguely recalled, martinis represented the height of sophistication—James Bond, the Rat Pack, long legs, tight capri pants, and bouffant hair.

Mary Kay liked to remind their tiny group of martini drinkers—the "Society," as Lynne, Beth, Carol, and Mary Kay called themselves—that the year this cookbook was written, Johnny Carson had just published *Happiness Is a Dry Martini,* featuring his bawdy drawing of a naked woman on the cover. Lynne would never forget coming across that on the bookshelf of her parents' modest Pennsylvania house, along with *Everything You Always Wanted to Know About Sex (But Were Afraid to Ask),* and wondering what her churchgoing, conservative parents *really* did with their nights after she went to bed.

Her finger traced DeeDee Patterson's quirky handwritten notes next to each recipe:

The Cosmopolitan—*Served 7/10/67 at cabin. Soothed ruffled feathers. Add splash more Cointreau.*

The Manhattan Martini—*B. Newell drank three, donated $500 to Bill's campaign. Makes a man feel like a man.*

The Dirty Martini—*Oooh! The Society's favorite. Sipped to "These Boots Are Made for Walking." Naughty fun!*

And the most powerful of all, the Classic Martini, gin, a whiff of vermouth, three olives on a toothpick. Elegance in a glass. *Cannot be topped,* DeeDee wrote. *Gets you whatever your heart desires.*

They'd tried them each with glee, finding DeeDee's observations consistently proved true. Thanks to the invention of flavored vodkas, they even went on to create their own— Persephone's Cosmos, Ginger-Pear, Chocolate-Raspberry Decadence, Lemon, and Clean Apple.

These were not mere drinks. They were potions, magical elixirs that transported them from their everyday occupations as mothers, a librarian, a nurse, a lawyer, and a teacher, to gloriously free spirits. Gorgeous, twirling, fabulous bon vivants! On some martini nights they ended up bobbing in Mary Kay's pool as a milky mist rose to meet the full moon. One winter, fueled by ginger brandy, Carol streaked naked out of the sauna, running smack into the Markowitzes cross-country skiing across Kindlewah Lake, and was so mortified she leaped into a snowbank for cold protection.

Then there was the early-summer evening thick with the sweet scent of Mary Kay's tea roses, when they lay on her green grass, head-to-head, hand in hand, forming a single large flower of women, strong and united, blissfully at peace.

Lynne closed the cookbook and studied the Kodachrome photo of the original Society perched in a semicircle on an elaborate memorial in the Old Town Cemetery that, thanks to their efforts, had been declared a national historic landmark. Their slim ankles crossed demurely, hands folded neatly in the laps of their short pastel dresses, sprayed hair swept into elegant blond or sleek chestnut updos, they were the picture of perfect propriety and breeding.

And yet, a keen eye would notice that behind each woman peeked the rim of a martini glass, a glimpse into what actually transpired at those conservation meetings when they weren't researching Marshfield's role in the Revolutionary War or preserving graveyards. DeeDee Patterson, trim, blond, and buxom, hardly the proper wife for a state assemblyman, sat front and center, a sly smile playing at the corner of her wide, red lips.

DeeDee, like many original members of the Ladies Society for the Conservation of Marshfield, was gone now, her beautiful remains entombed just beyond where she sat in the photo. Others had dispersed to warmer climes, but were they still together in spirit? Lynne hoped so, because she could not imagine eternity without Mary Kay, Carol, and Beth. Or, as they'd officially dubbed themselves during one particularly merry night of perhaps too many Cosmopolitans, the Ladies Society for the Conservation of Martinis.

Love you! She kissed the old recipe book and stuffed it back into the envelope along with the rest of the letters, resealed it, and pressed it to her chest. It was to these women, her closest friends, she would entrust the one task—the most important task, really—that bully cancer had refused to let her finish. She couldn't imagine anyone else handling the job—certainly not her husband.

For as much as she loved Sean, he would have been so hurt to learn that for decades she'd hidden this secret. But they would understand completely. They would set things right without Sean or the boys ever discovering the truth, so she could rest in peace.

Knowing this was the only way she could leave.

She hid the envelope under the protective safety of nightgowns and slips like a squirrel storing its treasured nut for her babies to find the following winter. One of the agreements they'd forged early on in the Society was that, should one of them pass, only a Society member would be permitted to clean out the personal belongings of another Society member. This vow was as sacred as never speaking ill of another's husband and—perhaps most holy of all—never adding "tini" to a drink simply because it contained alcohol. The addition of vodka no more made some lesser beverage a martini than the ridiculous addition of carats transformed a cubic zirconia into a diamond.

Martinis were sacred.

Downstairs, the brisket Beth had dropped off while Lynne was sleeping simmered in the Crock-Pot. "Thanks, kiddo," she whispered, yanking the plug.

As her next-door neighbor, fellow Society conspirator, and best friend, Beth didn't ask; she just *did*. Cleaned out the coat closet. Bundled up the recyclables and old newspapers. Scrubbed down the bathrooms. Stocked the refrigerator for Sean. Emptied the cat's litter box and took home two loads of laundry, returning them the following day clean and folded, picked up the prescriptions and made dinner three times a week.

Lynne was pretty sure she would have checked out long ago if it hadn't been for Beth holding on, refusing to give in, certain that if she turned her back for just one minute, Lynne would slip away.

And she was right, Lynne thought, bypassing the stack of letters that had taken weeks to write, along with the newly paid bills and envelopes containing spare keys, instructions, and various account passwords for Sean, who would never remember.

Chores over, duties done, she pulled herself onto a chair by the liquor cabinet over the refrigerator and let her fingers flutter across the bottles until they landed on the one she needed—a bottle of Hornitos tequila.

It was Carol who insisted that all their martinis be made of the highest-quality spirits. In her opinion, nothing less than velvety Jewel of Russia or Chopin would do for vodka, though Beth, who could be just as much of a snob, was satisfied with good old Smirnoff. Mary Kay didn't give a tinker's damn as long as it wasn't gin, which made her depressed, while Lynne was partial to Hornitos tequila simply because it reminded her of her honeymoon with Sean in Cancún.

She cracked open the tequila and added it to ice in the martini shaker along with a shot of Cointreau, some lime juice, limeade, and a dash of Blue Curaçao for color, following from memory DeeDee's recipe for the exotic blue martini—*turns strangers into friends and, therefore, turns failures into triumphs. Good icebreaker for tough crowds.*

Taking a taste, she was instantly whisked to the Mexican beach where she and Sean had frolicked, swimming in sparkling turquoise waters and lazing on the sand under the breeze of gently waving palm trees, steel drums playing softly in the background. She could still smell the coconut oil. She could feel Sean rubbing her tanned back and leading her by the hand to their secluded bungalow, where he proceeded to slowly and seductively untie each tiny bow on her bikini.

So fit. So young. So completely sure that their vitality and youth would last forever. Such a gift.

Having shaken vigorously, she poured out the drink and stood back to admire its dazzling aqua beauty. How could a drink that pretty, that sexy, play a part in something so lethal?

Mustn't think.

She grabbed a quilt off her hospital bed and went through the dining area, where family photos of better times dotted her china cabinet. Kevin and Kyle as naked babies splashing in the bath, her wedding day with Sean holding her as if he'd never let her go, the boys eager on their first day of school neatly dressed in matching khakis and wetted hair, the whole family blueberry picking, flying kites on Cape Cod, prom, graduation. Sean and the boys hugging her on Christmas morning, their last together. She carefully lay each on its face, putting them to bed.

Hers hadn't been an "exciting life" in terms of accomplishments. She hadn't earned a million dollars or become the next Laura Ingalls Wilder or married the prince of England, as her girlhood plans had presumed. But surveying the tiny house that she had decorated with her homemade curtains and colorful quilts of purple, red, blue, and green; her watercolors and oil paintings; and even her students' clumsy clay models, it had been a good life, rich with love and laughter. She was glad for the choices she'd made.

A zap of pain shooting up her spine pushed her back on track, even if the sliding door off the dining room to the screened porch didn't. Sean really needed to fix that thing. It was insane that they'd paid all that money to have it installed just over a year ago and already it was stuck. She tried to yank the door shut by forcing it back and forth, but it wouldn't budge. Screw it. One more thing she wouldn't have to worry about—again.

She collapsed onto the fancy Swedish divan Carol had sent her and let out a sigh, stretching her slippered feet as her aching body melted into its patented design.

Craning her neck to sip her martini, she spilled a bit on her hateful robe and concluded there was not much else Sean or anyone, really, envied about her situation. But if there was bitterness in this thought, the sunny tequila and Cointreau took care of that, the martini's blue fire rippling to her toes. She was getting warmer, though the air was colder. She pulled the quilt around her shoulders to stop the shivering.

Her first blue martini finished, she downed the second, poured a third, and decided it was now or never.

The oral morphine in the plastic specimen jar was thirty milligrams of instant death. If her oncologist, Dr. Bikashini, knew, he'd go ballistic, she thought, laughing to herself, slightly drunk perhaps. Old Bikashini had doled out the pain meds like a miser, drily explaining the dangers of developing a narcotics addiction. Right. As if becoming a junkie were a terminal cancer patient's biggest problem.

With a quick prayer, she knocked back half the entire specimen jar. It was incredibly bitter, as death should be. Gripping the edge of her divan, she managed to swallow the rest, chasing it with the martini. The rush of the morphine and alcohol was so intense she began to shake in panic. *Perhaps this is it! So soon? No, no, no.*

She decided she should call 9-1-1. Forget the embarrassment; just get the damn medics here to pump her stomach. But then what? The outcome would be the same.

Only worse.

Tears came to her eyes; she couldn't help it, thinking of her sons and her husband, even her abiding cat snoring on a nearby chair. The Brezinski boys next door ran out to play kickball in the dark as their mother flicked on the back light. A howl of wind blew dead leaves against the screens of her porch. Somewhere a dog barked.

Please, she begged God. *If it is Your will.*

Lynne had always passionately defended life, had fought for it with courage and determination. Until recently, she believed the end was God's to decide, not hers. But then years of poison and pain and the elimination of options that is the hallmark of terminal cancer treatment led her to one last conclusion.

She refused to accept an ending that would destroy her sons' memory of their mother as a healthy, strong woman and would drag her family into depression and inching despair and bankruptcy. She would not let cancer call the last shot. If there was nothing left to do, then she would go on *her* terms.

Shh, she heard Mary Kay whisper as clearly as if she were kneeling by her side, felt her stroke her forehead. *Let it be, honey, let it be.*

Lynne *did* feel sleepy and heavy, sinking deeper into Carol's soft sofa like a baby falling asleep in her mother's arms, the aroma of Beth's brisket snaking from the broken door, enveloping her in a motherly hug.

They were here with her in spirit if not in body. She knew they'd come. Lynne could sense them holding her, supporting her without judgment or pity as they had so many, many times before, buoying her with their wisdom and humor and boundless love. Her head began to buzz like the whistle of a teakettle. She was going under. This was it.

And so, because she could not bear to think of things that were too painful, of her sons and husband, whom she loved with all her heart, she slid under the quilt and remembered the first time Beth, Carol, Mary Kay, and she cupped their martinis and vowed to preserve and uphold the endangered cocktail—the night the Ladies Society for the Conservation of Martinis was formed—and let her friends carry her home.

Chapter Two

Alone, at last.

     Carol depressed the button on the custom-made blinds and shut out the honking horns of the Fifth Avenue rush hour below. Dimming the lights, she opened the cherry walnut doors to the private bar and, throwing protocol aside, proceeded to mix herself a very dirty martini, three olives, splash of vermouth.

She didn't often drink alone—at least, not in the office. As the only attorney at Deloutte Watkins specializing in fertility law, she and her clients didn't have much use for alcohol. She was in the business of making miracles. Not martinis.

Sliding into her large leather chair, she propped her feet on the desk and slipped off her $800 Stella McCartney pumps that fell with a soft thud onto the thick mauve carpet. The martini—cold, clear and powerful—rested gently between her long, delicate fingers as she slowly brought the glass to her lips.

She closed her eyes and braced herself for the initial shock of one hundred proof expensive British gin, relishing the satisfying jolt, the instant, if momentary, burst of headiness. As the effects of the martini rippled through her knotted muscles, untying them one by one, she let the truth sink in.

Lynne *did* it.

Carol cocked her head, impressed. "Dying with dignity" had become such a buzz phrase it was hard to take seriously these days. She would hope that, faced with debilitating illness and pain, she could spare her friends and family by quietly and civilly ending it all. It would be the right thing to do.

And yet, she couldn't imagine taking those final steps, allowing herself to pass that point of no return. She surveyed her collection of framed photos of dimpled babies in the arms of their overjoyed parents, clients who'd mortgaged their homes, begged relatives for loans, worked second jobs in order to afford the technology to create life when nature had failed its most basic duty. Intentional death was so counter-intuitive to the human drive.

She shuddered and took another sip, debating only briefly the pros and cons of reaching into her right-hand desk drawer for the ancient pack of Marlboro Lights she retained for emergencies. There were forty-three known carcinogens in the average American cigarette. Would lighting up be a form of dishonor?

Nah, she could hear Lynne say. *One's not going to kill you. Besides, I never smoked.*

True. Lynne never smoked. Carol removed a slim cigarette, thinking, not for the first time, how unfair it was that some people got away with smoking and committing all manner of sins without suffering any repercussions, while Lynne, so virtuous, had been inexplicably cut down.

Lynne had rarely indulged in anything forbidden except when the group got together for martinis. She was the last person you'd expect to develop a rare and particularly virulent cancer, not with her daily exercise and organic vegetables, all of which helped her fight for so long and so well. For a while there, it seemed, by gum, little Lynne Flannery had beat the damn thing on pure pluck.

But cancer waits. It lurks like a spider in its dark corner, pacing time until its victim can struggle no more, then descends quickly to deliver the final, lethal bite.

Unfair.

That was the word she and Beth and Mary Kay used over and over during that afternoon's round of phone calls, rehashing every detail until there was nothing more to say. Mary Kay had recounted how she and her boyfriend, alarmed that Tiffany had been given the night off, tried calling Lynne the next morning and, when there was no answer, rushed to her house where they found her cold body on the divan. They'd clucked their tongues over poor Sean up at the cabin after Lynne insisted he get a jump on the Columbus Day weekend traffic and leave on Thursday instead of Friday. They mused about the guilt he must have felt for letting her con him into leaving her side, how unfortunate it was that the boys had to learn from their college deans their mother had died.

Then they discussed the funeral plans, the menu, the flowers, and, at last, how weird it would be for Carol to return to Marshfield, the first time in two years. She hadn't been back since the dramatic departure that had made her the subject of gossip for weeks.

By the following week, it'd be over. Carol would return

to New York and get on with her life as if Lynne had never lived.

She watched the smoke mingle with her memories of her friend, rising to the heavens. "To you, baby," she whispered, presenting her glass for an invisible toast. "Wherever you are."

There was a soft knock. Since her secretary, Janis, would know better than to interrupt when the smell of cigarettes wafted from under her door, it had to be Scott.

Scott was the Deloutte in Deloutte Watkins, the saint who'd mentored her straight out of law school and rewarded her with an associate's position after she passed the New York Bar. When she and Jeff decided to move to Connecticut to raise their family, Scott stoically wished her well and promised there'd always be a spot waiting for her should she ever change her mind. As if she would ever think of returning to the law, she'd scoffed to Jeff.

But Scott knew her better than she knew herself. Once Amanda and Jonathan were teenagers with their own lives and activities, no longer eager for their mother to meet them at school or hold their hands as they crossed the street, Carol began to grow restless. Feeling useless and, she would later realize, probably clinically depressed, she called up Scott and, over an exquisite lunch of beef carpaccio salad, launched into a monologue about how her days had blurred into years of carpools and laundry and school committees, how she'd lost her identity, had lost her reason for getting out of bed. Much to her horror, she couldn't stop the words from flowing until Scott reached across the table, took her hand, and asked if part-time, two days a week in the New York office, one day at home, would fit the bill.

"Yes," she'd said with a sigh, nearly melting with gratitude. *"Yes."*

Now she was a junior partner, putting in twelve-hour days while Scott was a dashing widower, physically fit, though graying at the temples. So far, their dates had been quiet dinners and nothing more.

So far.

Scott pulled up a chair and tented his fingers, judiciously keeping his disapproval of her cigarette to himself. "How're you holding up?"

"Numb." She yanked down her skirt. "The funeral's a week from today, in the morning. I'm staying to clean out her closet with Mary Kay and Beth, but then I'm hightailing it out of there as soon as the last box is packed and taped."

"Not eager to return to the old stomping ground?"

"I'm looking forward to seeing my friends. That's it." She tapped an ash, the sickening apprehension returning as she considered what lay ahead.

She did not relish making an appearance in Marshfield and dealing with the stares and whispers. Few in town had not heard the rumors about how she'd stormed out of her seemingly solid marriage, simply abandoned her charming pediatrician husband and comfortable house for no valid reason.

"Worried about seeing Jeff again?" He regarded her without judgment. Scott was not one to let jealousy get the better of him. He was too much of a lawyer to succumb to such a barbaric emotion and he was too much of a *good* lawyer to consider the possibility of inadequacy.

Carol studied her cigarette. It would be so easy to nod and say, *Yes, it's Jeff.* Scott would see right through her, though, and then he'd ask more questions. There was no choice but to come clean.

"Not exactly." She took another sip of the martini, which unfortunately was growing warm. "The night I left Jeff . . . something happened."

"You said you had a huge fight."

"Right, but . . ." She was going to come off like such a jerk. An ache spread across her forehead, sign of impending doom. "Before that, though, there was an incident at the school board meeting."

Carol chose her words carefully. "I was extremely tired that night. It was the day the Barnegat decision was over-turned and, like I said, Jeff and I had been sniping at each other for months and not really talking. I'd been begging him to go with me to marriage counseling, but"—she took a last draw—"he couldn't stand the idea of outsiders weigh-ing in on our business. He insisted we should work it out ourselves, privately."

Scott remained silent. Carol stubbed out her cigarette, remembering how she'd been so helpless and alone.

"The last thing I needed was to be harassed by some overly earnest parent demanding another food ban. We were already fed up with eliminating peanut butter and vending machine candy and soda, anything with nuts. It was getting to the point of ridiculous.

"Anyway, this mother, Michelle Richardson, stood up at the meeting and started lashing out about how irresponsible the board was for condoning . . ." She paused because it seemed so silly. "Bake sales."

Scott grinned. "Bake sales?"

"You know, the usual standard fund-raising fare—

chocolate-chip cookies, brownies, cupcakes. The bread and butter, not to pun, of the PTA. I guess she wanted them to raise money by selling carrot sticks or apples instead of food loaded with empty calories. I don't know. Anyway, I lost it and burst out laughing. Then Michelle called me ignorant and said she had half a mind to file a lawsuit. So, I shot back a few choice epithets. Not my finest hour."

"What did you say?"

Let's see. What had she said, exactly? Carol leaned against her hand, remembering the look of shock on Michelle Richardson's face. "Entitled soccer mom. Trustfundarian. Something about suggesting she get a real job instead of bothering the board with hysterical causes that were totally pointless. You get the gist."

Looking back, what Carol saw was a crazed woman under pressure, her complexion splotchy from lack of sleep, eyes red from exhaustion. And that woman wasn't Michelle Richardson; it was her, Carol Goodworthy, hitting rock bottom.

She'd conned herself into believing she'd fooled everyone with her expensive suits and cool composure. Surely, no one knew that the dynamo who chaired the school board and commuted to New York to work as a high-powered attorney while still managing to deadhead her champion Barbara Bush roses and bake a mean strawberry pie was an absolute wreck. Carol took pride in being so disciplined that no one suspected that she hadn't slept with her husband for months, that she would spring wide-awake at two a.m. only to ramble around her big house like some sort of vampire yearning for rest. Much, much-needed rest.

If she'd been able to rest, if she and Jeff had been able to sit down and talk about what was going wrong in their marriage, the facade wouldn't have crumbled. She wouldn't have taken out her frustration on a well-meaning mother of five.

And now, because of Lynne's funeral, Carol was forced to go home and face Michelle, face all of them. What must they think of her? She rubbed the ache that had now blossomed into sharp, stabbing pain. What must they call her behind her back?

There was a chuckle and Carol snapped out of her reverie to find Scott at the sink washing out the ashtray. "What?"

"Bake sales." He shook water out of the dish and turned it upside down. "A life thrown into chaos over cupcakes. I'm sorry, Carol, but talk about pointless. Leaving your twenty-year marriage over a fight about something so inane—*that's* pointless."

"It might seem so now, but it wasn't then. When I got home that night, Jeff was pissed. He said I'd gone too far and that working at the firm had turned me into a cold, hard bitch who constantly cross-examined him, our children, even innocent neighbors like Michelle. Made me impossible to love, he said." She bit her lower lip, willing herself not to slip into the velvet trap of self-pity, a hole she'd visited far too often. "There was no one on my side, Scott. *No* one."

Except for her friends, she thought, correcting herself. After their fight, she went straight to Mary Kay's house, where an emergency meeting was called. Beth had sat on one side of her, Lynne on the other, while Mary Kay mixed her potent ginger martinis, famous for their healing and protective properties. Warmed by the vodka and ginger brandy, protected by friendship, Carol lowered her defenses and spilled about Jeff, about Michelle, about everything.

Beth, a librarian, dismissed Michelle as a troublemaker who'd tried to get Philip Pullman's books banned from her library because they sent a dangerous message to impressionable young readers. Lynne, then in her final remission, quietly pointed out life was too short to fight with your husband about idiots, while Mary Kay came right out and laid her cards on the table: Michelle Richardson was a control freak with an overblown sense of entitlement.

"Well, she isn't *all* bad," Mary Kay declared, her black curls bobbing in fury, her gray eyes flashing as she waved her martini glass like a queen's scepter. "If it weren't for her and her tedious PTA meetings, we may never have formed our little martini society."

Carol had forgotten that. It made her feel somewhat better.

But putting Michelle in her place couldn't change the underlying problems with her marriage, and when Carol confided that she and Jeff hadn't been sleeping together for months, the women wisely kept their counsel. Carol said the issue was her career. Jeff resented the disruption of their family life caused by her commute and overtime. He hated that she sometimes came in on the last train or spent the night in New York when she was in the thick of a case. It was hard on the kids, hard on him, he claimed. What was the point of having a wife if she cared more about her clients than her husband?

To their credit, Mary Kay, Beth, and Lynne never once slammed him or even went so far as to suggest Jeff was out of line. They simply listened and refilled her glass, assuring her that Jeff didn't mean what he said about finding her impossible to love. Of course he still loved her. She'd just misinterpreted because she was upset and tired.

They stood by her like always, unquestioning and forever loyal. Not her husband—*them*.

And that was when Carol decided her marriage was over.

"I'm on your side." Scott was leaning against her desk, arms crossed. His smile, turned up at one corner. He felt protective of her, though he was well aware Carol Goodworthy needed no man to fight her battles. Which only made him love her more.

"I know you're on my side." She didn't even have to think about it. From their very first interview when she was just fresh out of law school, Scott had been her advocate, her biggest cheerleader. "There was never any doubt."

"Tell you what." He pushed the martini glass aside. "To make the trip home easier, why don't you take the firm's town car back to Connecticut."

She started to protest, but he put a finger to her lips.

"Then, after you're done cleaning out Lynne's closet, I'll have the car drop you off at my place, where I'll have dinner waiting, along with an ice-cold martini and a hot bubble bath. You can pour out your grief in my antique claw-footed tub while I whip up my famous veal chops. How does that sound?"

The image of herself naked in Scott's tub caught her slightly off guard, though why it should was surprising. They both knew they were heading in this direction. They'd been mentor and pupil, then colleagues and close friends. Recently they'd begun to share long discussions after hours in his office that led to drinks at the corner café followed by casual dinners and slow strolls back to the firm. He'd held her hands and brushed his lips softly against her cheek as they hugged good-bye. He'd have gone further if he wasn't sensitive to the fact that she was still reeling from her shattered marriage. It seemed only natural that sex would be the next step. Scott Deloutte was not one to fritter away his precious spare time on platonic relationships with women, and Carol, as of the end of this month, would be officially divorced for one whole year.

It was time to move on.

"That sounds very nice. *Very* nice. However . . ." She ran her fingers over the thick silver Cartier watch on his wrist, under the cuff of his crisp, white shirt, the combination of which she found alluringly masculine. "There's a certain serious issue we need to address first."

"Oh?" He cocked an eyebrow. "If you're not ready, Carol, I . . ."

"Gin or vodka?"

"Pardon?"

"Are you a gin martini man or a vodka martini man? You've never exactly stipulated."

He paused, processing the concept that she was fine with them sleeping together. "Gin. It's the only way. James Bond notwithstanding."

Scott Deloutte was mature, kind, determined, and principled. More important, he shared Carol's passion for the law. He understood why she threw herself into her work and, better yet, appreciated her dedication, found it exciting and tantalizing. He would no more have asked her to choose between him and her job than he would have demanded she choose between him and her children.

He was everything she ever wanted or needed in a man. So what was her hesitation?

She returned his knowing look. "Then I'd love to come back to your place next Friday for a hot bath and your famous veal chops. Thank you."

"Good," he said, brushing a wisp of blond hair off her forehead. "I'll do my best to make it worth your while."

There was a tingling along her arms, shooting up her neck as his fingertips grazed her ear, and Carol concluded that maybe, just maybe, the ordeal of going home might not be so bad after all—if Scott and a martini were waiting for her when it was over.

Chapter Three

C arol had to admit there was a certain thrill in coming home.

Her excitement grew as the town car crossed the rusting metal bridge and she took in the breathtaking sight of the orange, red, and yellow fall foliage reflected in Kindlewah Lake, the ducks gathered on the rocky shore. Her old house was within sight, its graying dock peeking from behind a giant spruce. Boy, did she miss that place, the summers paddling around in the kayak, the winters skating on the ice.

There was the Marshfield General Store, where she used to stop for last-minute groceries on her way back from the city. She loved its rickety wooden floors; she loved that it sold everything from milk and homemade bread to pesto, shampoo, caviar, and fishing tackle. And there was the small elementary school where she had spent so many days as a room parent, the playground where Jonathan had split his lip, the nearby high school where both her children, she was proud to say, had graduated at the top of their classes.

Marshfield was a treasure, a Brigadoon tucked among farms and wooded hillsides too inconvenient from the Danbury train station to be overrun by New York commuters.

She would never forget the Sunday afternoon when she and Jeff, fleeing the hot confines of their Brooklyn apartment, had stumbled upon it after taking the wrong exit off I-84. Amanda was a baby in the car seat and Jonathan a mere twinkle in his father's eye. They hadn't realized their joyride had been a search for a haven to raise their family until they drove into Marshfield's town center and parked the car.

She and Jeff left Amanda sleeping as they sat on the hood of their old Toyota, admiring the town green with its snow-white gazebo, the lush hostas and pink-flowered rugosas lovingly tended by the local gardening club. They studied the white clapboard Unitarian church, the brick town hall, the library, and the hardware store and waved to an old man walking his terrier—the constable, they would later learn. They let the cool summer evening breeze, carrying its scent of freshly mowed grass, caress their skin and fill them with satisfaction.

"This is it, Carol. This is the place." Jeff inhaled the country air and covered her hand with his. "I could open a practice here. We could get a house by that lake we passed. Have another baby. The cost of living would be so cheap, you could quit your job and get out of the rat race."

Because she loved her husband, she didn't stop to wonder what it would be like to step out of the rat race, to cut herself off from the city that offered her the excitement and richness that fed her soul and nourished her mind. All that mattered at that golden moment was her daughter's childhood and Jeff's newfound contentment.

She squeezed his hand. "Let's do it."

With those three little words, she gave up everything. Twenty years later, she would take it back.

"It's right there." She directed the driver to the church into which people were filing. The whole town, it seemed. No surprise there.

Before she got out, she conducted a last-minute assessment of her armor. Black Donna Karan suit? Check. Blahniks? Check and check. Nancy Gonzalez tote? Check. Flipping open her compact, she swished her lips with another coat of gloss and pulled one side of her blond bob behind her ear. Together. Successful. And, most important, sane.

Keenly aware of what kind of entrance she was making, she waited for the driver to come around and open her door. "Thank you," she said politely, extending one long leg to the sidewalk.

"Carol!"

"Mary Kay! Beth!" She threw open her arms and rushed toward her oldest and dearest friends with the abandon of a giggling teenager.

The next she knew, they were in a huddle, the three of them, hugging and crying and laughing at once. Two years. Two whole years had gone by since she'd seen them. The last time, Lynne had been there too. It made their reunion so bittersweet.

"I can't believe how glamorous you are." Beth stood back and smoothed down her plain knit dress that hung too loose and too long. She'd always been so self-conscious of her generous curves, Carol thought, wishing she could convince Beth to cut that mane of hair and release the stunning woman within.

"I'm overdue for a haircut." Beth fingered her split ends. "It's just . . . Well, you could say it's been a hellish week. I've been working on the reception nonstop."

"You're amazing, as always." Carol wrapped her in another hug, thinking how Beth was the kind of friend who ignored trivial things like her clothes and hair not because she was a doormat, but because she was quite the opposite.

"I'm so, so sorry about Lynne," she murmured into Beth's ear. "I know how close you two were."

"My bestie," Beth said, her voice thick.

"And what am I? Chopped liver?" Mary Kay put her hands on her hips in faux indignation.

"Oh, come here, you." And Carol pulled her into their little group, Mary Kay's floral perfume making her light-headed with nostalgia.

"We're so glad you're back," Mary Kay said, giving Carol a squeeze. "This is where you belong."

Beth nodded. "She's right. It's not the same here since you left."

"Yeah. The school board meetings are *soooo* dull. No one ever tells off Michelle Richardson anymore." Mary Kay winked, teasing.

Carol broke away and sniffed back a few tears. "OK. Where's this Sam Drake I've been hearing about?" Mary Kay's serious boyfriend had to be incredibly tall, if what Beth said was true about him towering over her. Even in flats, Mary Kay was almost five-ten, her flippant excuse for not finding a husband being that she refused to date any man who couldn't eat an egg off the top of her head.

"He's inside, keeping a seat warm for me. You can meet him at Beth's house later and then give me your verdict." She paused for effect. "You know, over a few martinis."

Beth gave her a sharp nudge. "*Mary Kay*. This is Lynne's funeral. We shouldn't be talking about martinis."

"And why not? You don't think if Lynne were here, she'd be mixing up a pitcher right now?"

A bell tolled somberly, jolting them into silence, their casual banter vanishing under the weight of the heavy *bong, bong, bong*. They remembered, then, why they were there. To bury their friend. To say good-bye to Lynne.

"I guess it's time," Beth said. "You have your flats, Carol?"

Carol patted her bag. "Am I sitting with you two?"

Beth stared at her shoes, suddenly ill at ease. It was Mary Kay who stepped forward and took her by the elbow. "Actually, Jeff's saving a seat." She took a breath. "He's with Amanda."

Amanda, the daughter who had quit speaking to her after Carol left Marshfield, because she blamed her mother for destroying their family.

"That's nice," Carol said evenly. "It's good she came. Lynne loved her like the daughter she never had. After I left, I bet Lynne and Amanda must have talked on the phone every day."

"Granted, Lynne was very important to her," Mary Kay said as the three of them walked up the church steps. "But *you* are her mother."

They opened the heavy doors to a packed church, standing room only. An organ played "Abide with Me," an empowering hymn Carol remembered from her own upbringing. Lynne must have chosen it, since she planned the entire funeral down to the flowers that adorned her casket and the songs that should be sung.

> *I fear no foe, with Thee at hand to bless;*
> *Ills have no weight, and tears no bitterness;*
> *Where is death's sting? Where, grave, thy victory?*
> *I triumph still, if Thou abide with me.*

They tiptoed down the aisle, Beth joining Marc, who was sitting next to their son, David, home from MIT, who was next to Beth's parents, Chat and Elsie Brewster. Carol scanned the church, hoping to catch a glimpse of Amanda when someone next to her said, "Hey."

Jeff had stepped out of the pew, his blue eyes smiling sympathetically, and Carol felt the familiar jerk of her heartstrings. Nothing more than old habit, she told herself, trying to ignore how healthy he looked, younger and tanned, as if sawing off the old ball and chain had restored his muscle tone and improved his circulation.

Though he should have been going gray like Scott, Jeff's hair had somehow turned blonder. He reminded her of when he used to play every day at the New York Racquet Club where they were introduced by mutual friends and she'd quickly nicknamed him Vince Van Patten, although he claimed to never have heard of the California actor and semi-pro tennis player. He was too busy finishing his residency in pediatrics at Albert Einstein to have much use for TV sitcom reruns, he'd replied with such self-importance that Carol burst out laughing.

"I saved a seat for you between us." He waved his arm toward a gorgeous young woman in a slim black dress, her blond hair pulled severely into a clipped ponytail.

She was Amanda, obviously. But nothing like the blithe free spirit Carol remembered. The last time she'd seen her daughter was the summer before she left for her sophomore year at college, and she'd been entirely different. Not a care in the world.

Carol had mentally freeze-framed the picture so she'd never forget: Amanda in a blue sarong, her hair in straw-colored braids, daisies and yellow buttercups tucked in at the ends as she lay on the silver weather-beaten dock outside their house reading, her bare feet dangling in Kindlewah Lake as she hummed a tuneless tune.

"Hello, Mother," this strange new Amanda said, her gaze icy.

"Honey!" It was all Carol could do to keep herself from reaching out and gathering her baby into her arms. "It's so . . ." She extended a tentative hand.

Amanda flinched. "Don't," she whispered. "Not here."

Stunned, Carol sat and rested her Nancy Gonzalez bag on the wooden church floor while her daughter lifted her chin and stared straight ahead, refusing to otherwise acknowledge her mother's presence.

Carol made another attempt. "I'm so glad you came."

Amanda flipped through her program, ignoring her.

"Love the hair. I can't believe how grown-up you are. You look terrific."

Amanda inched down the pew.

How could her own daughter treat her so? How could she act as if they meant nothing to each other? What about the dollhouse she'd made and the fairy houses they'd built out of moss and twigs in the woods? What about the nights the two of them stayed up reading *Harry Potter and the Half-Blood Prince* side-by-side on the couch, dissolving into tears when Dumbledore was struck down? Didn't those moments count for anything?

She felt herself trembling and looked down to see her hands shaking in her lap. Jeff must have noticed this too, because he linked his arm in hers.

"Thank you," she said under her breath, fighting the tears that should have been for Lynne, instead of for her daughter.

He nodded encouragingly. "It's going to be OK, Carol. Give her time." He appraised her fitted black Donna Karan suit. "By the way, if I may say so, Amanda's not the only one who looks terrific."

She smiled and blushed, instinctively sensing Amanda's displeasure.

The music ended abruptly and everyone stood as Sean, Kevin, and Kyle proceeded up the aisle. Mary Kay's niece, Tiffany, trailed behind, head high and proud, though Mary Kay said she was overcome with guilt for leaving Lynne on the one night she should have stayed. That was absurd, especially considering the sacrifices Tiffany had already made, even taking a hiatus from her new nursing position in Boston so Lynne could have private care.

Carol made a mental note to find a moment after the funeral to praise Tiffany to the hilt. Though Tiffany was

Mary Kay's niece by blood and daughter by adoption, the two women shared much in common, including big hearts under their colorful clothes and thick perfume. Sometimes it was easy to take their abundant generosity for granted.

The family stopped before Lynne's coffin, white and strewn with flowers from her own garden—purple, orange, and red mums, the last of the yellow Shasta daisies, black-eyed Susans, and the fading pink roses of summer.

There was Lynne. She was really dead. She was really no more.

Next to her, Amanda began to weep and Carol brushed a hand against hers. This time she didn't flinch. It wasn't anything, really, a trifle, but to Carol it was a start.

The rest of the ceremony went by in a blur. Carol bowed her head and prayed, not to God, but to Lynne, wishing she was finally at peace. She hoped Lynne could see how much she was loved, how the whole town had turned out to say good-bye. It was inspiring to think one person, no one particularly special, rich, or famous—an elementary school art teacher—could touch so many, many lives.

Out of the corner of her eye, Carol absently admired Jeff's suit—an expertly tailored Brooks Brothers double-breasted with a slim silk dot tie. She entertained the possibility of a young girlfriend picking out his stylish accessories, wrapping his half-Windsor knot and brushing off his sleeves.

After all, she was getting closer to Scott. It was only reasonable that Jeff would have found someone else too. She observed how the muscles in his jaw flexed as he kept his emotions in check during the reading of "Adieu, adieu," the last line of John Keats's *Fairy Song*. She let herself drink in the smell of his Neutrogena aftershave that reminded her of their nightly ritual of lying in bed, her head on his shoulder, as he discussed his patients, unraveling his day.

What did she feel? Regret? Longing? *Anything?*

Carol realized then it didn't matter what she felt. Not anymore. They had been "torn asunder," to quote their wedding vows. They were two, no longer one. Spiritually, psychologically, and, most important, legally. So, that was that.

Lynne's son Kevin delivered a eulogy and then Beth stood up and delivered an emotional, if rambling, testimony about her friendship with Lynne. She recalled meeting her next-door neighbor while she was shoveling snow off her front walk and how they discovered they were both new mothers with babies about the same age. Those babies—Beth's son, David, and Lynne's twins, Kevin and Kyle—grew up together and became best friends, just like Beth and Lynne. Every week, she and Lynne went grocery shopping together. They shared clothes and divided and exchanged their perennials and occasionally Beth had to call on Lynne to remove the dreaded garter snake from her periwinkle patch.

Lynne had become such a part of her life, Beth said, she couldn't imagine going on without her, though she supposed that, like Lynne's husband and sons, she would have to adjust.

"It really is true that life comes with a guarantee of death, I'm afraid." Beth gripped the podium, her voice shaking with grief and, Carol suspected, an innate fear of public speaking. "I kept hoping if I loved her hard enough that I could keep her with me, but not even love, I've learned, can postpone the inevitable. Wherever Lynne is, I know she's in a better place and I hope you—Sean, Kevin, and Kyle—can find comfort in knowing she is finally out of pain."

By the time Beth returned to her pew, Carol had dissolved into tears, weeping over the totality of loss and the gnawing hunger of unremitting heartache.

The church was silent as local musician Jake Fenster hooked a Spanish guitar around his neck and began strumming a slow song that sounded familiar, although Carol couldn't quite place it.

Beth's husband, Marc, and one of Sean's brothers pushed Lynne's coffin down the aisle and everyone rose. Sean followed, along with the boys. Next came Mary Kay and Beth. Carol slipped out of her Blahniks with the four-inch heels, drew a pair of flats from her bag, and joined them.

Beth gave her a big, hard hug. "Ready to say good-bye to our girl?"

Carol's nose went hot. Trusting her Blahniks to Jeff, she joined the other pallbearers taking their positions by Lynne's casket. Kevin and Kyle stood in the front. Beth and Marc shored up the middle. She was next to Mary Kay, who said, "We'll get through this."

"We have no choice."

They lifted and adjusted the coffin's weight on their shoulders. It was heavy. Too heavy. Carol had to shift her feet to keep it from sliding off. She staggered a bit on the top step and for one brief, panicked second as her knees wobbled, she was sure she was going to drop it and ruin everything until Mary Kay reached out and steadied her with a firm grip.

"Link arms," she said. "We can do it if we do it together."

Carol entwined her arms with Mary Kay's and they proceeded down the steps, carrying Lynne toward the black open hearse and her final resting place in the Old Town

Cemetery, where she would join DeeDee Patterson and her sisters from the original Ladies Society for the Conservation of Marshfield.

Not until Jake walked behind them, strumming on his guitar and singing, did Carol peg the tune Lynne had chosen for her final exit.

"Wish You Were Here" by Pink Floyd. Vintage Lynne.

It was good to be home.

Chapter Four

What is it about funerals that leaves people so famished? Beth bustled about her dining-room table, refilling the hot mulled cider and checking on the state of the balsamic chicken wings, fast disappearing. She put down the pot and fetched the chicken-wing tray, pleased with how guests were loading their plates and returning for seconds. It had been a tremendous amount of work, setting out such a spread, but with rain streaming outside her windows and cold wind blowing, the menu of soups and warm homemade bread, chicken wings, and hot cider had hit just the right spot.

Of course, she'd had some help. Mary Kay ordered a raft of authentic smoked salmon from her native Alaska, and for that Beth had made her mother's special cream cheese with capers, red onions, and fresh chopped dill. Carol had brought from New York four dozen bagels that Tiffany sliced and put out, along with several bottles of good wine also from the back of Carol's town car.

Beth's mother, Elsie, provided a plate of cold cuts and crudités. Sean's sisters had assumed the arduous task of combining the fruit salad—cantaloupe, honeydew, grapes, strawberries, and pineapple—to go with a couple of batches of chocolate-chip cookies baked by Sean's mother.

But she had done the rest. With Lynne.

When Mary Kay came to the library last Thursday morning, Beth had been in her cluttered office, typing up the monthly newsletter announcing their reading list for the "cabin fever" book group series, the most popular of all their library clubs because it took place after Christmas, when snow and cross-country skiing were beginning to lose their white charms and folks were itching for companionship. *The Help*, by Kathryn Stockett, led the list. A big book, but most everyone had read it, so they'd be up to speed. She'd been tapping a pencil against her teeth, debating whether to include *Saving CeeCee Honeycutt,* by Beth Hoffman, or the latest Tracy Chevalier, when out of the corner of her eye she saw Mary Kay framing the doorway.

She was in her purple scrubs, the ones with the dancing teddy bears on the top, and her black curls were held back by a cheery bandanna in a matching pattern. But there was something else. Something off.

Beth hopped up from her desk, the pencil clattering to the floor. "Is everything OK?"

Feeling light-headed, Mary Kay slid down against the wall of Beth's office and crumpled into a heap on the floor, her torso bent over her knees.

"Oh, my God!" Beth gasped. "What's wrong?"

Mary Kay roused herself, and when she looked up at Beth, her eyes were glassy. "I'm so sorry, Beth. I don't know how to tell you."

What? Beth felt like she might crawl out of her skin if someone didn't explain right now exactly what was going on. And yet, *and yet*, through her racing panic she knew. In the back of her mind she sensed what Mary Kay had come to say.

"Lynne," Mary Kay began, her chest heaving, her hand gripping Beth's upper arm, her thumb pressing into her flesh so hard it would have been painful if Beth had bothered to notice. "She gave Tiffany the night off. . . ."

Don't. Beth fought the urge to slap her hands over her ears. She didn't want to hear anything about Lynne. Not like this.

"Tiff had no idea. Lynne had it all planned out right down to the notes she left." Mary Kay shook her head back and forth slowly, rolling it against the wall. "Beth . . . she's gone. She's gone forever."

No, no, no. Beth blinked back something in her eyes, her brain spinning for a logical answer to what obviously was a huge misunderstanding. Mary Kay might be a nurse, but even nurses could be wrong. Of course they could.

"She hasn't gone anywhere," Beth blurted out. "I just saw her."

Wait. When had she seen her? She searched her memory for the exact time last night so there'd be no doubt. She'd tried calling Lynne to tell her that she was bringing over the Crock-Pot, but the line was busy so . . . so, she'd brought it over anyway and plugged it in. Then she'd tiptoed upstairs and found Lynne asleep not on the hospital bed in the living room, but on her old bed in the master suite.

That was the problem. Mary Kay must have found the hospital bed empty and assumed Lynne had left.

"No, she's just sleeping upstairs. I checked on her last night and . . ."

Mary Kay tightened her grip. "Listen to me, Beth. You're not making any sense. I know this is awful to hear. It's awful to say. Drake and I . . . we found her this morning when we went to her house to check. She was on the back porch."

In this weather! It must have been close to freezing last night. What was she doing sleeping on the screened-in porch? "We've got to go get her." Beth tried to jerk away, but Mary Kay held on. "She'll catch her death of cold."

"Beth." Mary Kay refused to let go. "She overdosed on morphine. She committed suicide."

Suicide.

That did it. Beth just needed to hear the word. Her body quivered, her tongue suddenly as dry as sandpaper. The next thing she knew she'd curled into a ball on Mary Kay's lap and Mary Kay was holding her like a child, rocking her like a baby.

Suicide.

After all those years of surgeries and chemo and fighting to live, Lynne had taken her own life.

Rationally, Beth knew this shouldn't have been a shock. Hadn't Lynne repeatedly vowed that should cancer finally get the best of her, she would get the better of it first? But Beth had prayed Lynne would never actually go through with it, certainly not so soon, when she had enough strength to move around. There'd been no hint of suicide when Lynne called around lunchtime the day before to gush about the blue skies and unseasonably warm weather.

"Indian summer!" she'd exclaimed. "I feel *fantastic.* Gonna sit outside and soak up the rays."

It was the healthiest she'd sounded since her doctors brought up hospice, all other solutions having been ticked off, one by one. With morbid awareness, Beth realized Lynne had seemed so giddy not because of the blue skies and unseasonably warm weather, but because finally the wrenching decision was over. She had chosen to free herself of the pain. Permanently.

"I'm so sorry," she heard Mary Kay murmur. "You two had such a special bond. This is going to be especially hard on you."

Beth tried to respond, tried to form words, but couldn't. Her mouth was too dry and all she really wanted to do, to be honest, was burrow her face in Mary Kay's shoulder. How would she be able to face a world without her friend, without her daily calls and chats and laughter?

Who would loan her a few eggs, which Beth never seemed to keep in stock? Who would listen when David was screwing up one of his courses—and give solid advice she could use? Who would remind her it was time to cut back the raspberry canes or call to ask if she'd seen the bluebird nesting in the box Sean set up between their backyards? Who would tell her that everything was going to be OK? Because when Lynne said it, you knew it was true. Everything would be OK.

From now on, nothing would ever be OK. Beth felt as if she'd lost half of herself.

Mary Kay released her slightly and palmed away tears on her own cheeks. "This sucks, doesn't it?"

Beth laughed slightly because that was one of Lynne's favorite phrases. "Sucks big-time." A pit blew open somewhere inside her, directly under her diaphragm, a bottomless black hole as the truth sank in. Mary Kay must have come directly from Lynne's house.

"How did you get over here?" she asked, concerned that Mary Kay had been behind the wheel in her state. "Did Drake drive you?"

"He was still talking to the paramedics when I left." Mary Kay glanced up at the ceiling as if trying to recall. "I don't know how I got here. I must have driven, I guess, but I don't remember. All I remember is that I had to see you face-to-face. The two of us . . . we're all that's left of our group, our little Society."

"And Carol, don't forget." Beth crawled out of Mary Kay's lap and sat on the floor. "I wish she were here now, with us."

They sat like that, cross-legged on the floor of Beth's tiny office, neither of them saying anything. For how long, they had no idea. Beth couldn't erase the image of Lynne's last hours, of her taking the morphine and dying on the back porch while she, her supposed best friend, was merely a few feet away, scrubbing the sink or taking out the trash.

"I should have . . ."

"Shh." Mary Kay shook her head. "There are no should-haves. She did what she wanted to do. It was her choice."

If Mary Kay hadn't said that, Beth might never have left that floor, might be there still. *This had been Lynne's choice.* Even if Beth disagreed with it, even if this choice robbed them of precious weeks or days they might have had to-gether, in the end, all that mattered was that Lynne got her way at last.

It was a ring to grasp.

Beth set her lips firmly, wiped her eyes, and mustered the

Yankee resolve that had sustained her grandmother and great-grandmother and generations of women before them. "We need to send her off in style, then, don't we?"

Mary Kay grinned. "You got that right, tiger. Nothing is too good for our girl."

Beth gripped the wall and brought herself to a standing position, despite her weak knees. "I want the reception to be at my house. No slapdash Flannery thing or something impersonal that's catered. I want to cook it all. Everything. With my own two hands."

"Whatever you say." Mary Kay got up and plucked several tissues from Beth's box of Kleenex. "But first, I think we need to call Carol."

Beth blew her nose, fortified by the task she'd assigned to herself, to throw Lynne the most elaborate home-cooked spread Marshfield had ever seen. It helped to be *doing* something. Something that required sweat and hard work. "We can conference-call her from here and then I'm taking the rest of the day off."

"Wise idea. Me, too." Mary Kay removed the crumpled, wet tissues from Beth's hand and tossed them in the wastebasket. "And then?"

"Then I'll go to Costco. There's so much to buy."

"Like Lynne always said, when the going gets tough, the tough go shopping."

A reminder that Lynne could always be counted on to lighten the mood. Beth and Mary Kay exchanged smiles, thankful for the small touches that kept her memory alive.

After they put in the conference call to Carol, Mary Kay drove back to find Drake. Beth turned off her computer and slipped on her canvas coat. Grabbing her purse and flicking off the lights, she exited her office to the front desk, where the assistant librarian, George, pretended to be reading.

"I'll be out for the rest of the day," she said.

George placed a finger on the page. "Mary Kay told me about Lynne when she got here. I wish there was more I could have done. You know, I'll really miss her in our book club since she was the only one who didn't talk nonstop." They all knew Lynne. The whole library. The whole town.

Beth's eyes started hurting again. "We're planning a huge blowout reception at my house after the funeral. I'm going to Costco."

This needed no further explanation.

"See you Monday. Need anything?"

Beth considered what would be easiest for him. "We could always use an extra case of Coke."

"Will do."

The weather had taken a turn for the worse and Beth was glad Lynne hadn't stuck around for this, the rain and wind batting her car as she headed to Brookfield. It was a road she knew like the back of her hand. Twice a month, she and Lynne would head down to Costco to load up. You had to shop with someone at Costco; otherwise you'd be stuck with huge family packs of beef ribs or mega tubs of seafood salad.

When the boys were small, she and Lynne would turn it into a daylong excursion, hitting the store on Saturdays when meat was cheapest, letting the little guys run around and pick out cereals and snack bars. Meanwhile, they, the two mothers, would lean on their carts and talk, catching up on gossip or working out how to solve some family issue or another.

When Lynne got so sick she could barely keep down a cup of tea, Beth bought their groceries at the local Stop &

Shop. Kevin, Kyle, and David were in college, and the days when she used to accumulate milk in multiple gallons were done. Come to think of it, she hadn't been to Costco in about a year. She had never been without Lynne.

She would never be there with Lynne again. Ever.

Gripping the blue handle of the grocery cart in the cavernous Costco with its steel beams and blaring TVs, this realization left her paralyzed. *I am now alone.*

I am with you.

It wasn't so much that she *heard* Lynne say this as it was that Beth *felt* Lynne say this.

Beth set her jaw and pushed onward. Lynne would not want her to cry, not when a whole host of Flannerys and most of Marshfield would be showing up on her doorstep, famished. She tried to remember the menu she and Lynne had casually discussed, though she couldn't quite recall what Lynne had wanted, since she'd tuned out whenever Lynne mentioned her own funeral preparations. Beth preferred to believe Lynne would beat this thing and go on forever. But now she was at a loss.

Soup, she remembered Lynne saying. Make now and freeze for later.

Thank God for the deep freezer the group had chipped in and bought Lynne when the cancer returned. They'd set it up in the garage so well-intentioned neighbors could drop by and fill it with casseroles or garden vegetables without having to knock on her door and bother her when she was trying to rest. There would be plenty of storage.

Beth rolled her cart up and down the aisles and interpreted the sales as divine signs. Lemons were a bargain at ten cents apiece, so she decided to make her famous Lemon Buttermilk Cake. Turnips, carrots, leeks, onions, peppers. All went into making the soup stock. Garlic. Yes! She could make her Roasted Garlic Soup for the vegetarians.

Chocolate. One of the four food groups. Amanda had sent Lynne several bars of high-quality Callebaut Belgian she'd brought back from her junior year in France that Lynne had frozen, unable to eat even a nibble. Beth could make a flourless chocolate tart and then there were the apples on Lynne's trees. Definitely needed picking. Pie? Sour Cream Apple Coffee Cake? She'd decide later. Already she had enough to keep her busy through the weekend.

At home, she set the oven to 350, pushed back her sleeves, and scrubbed her hands thoroughly before cleaning the chickens and slamming them into pans, grinding pepper and sea salt over each, rubbing dried rosemary into the skin and stuffing oranges into their cavities.

Her heart pounded, sending blood that pulsed in her head, throbbing. She mustn't stop to reflect on what had happened. She *couldn't*.

Sean backed out of the driveway in his roofer's truck toward town, so she washed her hands, wiped them on her apron, and dashed into the rain to take his apples. They were Lynne's apples, anyway. They were for her, Beth thought, her arms aching as she plucked a high one. Cruelly, the branch snapped back, showering her with rainwater that ran into her eyes, stinging, fresh drops mixing with salt tears. For Lynne.

Crossing the soggy yard on her way back, an apple dropped from her apron and rolled into the burn pile, landing on the corner of a book she'd given Lynne last summer, *You, Too, Can Survive Cancer!*, half of it charred, its blue edges curled by heat. She nudged a melted amber plastic pill bottle with her toe, a sickening sensation rising in her throat. No. Not now.

In her kitchen, Beth dried off, put on the teakettle, and got down to business, shaving off the thick red peels of the McIntoshes, coring out their seeds, chopping them into even white bits, mixing butter and sugar, adding flour and cinnamon, and finally the sour cream and apples.

She thought of how Lynne had saved that tree when its leaves curled and the cankers appeared, how she'd whipped out her massive shears and sawed off the offending limbs disfigured by fire blight. Everyone told her it was too late, that the tree needed to be cut down and burned so it wouldn't infect the neighborhood. But Lynne had faith. She refused to give up and with the same determination she used to fight the disease within her, she nurtured that tree back to health.

And now it was alive and Lynne was dead.

Beth stuck the cake in the oven and got down to cleaning and dicing vegetables for the soup stock, stopping only to wash utensils or her hands, perhaps sip her tea. With the chickens done and cooling, the apple cake on the rack waiting for its crumb topping, she whacked forty cloves of garlic so they popped apart, drizzled them with olive oil, and roasted them for an hour, the first step for Roasted Garlic Soup.

With an expert eye, she measured warm water and sugar into one of her grandmother's ceramic bowls and added dry yeast that grew and bubbled. From death to life, she thought, amazed, as always, by the simple miracle of combining yeast, water, and flour to form bread. She slowly added the flour a cupful at a time, stirring. Finally, it became so thick she had to dump it onto the wooden board. She sank her fingers into the flat dough, massaging it, pounding until it turned spongy and sprang back.

From death to life.

But she couldn't bring Lynne back from the dead. There'd be no Lazarus trick for her. Beth kept on turning and folding, pushing the dough. Turn, fold, push, until her arms, already sore from picking apples, cramped in agony. *Turn, fold, push.* Tears spilled onto the dough's shiny, smooth surface. She didn't even bother to wipe them away. There was no point.

Flannery kin arrived next door in droves, gathering on Lynne's back porch and smoking in the rain. Lynne couldn't stand the smell of smoke, but that wasn't Beth's business now. It was Sean's house. Sean and the boys'. She would have to get used to that.

Marc came home later that night to find only the kitchen lights on. He put down his computer case and surveyed the scene: Beth crumbling brown sugar over the coffee cake, the stew pot with the chicken carcasses and vegetables bubbling on the stove, steaming up the windows, the seductive aroma of garlic in the oven, dishes everywhere piled on counters, on the sink. Beth wiped off her hands and came over to kiss him.

"For Lynne," was all she said.

"I know." He saw her pain in the heap of apple peels, in the scattered garlic cloves. "I'll order us a pizza," he said. "Unless you want to . . ." No. There was no point in asking if she'd like to go out.

"Can't stop," she said, wrapping the apple cake in foil and sticking it in a plastic bag. "Gotta go over to Lynne's and put this in the freezer."

Their house hummed with baking and cooking, day and night, leading up to the funeral. One early morning, around two a.m., Marc came downstairs to find Beth furiously zesting lemons, mounds of bright yellow shavings in a bowl. He was about to beg her to come back to bed, but she was so intent on whipping buttermilk into the batter that he reconsidered and made them a pot of coffee. The two of them chatted in the predawn hours about nothing and everything, about Lynne and about their son, David, about the book Marc was reading and where they would go if they could, at that moment, drop everything and just leave.

Italy, they decided, the classic, romantic Amalfi coast. Dramatic cliffs overlooking deep blue waters. Mount Vesuvius looming in the distance. They could travel by motorcycle, Beth on the back, her arms around Marc, hugging tightly as they wound through medieval villages by day and indulging in seafood, wine, and glorious sunsets by night when lights twinkled from houses set into the rocky hills.

Travel had always been something they'd fantasized about rather than actually done, going all the way back to their initial encounter in the travel section of Broadside Books in Northampton, Massachusetts, where they literally bumped into each other and then spent the rest of the evening talking until the store closed. Marc, a senior at Amherst, was researching the coast of Portugal, where he planned to hike part of his summer after graduating. Beth, a senior at Smith, was putting off her paper on German Expressionism by lingering over a picture book on the South of France and thinking how much she'd like to be drinking a Bordeaux in Provence rather than interpreting the use of bad lighting in *Nosferatu*.

They were an unlikely couple. Marc was adventurous, confident, a cosmopolitan New Yorker accustomed to hundred-dollar haircuts and late-night bar hopping, while Beth was bookish and quiet, a country girl from Connecticut who was happiest alone in her room on her bed, a novel propped against her knees, a cup of tea and a plate of cookies nearby.

Before he met Beth, Marc had intended to explore the far reaches of Asia and India while writing sweeping international novels in the vein of Somerset Maugham. Marriage and kids were not in the cards. Even a serious girlfriend was a luxury he couldn't afford.

To his surprise, he fell so hard for Beth's sweet nature and her nurturing spirit that the summer he was supposed to hike the coast of Portugal he spent making love to her in his Northampton apartment. That fall, they eloped and the spring afterward moved to her hometown of Marshfield because Beth was pregnant and they were flat broke.

With no real professional experience and a family on the way, Marc ended up working for Beth's father, Chat, at Brewster Insurance, a job that paid the bills but barely anything more. It was a far cry from the future they'd discussed that day in Broadside Books. It was a daily grind of mind-numbing insurance claims and Rotary Club dinners.

Beth told herself it wasn't one hundred percent her fault that they'd ended up this way—after all, it takes two to make a baby—but she couldn't help feeling largely responsible, since they had returned to *her* town to be near *her* parents. And though he never said as much, they suffered through episodes when Marc became dark and moody, when he descended to the basement to write and didn't emerge for days.

That's when she worried he might do what Carol did and run away.

It was awful to admit, but Carol and Jeff's divorce had been like a stone dropped into a tranquil pond, sending ripples that rocked the people closest to them. Mary Kay broke up with the guy she'd been dating for four years. Lynne, who'd received a clean bill of health the June before, developed a strange cough that turned out to be malignant tumors in her stomach and liver. And Marc grew more and more distant, spending his weekends writing or going off on long hikes by himself.

Which was why their middle-of-the-night cooking session was such a gift. As they chatted about Amalfi, it was as if time reversed and they were young and energetic again, full of hope and plans back at Broadside Books. Marc opened up about quitting Brewster Insurance once David's student loans were paid and floated the idea of subleasing their house for a year so they could take off.

Someday soon, she thought to herself, *I will get you out of here. I owe you that much.*

Marc gathered up the extra lemon shavings and placed them in a mason jar, covering them with 100-proof vodka to make limoncello. "In honor of Amalfi," he said, setting the jar far back in a cabinet so it could marinate for a month or more. "If we can't go to Mount Vesuvius, Mount Vesuvius can come to us."

She loved him at that moment, loved him more fully than when he'd wrapped her in his arms twenty-some years before and proposed under an August blue moon. They had been mere children then. Innocents. Life had been a playland of few obligations—no unpaid bills, no teenagers keeping them up nights with worry, no friends dying.

Anyone can fall in love in the dewy grace of youth, but it takes true grit to negotiate the crags of middle age and still manage to uncover new levels of passion. What she knew that day as the sun rose and she and Marc finally went to bed, was that riding over the rough spots had been worth the aggravation.

She wondered what would have happened if Carol and Jeff had held on tight and ridden over their rough spots too.

That was days ago and now here she was, refilling the coffeepot in the sink for the guests at Lynne's funeral reception, when Mary Kay waltzed into the kitchen carrying a full plate. "There you are!" She set down the plate and turned off the water. "OK, Cinderella, put down your broom. I snagged some food before there was nothing left. Sit down and eat."

She couldn't stop. There was too much to do. "Just let me make this coffee."

"There's plenty of coffee out there. I just checked." Mary Kay removed the pot from Beth's hands and stuck it back in the maker. "Besides, we need to wind this down so we can go next door and clean out Lynne's stuff. Carol's gotta get back to the city."

"So soon?" Beth peered into the living room. Carol seemed in no particular hurry. Her head was thrown back, laughing at something Jake Fenster was saying. Bitsy Kramer and Sue Allen from the PTA were with them, laughing too, as if nothing had changed. "I was just thinking of her, hoping that . . ."

Mary Kay took the opportunity of Beth's open mouth to

shove in a bite of artichoke salad. "She wouldn't turn around and head for the city, right?"

Something like that. Beth chewed. The rice salad was too salty. Next time, she would remember to use plain brown instead of a mix. "It's just that she left so abruptly last time. And then never returned. Remember how we packed up her stuff and shipped it to New York while Jeff was at work?"

"Like she, too, was dead." Mary Kay folded salmon on a cracker and added a spoonful of the cream cheese. "Now, be a good girl and open up."

Beth did as she was told. The salmon was fantastic, freshened by the dill. There was another peal of laughter from the living room. Carol's trademark giggle. "Now it's like she never left. I even saw her in a heart-to-heart with Michelle Richardson over in the corner. They had their heads together like nothing had ever happened."

Mary Kay studied the plate, trying to choose what to feed Beth next. "Did Jeff show?"

Beth wiped her lips. "Not yet. I think he had to take Amanda back to the train station or something."

Mary Kay rolled her eyes. "After all Lynne did for her? Hmm. I don't know about that kid, though it was nice to see the three of them together at the funeral. Did you catch how Jeff had his arm around Carol?"

Beth went quiet. "To be honest, I didn't see much of anything at that funeral. It's such a blur now, I barely remember standing up and speaking."

"Well, you did great," Mary Kay said. "How about one of those chicken wings?" she asked softly. "That balsamic Dijon sauce of yours made such a difference. Is that rosemary?"

"Tarragon." Beth was back to the sink, washing, trying not to think as she glanced out the window and saw a strange figure coming down the street.

"Come on, hon. Quit with the cleaning up already."

"No. Look." She pointed at the sight of Jeff, the collar of his trench coat yanked to his ears to keep out the rain, hustling down the driveway carrying a pair of black high-heeled shoes—Carol's, from the funeral when she took them off to carry the casket.

Mary Kay joined her. "What's he doing?" Jeff stopped, reconsidered, and headed back toward the road.

"Looks like he was bringing Carol's shoes."

"They should be in a plastic bag. They'll be destroyed in this weather."

"Yes, but . . ." That wasn't the point, Beth thought. "Now he's heading to his car. Why doesn't he just come in?"

"Maybe it's too awkward for him, what with everyone in town here. You know, Carol got to run away to New York but Jeff had to stay and answer all the questions. He still can't go out to dinner with another woman without tongues wagging."

"I'm glad he didn't bring a date today. That would have been too much, him with someone else and Carol and Amanda all under the same roof."

Mary Kay ran a finger under her lower lip. "I know for a fact he's not seeing anyone. It'd be all over the hospital if he were."

Which was more than Beth could say for Carol. "Even if Jeff isn't seeing someone, Carol is."

"Pfffewh," Mary Kay snorted. "You mean Scott Deloutte? He's just a partner at her firm."

"More than a partner," Beth said, resuming her dishwashing as Jeff pulled away from the curb in his BMW. "They've been seeing a lot of each other outside the office and Carol mentioned that tonight she's going to his place to, as she put it, unwind and deconstruct."

"Deconstruct, huh?" Mary Kay put a hand on her hip, trying to make sense of that, when Carol bustled in, flushed and bright-eyed.

"Hey," she said, depositing her saucer and coffee cup in the sink, "shouldn't we be heading over to Lynne's? It's almost three."

The two women exchanged silent signals to continue the conversation later as Carol pulled on a pair of jeans and undid her skirt, quickly sliding it easily over her slim hips. "All these years of speculating what Lynne hid for us in her drawers and at last we're gonna find out." The skirt dropped to the floor. Carol picked it up and stopped, skeptical. "Hold on. You two were just talking about me, weren't you?"

Beth, who couldn't lie to save her life, blinked in embarrassment. Mary Kay, who harbored no such hang-ups, trilled, "Don't be silly. We were talking about martinis."

"Martinis?" Carol cocked a brow, intrigued.

"I was asking Beth if we should mix up a pitcher before we head over there. You know, for old times' sake."

"And fortification," Beth added, thinking she could use a boost, the exhaustion from Lynne's death and arranging the funeral suddenly hitting her like a lead balloon.

They decided on Persephone's Cosmopolitans, a martini they invented to celebrate Lynne's remission, the night she first hinted that there might be a secret hidden in her drawer.

The Gift of Spring:
Persephone's Cosmopolitans

The cosmopolitan—traditionally vodka, triple sec, cranberry juice, and lime—would hardly be considered a martini by the impossibly high standards of most traditionalists. However, it is hard to find a merrier cocktail than a cosmo, which was developed in the wild and fun-loving bars of Provincetown, Massachusetts, where the only welcomed mind is an open one. Sweet and pink, in our opinion it desperately needed a tweak from its 1970s style. Therefore we substituted pomegranate juice for cranberry and sprayed each glass with the very faintest misting of rosewater for a particularly delightful taste.

Hades, god of the underworld, tricked beautiful Persephone into remaining in his deathly hollow by enticing her to eat several pomegranate seeds. But every spring, when she rises from the dark, cold world of death to rejoin her grieving mother, Demeter, thereby ushering in the joyful season of summer, we celebrate by drinking a cosmopolitan dedicated to her spirit.

For nothing lasts forever. Not even death.

Chapter Five

What was hidden among Lynne's private belongings had been the subject of constant speculation since Carol, Beth, and Mary Kay made the promise that they—and they alone—would clean out her stuff after she died.

Not that the women often discussed what would happen "afterward." It was much easier, they had found, to pretend the cancer would blow away. *Poof!* That one morning Lynne would jump out of bed and be her old feisty self, so vibrant and full of life.

Oh, to see that Lynne again instead of the pale and thin shell she'd become. The women never stopped believing she would kick cancer to the curb and reappear better, brighter, even sassier than before.

Then the miracle they'd been praying for came true. One glorious day in June as Mary Kay was driving Lynne back to Marshfield after a visit to her oncologist at Yale in New Haven, Lynne called Beth with fantastic news that the vigorous chemotherapy protocol had been worth the torture. All her scans came up clear, including the blood tests. No evidence of tumors anywhere, no protein tracers either. The cancer had simply vanished.

"You're cured!" Beth screamed into the phone. "You did it!"

"Well," Lynne said with hesitation, "*cured* isn't a term that's used in cancer treatment. More like remission."

Who cared about vocabulary at a moment like this, Beth thought. "Whatever. Tonight we're getting together to celebrate. The martinis are on me."

Later, they gathered at Mary Kay's house on what turned out to be an unusually warm early-summer evening. The roses were in full bloom, saturating the misty air with heady, seductive perfume. Frogs croaked in the distance. Fireflies rose from the tall grass near Kindlewah Lake and a full moon drifted in and out of clouds above.

It would be their last pleasant gathering before the emergency meeting at Mary Kay's house when Carol left Jeff, before Lynne's cancer returned with a vengeance.

Carol, Mary Kay, and Beth had bobbed in the pool, holding their glasses aloft in a toast to the health of their girl, Lynne, curled up on a chaise longue like a queen.

She saluted them in return with a glass of weak iced chamomile tea, the most potent potable left in her limited repertoire. "I have something to say and I need the three of you to make me a promise."

"Same time, same place, next year," Beth declared, refusing to abandon the myth that Lynne was cured permanently.

"I need you to promise that when I go . . ." Lynne paused

to make sure Beth didn't protest. "You will clean out my things. Not Sean, because it'll be too painful for him. Not his sisters and, please, God, not his mother, because I can't stand the idea of them rifling through my personal belongings. But you, because you are my closest friends and I trust you to keep my secrets secret."

What secrets?

Lynne refused to say and, unwilling to upset her, they didn't press, although that didn't mean their curiosity was any more quelled. Whenever they got together, the three of them, the topic inevitably came up. What could be so risqué that Lynne needed to keep it out of the hands of her mother-in-law? Sexy lingerie. Sex toys. A sex video. Always, their minds ran to sex, and yet those things were so not Lynne. And if she did have them, who would give a flying fig?

Now, a little over two years later, here they were in Lynne's peach-painted closet, the answer hidden in their midst.

Beth dropped her empty Tupperware tub on the carpet and surveyed the task at hand—a bureau to clean out; racks of shoes to sort; dresses, skirts, blouses, pants, jewelry, and even a wedding gown to pick through; and, on a shelf above, purses and sweaters. "Honestly, I don't know if I can do this. I'm not sure I have the energy."

"You've done enough, Beth," Mary Kay said, resting the thermos of cosmopolitans and set of glasses on Lynne's bureau. "Why don't you sit there while Carol and I do the heavy lifting. You can give us directions."

Carol unfolded a small stepladder and made a beeline for her pet favorites, the handbags, on a high shelf. "We have to work fast anyway so we get it done today while Sean and the boys are up at the cabin."

Sean and his sons had left a half hour before to mourn in private. Downstairs, various relatives from Sean's side of the family were helping themselves to the house, watching football and shouting at the TV. It was awkward being a floor above in the closet with the Flannerys underneath. The women felt about as welcome as mice in the attic.

"I'll do the shoes," Beth said, kneeling on the floor. "At least I can sit."

The women settled into a quiet routine, chatting about the funeral and complimenting Beth on her chicken wings and soup as they sorted. Clothes in decent condition were neatly folded and placed in boxes for Goodwill. Old jumpers, the ratty robe, sneakers, and anything else that had seen better days were thrown in a black garbage bag for recycling. Keepsakes like the wedding dress, veil, and jewelry were conundrums, since Lynne didn't have a daughter. Beth decided to save them in the Tupperware for Kevin and Kyle, if they should be so blessed as to have girls.

The conversation eventually turned to Michelle Richardson, who'd taken Carol aside at the end of the reception. "I was certain she was going to chew me up and spit me out, but she didn't." Carol removed old receipts and lipsticks from one of Lynne's bags, mementos from a normal life. "She apologized for overreacting and was almost self-deprecating. I was so surprised."

"Really?" Beth debated whether to toss a pair of jeans, slightly faded but otherwise wearable. "You know what Marshfield's like, how decent most people are. Mary Kay and I were joking about the school board meetings being boring since you left, but there's a nugget of truth there, too. Everyone's sorry you left, Carol. You were such a big part of the community."

"I guess I had to go away and come back to understand that." Carol added a brand-new Anne Klein hobo bag to the box, the $150 price tag still clinging to the strap. "Lynne's going to make someone at Goodwill *verrry* happy."

There was a beautiful symmetry in three old friends coming together after years apart to close out Lynne's life, Mary Kay thought as she worked through the dresser. They were long past the age when they needed to boast about their kids or brag about their husbands. It was pleasant enough to be alive, together, as a soft rain patted on the roof. She felt Lynne's presence, too, in the paint-splattered smock hanging on the door near her tiny Chinese slippers, in the faint smell of her trademark Happy perfume. To this day, Mary Kay could not walk past a Clinique counter without thinking about Lynne.

"When this is over, we should take a vacation together," Beth suggested, saving a soft flannel shirt for her own personal rag pile. "Maybe a long weekend at the Cape like we did that one April. Remember that? It rained the entire time and I got a shell splinter in my foot."

"How about a cruise?" Finished with the top shelf, Carol stood on her tiptoes to make sure nothing was caught in the back.

"A cruise could be fun," Mary Kay said, gathering a bunch of T-shirts. "You can get great deals right before Christmas."

"That reminds me of Lynne." Beth grabbed a handful of empty hangers. "She used to talk about the day when we could go on cruises together after our husbands died, wearing elastic-waist pants and eating as much as we wanted and not caring one bit."

"Paperback novels on the lido deck, right?" Carol said. "Long naps in the afternoon. No pressure to do anything athletic."

Beth dumped the hangers and slid more off the rod. "Piña coladas at sunset. Shopping for souvenirs at the ports of call. Does that sound like bliss or what?"

Mary Kay was about to agree when she opened the lingerie drawer, lifted a nightgown, and uncovered a large orange envelope marked with the date of Lynne's death and addressed to *The Ladies Society for the Conservation of Martinis*. Her heart stopped beating. "Guys?"

"I don't know if we'll bring any guys," Beth said, separating the padded hangers from the wire ones. "More trouble than they're worth."

Carol climbed off the step stool, a sweater draped over her arm. "What's that, Mary Kay?"

Mary Kay held up the envelope. "It's for us."

The coat hangers fell out of Beth's grip.

"Well, open it," Carol said excitedly. "This might be the big secret."

With shaking fingers, Mary Kay undid the clasp and removed the original *Best Recipes from the Ladies Society for the Conservation of Marshfield, 1966*, its cover yellowed and stained with drops of martinis long past. "So that's where this went."

She handed it to Beth, who pressed it to her chest. "Is that all?"

"No, there's more." Reaching in, she pulled out three sealed business-size envelopes. The first was addressed simply to *The Society*. The second to *My Mother*. And the third . . .

" 'To My Lovely Baby Girl, Julia.' " Mary Kay teetered slightly. "My baby girl, Julia? What does that mean?"

Carol and Beth, equally at a loss, shook their heads. "Does that . . . Did she? . . ."

Beth covered her mouth as it slowly dawned on her Lynne's secret wasn't something naughty but something earth-shattering. "Oh, my God." She plunked herself on the Tupperware tub. "That must be why she didn't want Sean or his sister or his mother cleaning out the closet."

"Your house," Carol said firmly. "Let's get rid of this stuff and then go to your house, Mary Kay, where we can read the letter in private without the threat of Flannerys barging in."

"What about the martinis?" Mary Kay eyed the thermos and glasses on the bureau. "We haven't even touched them."

Carol smiled. "We'll drink them at your place. It'll be just like old times, all of us in your living room, shoes off, hanging out, trading secrets. In this case, big secrets."

Beth sealed the Tupperware with a declarative burp. "Carol's right. I hereby call for a reconvention of the former Ladies Society for the Conservation of Martinis to discuss very important business. All in favor say aye."

"Aye."

And with that, the Ladies Society was back in session. Minus one.

It was great to be in Marshfield. There, she admitted it.

For most of the day, Carol had been resisting the love

emanating from her former neighbors and friends, even her ex. When Jake Fenster moved her to tears with his Pink Floyd arrangement, she told herself it was simply grief. When Michelle Richardson held out the olive branch and confessed that "the school board's been in disarray since you left," Carol passed off her gratitude as relief.

And when Jeff linked his arm in hers and told her everything would be fine, when she drifted off into memories of them lying together in bed at the end of a long day . . . Well, the fact was she didn't have an excuse for that.

But now, once more in Mary Kay's library with Beth, if not Lynne, a fire crackling in the fireplace, a lovely rosewater and pomegranate cosmopolitan before her, Carol was overcome with a serious case of nostalgia.

She missed them.

She missed the Society meetings, this room with its red walls and white bookshelves, their private conversations. She missed being in a small town where people used to stop her on the street to congratulate her on Jonathan's winning goal at last Saturday's lacrosse game or to ask how Amanda was doing at Parsons.

How could she ever return to New York, where not even her colleagues knew (or cared) that she had children? Having spent the morning dreading her return to Marshfield, now she was dreading her exit even more. Like Jeff used to say, she was a human roller coaster: never flat and one heck of a ride.

Mary Kay lifted her glass, pink and perfect. "It's so good to see all of us together, and I don't know about you, but I feel that Lynne's here with us."

Beth patted the seat next to her on the couch, Lynne's

reserved spot, her back against the blue embroidered pillow. "Right here."

Carol put a hand over her heart. "And here. Within us. Always."

"Always," Mary Kay agreed, holding her glass a little higher. "To our girl. Who will live in our hearts forever."

"Forever," they chimed in unison, their glasses clinking.

Each took a sip of her Persephone's Cosmopolitan—a heavenly mixture of pomegranate juice, Cointreau, vodka, lime, and the secret ingredient—rosewater. Like drinking the season of spring from a glass.

"OK. We ready?" Mary Kay slipped on her funky half-glasses—black mother-of-pearl—opened the envelope, and removed the letter. Reading a line or so, she took a deep breath and began.

To My Beloved Society Sisters—Mary Kay, Carol, and, especially, my best friend, Beth: Hi.

I know that seems inadequate in light of what's happened. Or what's going to happen, I suppose. And that's why I want to begin with, "How's tricks?"

Mary Kay stopped reading and looked over her glasses. "Is that classic Lynne or what?"

"Always with a wisecrack," Beth said. "Here we are broken up, and she's cracking up."

If you've found my letter, then you've upheld your promise as I knew you would. Thank you. You guys always did have my back. Someday, I hope to repay the favor.

Mary Kay took another sip, to calm her nerves, and went on.

> *There is so much I need to say to each of you and, yet, sitting here with my pen over the page, words seem inadequate to express my feelings of deep, deep love and gratitude. Let me say that had it not been for our little group, these last few years would have been unbearable. Even separated as we've been lately, you have been my sisters, my advocates, my sustenance and support. It's not just that you, Beth, checked in on me daily or that you, Mary Kay, went with me to every single doctor's and chemotherapy appointment or that you, Carol, did what you did. (And you know what you did—we'll keep it between us.)*

Beth said, "What did you do?"

Carol tasted her martini. "Nothing much."

Mary Kay gave her a look, indicating that she knew full well what Carol had done and that it had been significant.

> *It's that you brought fun back into my life. You danced with me in the moonlight and helped me survive mothering twins. Thank you. I love you all more than you know.*

Beth got up to fetch a box of tissues from the powder room down the hall and returned, dabbing her eyes. "She would have to say that, wouldn't she? I'm going to be a blubbering mess if Lynne keeps this up." She sat, and Carol gave her an encouraging pat.

OK, here's the big news that I've been keeping secret and before I go on, you guys need to know that I came close, really, really close, to telling you a billion times. I only held my tongue because of Sean and the boys. I could not risk them finding out. It would have destroyed my family. It would have destroyed me. So when you read this, please keep an open mind and know that I did what I did for the right reasons, if not the right ends.

When I was eighteen, I gave birth to a daughter and I named her Julia.

Whew. That was amazing to write.

Mary Kay stopped reading.

"So it's true," Beth said, wondering how many more shocks her system could take after Lynne's suicide and now this. "She really does have a daughter."

"And we had no idea." Carol scooted farther into the couch. She would never have been able to carry around a secret like that without telling someone.

Mary Kay went back to the letter.

Julia was the most beautiful baby in the world. Tiny fists. Pink cheeks. The sweetest strawberry birthmark on her forehead. She weighed eight pounds on the dot when I delivered her at St. Jude's Hospital in Mahoken, a steel town in eastern Pennsylvania. I saw her for exactly five minutes before she was taken from me and I was never allowed to see her again. I begged to hold her, but they said I had to sign papers relinquishing all parentage first. So I did. Then they gave me something to make me sleep and when I woke up, she was gone from the hospital.

The three of them gasped in unison. Mary Kay snatched a tissue. "That's a crime, is what that was."

"A contract signed under duress is not a valid contract," Carol said, chewing the inside of her cheek as she often did when she was suppressing her indignation.

This might come as a shock, but that's because for many, many years I forced myself to pretend Julia didn't exist—as my mother insisted.

My mother was a good person, but she was other things as well, above all, fervently Roman Catholic. I lived in fear of getting pregnant, which was probably why I didn't go to the doctor until I was four months along. The father of my baby was not in the picture. He was slightly older than I and "passing through" my hometown of Calais, PA. (Sounds way more exotic than it was—a mining town about 40 min. northeast of Pittsburgh.) I was a teenager in the hicks, itching to get out of Dodge and he, I mistakenly believed, was my ticket out. It's an old story, the stuff of TV movies. When I found out I was pregnant, he had already left and I never felt more alone or scared. There was no one to turn to but Mom.

That's why I agreed to her "solution." She arranged for a private adoption through a local lawyer whose name I never knew. Then she sent me to live with my aunt Therese Zahm clear across state in Mahoken so people back home wouldn't find out I was pregnant. (As if!) Julia was born on December 3, the winter after I graduated from high school. The lawyer, I was told, came to the hospital along with a professional nurse. They brought the legal papers that I signed and I could hear my baby girl crying down the hall as I slipped into a drugged sleep. Despite years of cancer and cancer treatments that left me nauseous, aching, and blistered, that night remains the worst of my life. I dream of it to this day.

My mother said it would be for the best, that I would thank her years later.

She was wrong.

"And I used to think *my* mother was a piece of work when I was a teenager," Beth said. "Elsie seems like Carol Brady in comparison. To force a girl to give up her baby on the spot . . ."

Mom's plan was for me to return home that Christmas. She told everyone that I'd been at a junior college in the Poconos and, for a while, I played along. But then I started crying for no reason and wandering around at night, restless. On one of those nights, in the spring after Julia was born, I managed to get down to Pittsburgh with a plan to hop a bus to Boston, where my best friend from high school went to college. I made it to Scranton, but from there could only afford to go as far as Waterbury, Connecticut. Luckily, I found a job waitressing and a few months later met Sean at the diner where I worked and, well, you know the rest.

You also know Sean and how conservative he is and what a blow it would be for him to find out that the woman he loved kept a huge secret throughout his marriage, that she lied to him and to his sons, not only about their half sister, but also about their grandmother, whom they were raised to believe died when I was a teenager. Which, in a way, she did.

Carol put a hand over Mary Kay's. "That means Lynne's mom doesn't know her daughter is dead."

"Or that she was even sick, I expect." Mary Kay turned to Beth. "Did she ever say anything to you about her mother?"

Beth, more confused than either of them, could barely whisper. "No."

After I got sick—or maybe it was when Kevin and Kyle were no longer children—I started thinking about Julia more and more. I became obsessed with finding out what happened to her, if she landed in a nice family, if she was loved, if she had red hair! So I made a few calls, first to the hospital in Mahoken to no avail. The hospital's records were sealed—even though I'm the biological mother! I checked with Northampton County Orphans Court and found the same thing. The clerk told me in all likelihood the birth certificate had been changed to remove my name and replace it with the names of the adopting parents. So there's no record tying me to Julia whatsoever.

Mary Kay put down the letter. "Dear Lord!"

I guess by now you know where this is going. I am asking you the huge favor of picking up where I left off in my search for Julia. Believe me, I do not make this request lightly. I'm fully aware that it is a tremendous burden and interruption in your otherwise hectic lives. All I can say is that I trust no one else but you. We have been through so much—marital problems, job changes, cancer . . . teenagers! I know you guys will take this letter seriously and fulfill my

*last request. That alone gives me tremendous peace as I pass
from this existence to (hopefully) another.*

They felt deflated, flattened by the loss Lynne had been
mourning for so many years while they had gone on with
their routines, drinking martinis and bitching about their
petty problems that couldn't compare to being forced to hand
over a baby, to running away from home and being cut off
from family. Beth rested her head on Carol's shoulder as
Mary Kay finished the letter.

*The first step in your search is definitely to contact my
aunt Therese, who continues to live on Notch Road in
Mahoken—by Allentown—and my mother, Eunice, something I haven't been able to bring myself to do since I took
that bus to Waterbury. I kept meaning to call her when I
was in remission, but to do so would have meant welcoming
her into my new life and introducing her to Sean and the
boys, thereby raising all sorts of questions. Frankly, that
would have been more toxic than the chemo.*

*My father was Carl Swann. He died in 1976, but
Mom lives in the Beckwood Landing Assisted Living
Center outside Calais. (A quarter mile off Route 66. I'm
sure Carol will figure it out, what with her map skills.)
You'll find, enclosed, a letter I've written to her in a sealed
envelope marked "My Mother." Please tell her I love her
very much and that I left this earth with no hard feelings,
only loving memories. She might know, better than anyone,
what happened to my daughter. If she hasn't slammed the
door on your faces, ask her if she remembers the name of the
lawyer.*

If you locate Julia, please give her the other envelope, my grandmother's gold earrings (they're in a box on my bureau), my wedding dress, and a hug, a mother's hug from deep down. Please tell her I love her so, so much and that while I could not watch over her in life, I will do my best to watch over her in death. Our physical beings might pass away, but our love never does.

Needless to say, time is of the essence. Neither my aunt nor my mother was aware of my illness . . .

Mary Kay tapped the paper. "So that answers our question."

. . . which means you will have to tell them of that, and of my passing before they find out some other way.

Beth let out a groan. "I'm not very good at that. It was hard enough calling you, Carol, with the news Lynne had died. I can't imagine notifying total strangers."

"It'll be OK. I'll be there and Mary Kay, too," Carol said, foretelling the next line in Lynne's letter.

This is why I hope the three of you can clear your schedules and do this as a group. It'll definitely be more tolerable, might even be fun!

Right now, I'm sitting here, picturing you guys taking a road trip across Pennsylvania, crowded in Beth's new Highlander, no husbands, no jobs, no kids, cranking the tunes, talking and laughing and winding down the day with martinis. And martinis are a must. I insist on a different one every night! After all, this is what we're all about, right, ladies? Don't forget our mission statement to preserve and protect the endangered cocktail. If we don't make the sacrifice, who will?

So, while I won't be with you physically, trust that I'll be there in spirit as you drink your spirits. Have one on me and good luck.

To paraphrase the Boss, everything dies, but maybe everything that dies comes back. And the Boss never lies.

Until then,

Love,

Lynne

"Can I see that?" Beth, her body aching in a strange new way, took the letter, biting a nail as she reread it word by word.

Mary Kay finished her martini and set the glass down declaratively. "Man, am I ever gonna miss her. That letter was so Lynne, so bursting with her kick-ass attitude."

Carol was silent, analyzing this assignment that would be no small feat indeed. It would require nerves of steel, breaking the news to Lynne's aunt and, especially, Lynne's mother. Then there was the challenge of locating Julia—a virtual impossibility, considering the legal obstacles—not to mention the exhaustion from driving hundreds of miles.

She would have to cancel her date with Scott so she could go back to her own apartment and pack, make arrangements for work. Carol realized she should have been disappointed by this—actually, she *had* been looking forward to their night together on the drive to Connecticut that morning—but now, after being home, after sitting through that wrenching service and finding this letter, the absolute last thing on her mind was sex. Sleeping with another man besides Jeff would be emotional enough without thoughts of death and lost babies rolling around in her head. No, tonight was not the night. It would be unfair to Scott. "I think we should leave tomorrow bright and early," she said.

Beth lifted her head from the letter. "Tomorrow? Can't we hold off until Monday?"

"I'm concerned about her mother and aunt finding out. With the Internet these days, news travels in a flash. What's to prevent someone in Lynne's hometown from coming across Lynne's obituary online and contacting her mother?"

"I hadn't thought of that."

"Makes sense to me," Mary Kay said. "All I have to do is convince my supervisor that this is a personal crisis, and with my saved vacation days, I'll get the week off. How about you, Beth?"

"The library? They won't care. George can take over."

Mary Kay turned to Carol. "I bet for you it's a big deal, what with that fancy law job."

"Another lawyer will cover my clients. Besides, I happen to have an in with the firm's founding partner," she said, smiling to herself. "Not like I don't have some pull."

"Yeah, I wanna hear more about that pull," Mary Kay said. "You can fill us in on the *loooong* drive across Pennsylvania."

So they hammered out logistics. Carol would rush back to New York, pack a bag, call her clients, and work with the firm to rearrange her caseload. The next morning, she'd hop the MetroNorth to Danbury, where Beth and Mary Kay would pick her up in Beth's car, as Lynne suggested. If all went according to Beth's scheduling, they could be in Pennsylvania by noon on Saturday.

It was done. By the same time the next day, they would be on the road, searching for Lynne's long-lost daughter.

Chapter Six

Dawn broke through the high windows in Mary Kay's bedroom as she quietly slid out of bed, leaving Drake peacefully asleep on her Egyptian cotton sheets, his broad back rising and falling softly. She kissed his shoulder and snuck into the shower, mentally ticking through a list of last-minute errands.

She was running late. The plan was to meet Carol at the train station around eight and already it was almost six thirty. Thankfully, she'd packed the night before, tucking away flatware and tablecloths into the cooler that held various mysterious bottles for their journey, along with her antique silver shaker and bright Capri hand-painted martini glasses.

Just because they'd be on the road was no reason to settle for plastic cups. But that was Mary Kay. Why settle for less when you can have more?

After her shower, she toweled off, applied her makeup, and opened the peach-colored packet of birth-control pills, turning the dial to the next dose, pushing it through the foil and promptly dropping it into the sink.

Turning on the faucet, she sighed and watched the little green pill swirl down the drain. She remembered an article she'd read about the groundwater being contaminated with estrogen and other hormones that had been flushed away. Could it be that she was but one of a legion of women who secretly wasted their birth control?

"Why do I even bother *pretending* to take them?" she asked herself, knowing full well the answer.

Because she wanted Drake to think she could get pregnant—even if she couldn't.

The ruse had started quite by accident. When they first started sleeping together, Drake came across an old packet of her birth-control pills and made a comment about how interesting it was that she still needed them at her age. Mary Kay had been slightly taken aback because she didn't think of herself as being *that* old.

OK, so she had crossed the big 4-0 and was a full five (pushing six) years older than Drake. But as a nurse midwife she'd helped plenty of women her age deliver their babies. It was funny that Drake didn't know this.

What was more striking, however, was how pleased, almost animated, he became after stumbling across those pills, as if he were seeing her in a whole new light. Overnight, their relationship bloomed from casual to serious. They started spending weekends together, going for long walks and hikes. While Drake taught her how to belay down a rock face and build cairns, they hashed out those deal-breaking commitment issues like religion and money and whether it was ethically wrong to have more than two kids.

Turned out, Drake loved children. Not only did he work with them in his profession as a child psychologist, but in his spare time he helped abused kids regain their self-esteem by leading them on wilderness adventures. Mary Kay had never met someone so giving, so eager to make the world a better place.

She was literally head over heels and before she knew it, the prospect of losing him filled her with panic. By then she didn't have the heart to tell Drake the real reason she used to take birth control wasn't to prevent a child—but to spare her life. After being diagnosed with scarred fallopian tubes and, therefore, at a high risk of ectopic pregnancy, Mary Kay was prescribed the Pill, which she used to take religiously until she figured that, after forty, it was doing more harm than good. Now she just washed them down the drain.

It had been hard going, coming to terms with the fact that she would never experience the miracle of life growing within her. But as the years went on, she'd made peace with her body. To have to revisit all that with Drake would mean ripping open old wounds, and Mary Kay found it much easier to simply pretend everything was A-OK. Yes, sometimes it made her blue to realize they could never conceive a baby of their own, but she took comfort in the knowledge that she *had* been a mother in every meaningful way—to Tiffany.

Tiff was all Mary Kay had left of her older sister, Ellen, who, along with her husband, had died in a car crash outside Hartford. Mary Kay was working as a nurse in the Alaskan outback when she got the horrible call. She immediately dropped everything and ditched her old life four thousand miles away to raise her niece in the only home she'd ever known, Ellen's pristine Victorian, commonly referred to in Marshfield as the Patterson House.

She and Tiffany had been a team ever since. Mary Kay threw herself into the brand-new role of single motherhood with her customary gusto, legally adopting Tiffany as her own, joining the PTA and volunteering as a room parent, reading to her every night and making sure Tiff practiced her piano daily as Ellen would have demanded. Mary Kay also taught her how to ride a bike without holding on to the handlebars and how to walk a certain way so boys followed like dogs, imagining with glee how Ellen would have been appalled.

And when the big day arrived, Mary Kay designed Tiffany's prom dress, sniffing back tears as her niece descended the stairs in a strapless pale lavender satin gown, her dark hair piled high, Ellen's amethyst necklace at her throat, looking every inch like her mother, right down to her sweetheart chin.

Those were magical years.

So devoted was she to ensuring Tiffany enjoyed the best childhood possible, Mary Kay had sworn off men until her daughter left for college. It wasn't that hard, actually, since so many guys who crossed her path seemed to be jerks. But when Drake came along, it was a different story. By then, Tiff was completely out of the house, working as a rookie nurse at Mass General, and Mary Kay was ready to release all the sex, love, and passion that she'd bottled up within her. The timing of Drake's arrival couldn't have been better.

The irony was, of course, that when Drake finally did ask

her to marry him—on the night before they found Lynne—she couldn't accept his proposal. It was impossible to be his wife when for two years she'd misled him about her ability to bear children. She loved him too much for that.

Be careful what you wish for, she thought sadly as Drake sauntered into the bathroom in nothing but his cotton drawstring pants.

"Thought you could slip away without saying good-bye, eh?" He came from behind and wrapped his arms around her waist, kissing her neck.

She checked his reflection in the mirror, admiring how the slight brown hair on his firm abs narrowed to a V. It was pathetic how thrilled she was by the superficial aspects of their relationship—that he was taller than her, that other women turned when he passed and waitresses flirted with him right in front of her. She found secret pleasure in knowing that while they might wonder how he was in bed, she *knew*.

Recapping her mascara, she said, "I didn't want to wake you on a Saturday when you could sleep in."

"You were trying to sneak off; don't deny it." He ran his hands over her smooth white shoulders. "Three, maybe four whole days. How will I stand it without you?"

"Takeout?"

"Man cannot live by Thai alone."

She dropped the mascara into her makeup bag and zipped it shut. Turning, she kissed him lightly on the cheek and said, "Oh, I think you'll manage just fine."

He lifted her hand and frowned at her unadorned fingers. "Hey. What gives?"

Her knuckles curled slightly in apprehension. "Since I

haven't told Beth and Carol yet, I thought I'd wait until I got back," she fibbed.

He wasn't buying it and looked so disappointed she figured what the hell. Fetching the small black velvet box from the table by the sink, she said, "Would you do the honors?"

"Gladly." He slipped the ruby and diamond engagement ring on her finger slowly and pressed himself into her with a soft kiss. "I love you, Mary Kay. Come back and be my wife."

"It's not that easy."

"Actually, it is. It's just a matter of saying yes."

⁓

Beth was almost ready, except for a few things she was standing on tiptoe to retrieve from her kitchen cabinet. Olive oil. Oregano. Maybe a bottle of balsamic vinegar. In other words, the essentials.

Marc slid his laptop onto the kitchen table and carried his cup to the coffeemaker for a refill. "You know, Beth, there are these inventions called restaurants where they cook the food for you."

"As if." She debated basil and maybe turmeric, in case they wanted to do an Indian something-or-other. "Carol said she'd reserved suites and most of them have kitchens, albeit poorly stocked ones." Should she bring the salad spinner? Definitely a whisk. "Besides, we're trying to save money, remember? And this trip is going to be expensive enough."

"Don't worry about the money." He leaned against the sink and sipped his coffee, watching her pack away the spices. "You worry too much."

"I worry because we don't have any."

"We have enough."

"Maybe I should let Carol and Mary Kay do this without me," she told Marc. "I'm sure they could handle it just fine by themselves." She pulled a jar of basil out of the cabinet. "Besides, what about my dad? What if he needs me?"

Beth's father, Chat, had undergone cardiac tests shortly before the funeral and was slated to receive the results Monday. Beth had planned to accompany her parents to her father's appointment, to hold her mother's hand and talk rationally with the doctors since Elsie found it difficult to remember what questions to ask.

"My brain flies out the window when I'm under stress" was her mother's pat phrase. "You'll have to do the thinking for me, Beth."

Already, Chat had survived two heart attacks and Elsie was at sixes and sevens about the prospect of number three. She'd spent a lot of time on the phone to her eldest daughter, Madeleine, who was not a doctor but whose A+ in high school biology somehow crowned her as the family medical expert.

In Maddy's opinion, Chat should be seeing specialists in New York, not squandering his time and money with rinky-dink Grace Hospital. Grace was fine for the occasional broken toe or bee sting reaction. But with Manhattan so close, it was simply imprudent not to seek the best possible (and most expensive) care, especially when it came to the heart.

It had been Beth who had talked her parents into sticking with Grace because it was closer to home and friendlier. She couldn't imagine her father dealing with the red tape at one of those mammoth urban medical centers, having to tolerate arrogant physicians, teams of residents, and crowded waiting rooms. Elsie agreed, mostly because she hated driving into the city.

After much debate she sided with Beth: Chat would have his tests at Grace.

Maddy was outraged.

Now, after all that wrangling, Beth wouldn't be there Monday for the results and Maddy, helpless out in L.A., was urging Beth to reconsider the trip.

"This is our father," she'd wheedled shortly after Beth returned home exhausted from cleaning out Lynne's closet. "Our *father*. What could be more important? You know Mom's not equipped to deal with bad news. You need to keep her on an even keel."

Beth had to begrudgingly admit that Maddy was right, leading her to toss and turn all night debating whether to stay or go. Even as they were preparing to load the Highlander, she still wasn't sure.

Marc picked up her suitcase and carried it out to the car. "You don't want to stay home. Lynne was your best friend. If anyone should go on this search, it's you."

She followed with her box of cooking stuff, willing to be talked into a position. "But what about Dad? Like Maddy said, Mom can't handle bad news alone. She'll flip out."

"You're a cell call away, available around the clock. And if it makes you feel better, I'll take off Monday and go with them to see your father's cardiologist. Your parents trust me more, anyway."

She slid the box of cooking stuff into the trunk and punched him lightly on the shoulder. "If I didn't know better, I'd say you're trying to get rid of me this weekend."

"You don't know better. I am." He closed the hatch.

"Don't get into trouble while I'm away," she said with a smile.

"As soon as you get in the car, I'm planning to e-mail a query letter to each agent on my list. For all you know, by the time you get back I'll be an author with a publishing contract."

It was a nice thought, if a total fantasy. Wrapping her arms around his neck, she whispered, "I believe you will."

He held her and smiled. "You've never lost faith in me, have you?"

"Not for a nanosecond."

"Man"—he squeezed her tightly—"am I the luckiest guy or what?"

She kissed him on the nose. "Or what."

The autumn fog after the rainy night had barely lifted from the deserted Danbury Station when Carol stepped off the train, towing her orderly black bag and matching computer case. She subdued a flutter of anticipation as she scanned the parking lot, checking for the familiar car. Not here yet.

Finding a wooden bench, she sat and applied a coat of neutral lip gloss to complement her ribbed cream-colored turtleneck and camel peacoat. Her blond hair, pulled neatly into a ponytail, was deceptively casual, since it was designed to show off her ultra-sexy hammered gold earrings that had cost Jeff a small fortune. A bit over-the-top for a Saturday morning at the Danbury train station, but so what?

She tried not to think about Scott in New York and how

disappointed he'd been by her abrupt change in plans, though he rallied to her cause, as always.

"If Mohammed can't come to the mountain, then the mountain must come to Mohammed," he said when he showed up at her door after the funeral, an artichoke and olive pizza in one hand and a bottle of an excellent petite sirah in the other.

She was in nothing but old sweats and a towel, her face bare, but that didn't stop her from throwing her arms around his neck and kissing him for being such a saint. Lesser men would have taken advantage of her vulnerability. Not Scott. He slowly removed her arms and took her in his instead, holding her with such quiet tenderness that she burst into sobs.

Then he led her to the couch, poured the wine, and handed her a glass, all the while listening earnestly as she recounted her day, from the joy of reuniting with Mary Kay and Beth to the sadness of seeing Lynne's white coffin strewn with her own flowers. She related how making up with Michelle had been no big deal and how shocking it was to find Lynne's letter and the secret that would upend their lives for at least the next few days.

The only thing she didn't mention was Jeff.

"It couldn't have been easy seeing him again," Scott said, exposing the elephant in the room. "You were married for twenty years." He passed her a slice of pizza on a paper napkin. She picked off an artichoke.

"It's over," she said. "He's OK. I'm OK." She shrugged and laughed, perhaps a little too loudly.

Scott said, "As long as you're sure."

"No question," she said, and meant it. It barely even

fazed her when Jeff had called her after the funeral to say he had her shoes and asked if it would be better to mail them to her office or apartment.

"Why don't you hand them over in person?" The offer surprised her as much as it shocked Jeff.

"What?" he asked, confused. "Really, it's no problem for me to take them down to the UPS place."

"I'm arriving on the eight a.m. train to Danbury to meet Beth and Mary Kay. There's something we have to take care of . . . for Lynne. We could do a quick pass-off."

So, they made an arrangement to meet in the parking lot and here she was, dressed to the hilt, proving she was as fine as frog's hair. Never better.

Twenty years.

Jeff's black BMW pulled up to the station. The passenger window lowered and he leaned over. "Hello," he said.

"Hey." She smiled.

He got out and opened the door. "*Entrez-vous.* There's a triple venti latte waiting for you, light soy. I figure while you're waiting for Beth and Mary Kay, you might as well get coffeed up."

Coffeed up. Their term for their morning ritual of getting up before the kids and welcoming the day with French roast and the *New York Times* in the sunroom overlooking the lake.

Jeff took the bag from her hands and laid it in the trunk and then got back behind the wheel, parking so they'd have an unobstructed view of the station.

"Your shoes are in the back." He gestured to a white plastic bag from which protruded two black stilettos. "I had no idea you'd be a pallbearer. It was a touching choice on

Lynne's part." He sipped his own coffee and fiddled with the heater.

"You didn't show up at the graveyard. How come?"

"Amanda." He seemed slightly embarrassed by this. "She insisted on making the noon train, so we had to hightail it out of there. Midterms."

This was a white lie and they both knew it. The truth was Amanda couldn't stand to be around her mother. Carol glanced out the window, resolving not to let this latest rejection get to her. If only there were a way to reach her daughter.

Jeff touched her coat lightly. "Don't give it another thought. You know how kids are."

Changing the subject, he said, "You look good, Carol. Healthy." If he noticed the earrings, his fifteenth wedding anniversary present, he chose to keep that to himself. "How've you been?"

"OK. Considering."

"It was a nice funeral."

"Yes. Lynne gave it a lot of thought."

"Nice flowers. Were they from her garden?"

"I think so." *God, this was awful.* She didn't know how to hold a decent conversation with her own ex. Why must they always be so stiff and formal? She wished they could talk, really talk.

But all she could say was, "I'm glad it stopped raining."

Jeff checked out the window. "Me too, except it's been a pretty dry fall. Lots of fire warnings."

"Jeff . . ."

"Carol . . ."

Carol blushed. "Sorry. You go."

He breathed in and out deeply. "Look, I know this is probably not the best time, coming on the heels of Lynne's death."

She gripped her latte so tightly the thin cardboard began to buckle.

"But ever since the divorce, I've been thinking."

"Yes?"

"There are so many memories I have, so many great memories of our family."

She felt her stomach stir and chalked it up to the fact that she hadn't eaten yet.

"I hate to leave, but . . ."

She blinked in confusion. *Leave?*

"How do I say this? I thought you should know that I've taken steps to sell the house. Already we have two offers and I haven't officially put it on the market."

The coffee nearly slipped from her hand. Sell the house?

That house represented their entire family history, from the gardens where Amanda and Jon had hunted for Easter eggs in their adorable spring outfits to the backyard where they threw the annual neighborhood Fourth of July party with greased watermelon races in the lake and fireworks over the waters of Kindlewah.

Together, they'd stripped the wallpaper and repainted the kids' rooms and knocked down a wall to build a nursery for Jon. They'd added a balcony for Amanda and repainted every inch of that molding. That house had been their labor of love. Their *home*.

She replaced the coffee in the cup holder, afraid her unsteadiness would lead to a spill that might ruin the camel coat. "Why now?"

"The judge wanted us to do it a year ago. The only reason we held off was because of the kids."

"And now they're OK?"

"I'm sure they will be. They've already moved out. Jonathan's clear across the country in Portland and Amanda
keeps talking about going back to France after that incredible
junior year she had." He ran a hand through his straight
blond hair. "As hard as it is to believe, they're adults now."

"But it's our house, Jeff." Carol searched for concrete
arguments as to why he shouldn't sell it and, much to her
distress, couldn't think of one. "Where will everyone go for
Christmas?"

He shrugged. "How about your place? Carol, think
about it. With your half of the money from the sale, you'll be
able to put down a sizable deposit on a pretty decent Upper
East Side co-op."

She didn't want a "pretty decent" co-op on the Upper
East Side. "What will you do? It makes no sense selling a
house here and then buying a smaller one. And it's not like
Marshfield's overrun with apartments."

"Well, that's the thing." He studied his gloved hands.
"Like I said, I'm ready to leave."

This took a second or so to comprehend. Oh, my God,
she thought, quelling a wave of alarm, those weren't euphe-
misms. He was actually talking about going away. Away
from the kids and their home—away from *her*.

"You mean, you want to leave Marshfield."

"Yes. That's the idea."

She thought back to that sultry summer afternoon when
they stumbled upon the village that would soon become
their home, the glow of the setting sun on Jeff's handsome

face as he talked about Marshfield being a place where they could grow old together, where their grandchildren could run through fields and catch butterflies.

"I might come back. Someday. But look, I'm only fifty, Carol, and there's so much I want to do. Murray Schwartz has been working with Doctors Without Borders in Africa, and this winter he's going to Haiti. He's asked me to come along, and . . . you know, it's a once-in-a-lifetime opportunity."

Carol's mind suddenly went black. All she heard was that Jeff was selling their house and leaving her alone in New York. Their family truly was shattered, as Amanda said.

And it was Carol's fault.

There was a beep and they both startled. Beth and Mary Kay were a mere few feet away, waving at them from the Highlander. "I better go," she said, grabbing her shoes from the back.

"So I have your OK to take the best offer?" He hustled out to fetch her bag from the trunk.

"I'm not sure."

"You're not sure? I don't mean to be pushy, but you've been grousing for months about not having enough money to start your new life. Now's your chance."

"I know, but . . ."

"But what, Carol?" He wasn't mad as much as mildly annoyed, which was about as agitated as Jeff ever got. "This is the final part of the divorce agreement you requested. I didn't want to get divorced. I was perfectly satisfied with how we were." Though increasingly upset, he kept his voice appropriately low. "You were the one who felt trapped, remember?"

Carol winced. Had she said that . . . *really?* What had she been, a 1970s housewife?

"Do you know how hard it's been adjusting to life after you split for no reason? How depressed I've been? Now, when I finally find something that'll let me put my talents to productive use and go forward, you're holding me back." He gave the trunk a hard slam. "That's rich."

She hadn't realized the suffering she'd caused Jeff, her entire family, by simply pursuing her own dreams. And she couldn't help but resent him, slightly, for making her feel guilty.

Even if he was right.

It was so confusing. She missed their life together. She loved her work. She loved her children. She longed for the peace and quiet of Marshfield, and yet she relished her independence in the city, too.

And then there was Scott, so fantastic in his own right.

It was too much at once. She couldn't think straight.

"I apologize," she said, racking her brain to come up with a stall tactic. "Let's talk to the kids before we make any rash decisions. Even if we overrule them, at least they'll have a chance to register their opinions."

Jeff mulled this over. "Good idea. I'll get in touch with Jonathan. Should I call Amanda, too?"

She wasn't certain he was aware that Amanda refused to take her phone calls. But this would be a legitimate reason for them to talk. "I'll handle Amanda. I'll call her this evening and get back to you."

"How about six p.m. Sunday night?"

Carol pulled out her iPhone and made a note. "Six p.m. it is."

"And then? . . ." He cocked his head gently.

"If Amanda agrees, you can sell the house. If that's what you want."

"Thank you." He held out his hand and they shook. "Have a safe trip."

They said good-bye and she watched him get into the car and pull away, feeling as if a coffin were closing once and for all on the life she'd left behind.

Chapter Seven

"Wow! Can you believe we're actually doing this?" Mary Kay, riding shotgun, gave Beth behind the wheel a little pinch.

Beth rubbed her arm, feigning pain. "Ow!"

"Sorry. It's just that I'm so excited to get away. Think about it. No men or bosses. Only the open road and the three of us." Mary Kay spun around, her black curls bouncing to keep up. "Aren't you excited, Carol? Two years we've been apart and now we're together again like nothing's changed."

Carol was staring out the window in a daze, her laptop open before her.

Beth flashed Mary Kay a knowing glance. Carol had been lost in thought all morning, ever since she said good-bye to Jeff at the train station. Supposedly, he'd stopped by to drop off her shoes, but Beth wondered if there was more to the story.

Switching lanes, Beth said, "You know what happened

to me this morning? I woke up and realized this would be my first day without doing something for Lynne. I didn't even want to get out of bed."

Carol closed her laptop and put it aside. "They say that's the hardest phase of grief, when everyone goes home and life gets back to normal."

"Except, then I remembered our trip." Beth held up her finger. "And I thought, aha! Today won't be so bad after all."

"Because we're anything but normal, right?" Mary Kay said.

"Exactly." Beth smiled. "Leave it to Lynne to know exactly what we'd need. Could you imagine what it'd be like if you went back to New York, Carol, and Mary Kay and I got on with our same routines? It just wouldn't feel right."

"And this way," Mary Kay said, "we can toast Lynne every night." She patted the red Igloo cooler.

Carol leaned forward. "You didn't."

"Sure, I did. Lynne told us to. Didn't she, Beth?"

Beth agreed. "Right there in the letter. Martinis are a must."

Carol opened the cooler and examined the extensive collection of oddly shaped bottles, a copy of DeeDee Patterson's cookbook, and Mary Kay's hand-painted martini glasses. "It's an entire bar."

"Only the essentials," she said matter-of-factly. "Gin. Vodka. Vermouth. Though where would we be without Domaine de Canton and limoncello, not to mention good old Cointreau? And Framboise, of course."

"Of course." Carol removed a dark bottle of Godiva chocolate liqueur. "And this?"

"For chocolate-raspberry martinis. Don't tell me you've forgotten?"

"I *love* those," Beth gushed. "Marc and I make them every Valentine's Day."

Personally, Carol thought they were way too sweet, even if it was hard to resist the hard dark chocolate coating around the rim of the martini glass—a technique that set the professionals apart from the amateurs. "Maybe I should try one on Scott."

"Yes, do tell us about this Scott," Mary Kay said, replacing the chocolate liqueur and closing the Igloo securely, as if it were carrying precious cargo.

"There's not much to say." Except there was. "We've known each other since forever, before I met Jeff even." This, in Carol's mind, exempted him from the status of home wrecker. "He's about five years older than I am, and he's a widower. His wife died long ago from a brain aneurysm."

"His résumé is fascinating, I'm sure," Mary Kay said, resting her chin on the back of her seat. "But what about the guy himself? Does he have a good sense of humor? Is he cheap? Extravagant? Eats crackers in bed?"

Carol's lips twitched. "Gee, Mary Kay, why don't you come right out and ask if the sex is good?"

"All right. Is the sex good?" Her gray eyes twinkled.

"I wouldn't know."

"You wouldn't?" Mary Kay frowned. "That's no fun. You know, I'm only on this trip for the sex. Isn't that true, Beth?"

Beth, trying her best to pass a hog of a tractor trailer, said, "I'm here for Lynne."

"Granted. But if Lynne were here, you'd have to admit, she'd have come for the sex too."

"Knowing Lynne, sure." Beth passed the tractor trailer at last and slowed, her heart thumping in her chest.

"Well, I hate to be a party pooper, but we haven't slept together," Carol said. "We were supposed to the night of the funeral—Scott had a whole evening planned with a home-cooked dinner and a bubble bath—but it didn't quite work out. Kind of wasn't in the mood after . . . you know."

"Seeing Jeff?" Mary Kay raised an eyebrow.

"No! I wasn't in the mood after burying Lynne."

"Oh."

Beth said, "Pay no attention to the woman behind the car seat, Carol. She's just stirring up trouble 'cause she's bored."

"Mom?" Mary Kay whined. "How much longer until we get there?" She slipped off her leather gloves to get a Diet Coke out of the cooler and all of a sudden Carol's relationship with Scott was jettisoned to the back burner.

"Mary Kay!" Beth exclaimed. "You didn't!"

Mary Kay checked her seat. "Uh-oh. What did I do wrong now?"

Carol wedged herself forward. "Don't tell me she's started drinking already."

"Look!" Beth flapped her hand toward Mary Kay's lap. "Oh, my God! Why didn't you tell us?"

Beth had never seen Mary Kay turn such a shade of crimson; a shot of red ran right up her long neck and blossomed on her cheeks as she shyly displayed her fabulous engagement ring. "This? This is nothing."

"That's not nothing," Carol said. "That's a huge ruby

surrounded by a bunch of diamonds in a platinum setting. Unless things have changed since I got married, I'd say that is one bona fide engagement ring. A hunk of bling."

" 'Hunk of bling,' " Mary Kay said. "I like that."

"When did this happen?" Having nearly sideswiped a VW Bug, Beth gripped the wheel and satisfied herself with waiting until they stopped so she could inspect further.

"The night Lynne died, before we knew. It didn't seem right to flash it around while everyone was in mourning."

"It's gorgeous." Carol undid her seat belt and craned for a better view. "It's you to a T, Mary Kay. Colorful. Bright. Over-the-top."

"I'll take that as a compliment. Drake designed it himself using a stone from his late mother's ring."

"I don't know which is better," Carol said. "That you won't have to deal with a mother-in-law or that you've got her ruby."

"Mother-in-law jokes already. Low." Mary Kay shook her finger playfully.

Lynne would have been so pleased, Beth thought. She adored Drake.

Carol said, "So when's the big day?"

Mary Kay let the ring catch the morning sun, turning it this way and that, as if she'd never really noticed it before. "Um, not sure."

"What about a Christmastime wedding?" Beth suggested. A winter wedding was so romantic. "In the evening, arriving by sleigh."

She could see the old church on the town square now. White candles flickering against the dark glass, pine boughs and red poinsettias. Snow falling lightly outside as carolers serenaded Mary Kay as she walked down the aisle wearing a white satin cape trimmed in faux ermine and carrying a big bouquet of red roses. (Beth had seen something like this once in the *New York Times* Sunday "Style" section.) The bridesmaids could wear dark wine-colored dresses. . . .

Beth surreptitiously checked her soft upper arms and cringed. Definitely with sleeves.

"I don't know about a Christmas wedding," Mary Kay said. "That's right around the corner."

"You know what they say. Where there's a checkbook, there's a way," Carol said.

"Actually . . ." Mary Kay paused. "I don't know about a wedding. Period."

Beth slammed on the brakes, nearly missing the turnoff to Routes 6 and 209. Thank God she saw that. There wasn't another exit on I-84 for miles. "What do you mean? You said yes, didn't you?"

Mary Kay was silent. Beth and Carol exchanged quizzical glances in the mirror.

"Not yet."

What?

"But you're crazy about him," Beth said, totally baffled. Whenever Mary Kay got into her second martini, she'd moan and groan about how there were no decent men in Marshfield and how she'd sacrificed her youth and beauty for Tiffany's sake. Now along comes Mr. Right with his Ivy League pedigree and super-nice manners and she turns him down?

If Lynne were alive, she'd give MK a kick in the pants.

"You're living together. Why in hell *wouldn't* you say yes?"

Mary Kay folded the gloves in her lap. "It's a big decision and I want to be sure. Drake gets that."

Beth didn't. "You have to accept, MK. You can't let that guy slip from your fingers. He's one in a million. Lynne said so herself. And you know Lynne. She was an excellent judge of character."

A hand pressed into her shoulder. Carol gently signaling for Beth to back off.

"I'm sure Drake's not going anywhere," Carol cooed. "And I understand, Mary Kay. A lifelong commitment is about as serious as it gets, next to whether to seek a divorce. Take it from someone who screwed up both. Besides, it's not like anything's going to happen to you guys between now and when we get back."

Beth exhaled, begrudgingly willing to give Mary Kay the benefit of a long weekend. "That's true."

"And in the meantime, we have a big job ahead of us," Carol continued. "We can't be meandering down the highway mooning over boys. We're here to carry out Lynne's last wishes. We need to be girl-focused."

"Amen, sister." Mary Kay was glad they were off the Drake subject. "Three women, a mission, and a cooler full of martinis."

"We are women. Hear us roar," Carol chimed in. "Don't dare kick us out the door! Or however that song goes."

Beth shook her head. "Honestly, if you two are going to be like this all during the trip, sober, then I am seriously considering throwing out that booze right now."

"Who said anything about sober?" Mary Kay asked. "Did you, Carol?"

"Perish the thought."

Beth flicked her blinker to take a left into a picnic area. It was hard being the only adult in the car.

The picnic area was in the Delaware Water Gap National Recreation Area, a perfect spot to stop. Beth put out a lunch of leftovers from the reception—assorted crudités; a mint yogurt dip; cut strawberries, melon, grapes, and fresh pineapple; a baguette and Boursin cheese; the last of the chicken wings. She'd also brought along a pitcher of the mulled cider, now ice-cold, that she poured into plastic cups. Martha Stewart could eat her grits.

Overhead, the sunlight streamed through dappled autumn leaves onto the worn cedar table engraved with various declarations of love. With the Delaware babbling and rushing in the background and the day unseasonably warm, it was very pleasant.

Mary Kay helped arrange the vegetables as Carol walked off to call Amanda. Once she was out of earshot, Beth weighed down the napkins with a bowl and said, "OK, what do we make of that?"

"Of what?" Mary Kay bit into a carrot.

"Of Carol wondering if she made a mistake leaving Jeff."

Mary Kay chewed. "She didn't say that, did she?"

"Not in so many words . . ." Beth squinted into the sun, checking on what Carol was up to, wondering why she was pacing back and forth. "It's obvious Jeff dropped some sort of bomb in the parking lot. Did you see the way she acted when we picked her up? She was lost in la-la land. I'm thinking maybe they finally had that honest and open discussion about their marriage—the one they *should* have had before Carol flew off like a bat out of hell."

"Open? Those two? They couldn't open a pickle jar."

Mary Kay laughed at the absurdity. "They're like those cartoon gophers Mac and Tosh. After you! No, after you! They essentially excused and pardoned themselves into a polite divorce."

"This is why you have to fight for your marriage, fight as if your very breath, your soul, depends on it," Beth said rather dramatically. "You don't declare surrender like Jeff and Carol did."

They were silent for a while. Then Mary Kay said, "Is this your way of slipping me some marital advice?"

"I'm just saying." Beth went back to setting out the last of the chicken wings.

"Because at my age I'm pretty sure I know what it takes to keep a marriage going."

"Maybe that's why you're too scared to try."

Mary Kay snatched a napkin from under the bowl. "Is that what you think? That I'm scared? Excuse me, but as someone who used to live among grizzlies up in Alaska, 'scared' is not a word in my vocabulary."

Carol returned, clutching her camel coat, lips tight and bloodless.

"How's Amanda?" Beth asked, trying a different approach as she offered Carol a plate of wings.

Carol took one wing and a few measly grapes. "She didn't answer, so I left a message."

"Ah." Mary Kay forced a smile. "College students are so busy, what with running here and there, to classes, hanging out with friends. When I was in college I never called my parents, except maybe to ask for money."

"That was back in the day of the hall phone—remember that?" Beth stabbed a piece of melon, keeping the tone upbeat. "At Smith, it would ring off the hook on Sunday nights and one girl after another would fly down the hall screaming that it was for her. Now, with cell phones, I bet those dinosaurs are long gone."

Frowning, Carol pushed aside her plate and leaned on her hand. "I'm afraid I'm not very hungry."

Mary Kay reached out and took her wrist. "What is it, baby cakes? You've been glum all morning."

Carol traced her finger around the K+K 4evah 2getha carved into the table. "Jeff wants to sell the house."

Mary Kay cleared her throat. "And you don't want him to?"

"I do . . . and I don't. I mean . . ." She picked at the engraving. "It's what we should do. When we got the divorce, we were supposed to divide up all the assets, but we wanted to keep the house for Jon and Amanda. It's the only home they've ever known and we felt they needed time to adjust. On the other hand, I needed cash to buy my own place in New York. So the agreement we worked out was that I would rent and he would sell the house a year after the divorce was made final."

"Which is now," Mary Kay said.

"Right."

"And how are the kids taking it?"

"Don't know, yet. Unfortunately, we don't have much wiggle room. There are two offers on the table and we haven't even put the house on the market. Could be Amanda and Jonathan spend Christmas with me, which will be hard. Our Christmases were so magical in Marshfield. Those bonfires and midnight ice-skating and . . . Well, there's no use getting worked up over what I can't control."

Carol slumped, appearing very small.

Softly, Mary Kay said, "Look, there's no need to rush, right? If those buyers want your house, they'll stick around. Might even throw in a few more grand. The issue is whether this is what *you* want."

"What I want? That doesn't matter. Not anymore."

"It matters. Absolutely. That's why you left Marshfield. Because no one was taking into consideration what you wanted. Jeff's career, the kids' needs—hell, the family dog had top priority. Who could blame you for snapping?"

Carol lifted her head and nodded. "It wasn't that I didn't love them. It was that they didn't love me."

"Don't be silly. Of course, they loved you," Beth insisted. "How could you think for a minute that they didn't?"

"They *depended* on me, which is different. And that's fine, except maybe once in a blue moon they could have turned the tables and supported me in return."

"That's why you have us," Beth said. "We'll always support you."

"Like Spanx." Mary Kay snapped the elastic waistband of hers. "Whether you sell the house or not, stay in New York, return to Marshfield, or relocate in Scandinavia if that flips your switch, we've got your back."

"Really?"

"And if selling the house isn't what you want, then it's not going to happen."

"Not on our watch." Beth punctuated this with an empowered crunch of celery.

Carol exhaled. "Have I told you how great it is to be with you guys again? New York is exciting and everything. I love being in a city where I can get the newspaper at two a.m., see a first-run movie when I want. But nothing compares to having honest-to-God girlfriends. And that's what I don't have these days." It was embarrassing to admit, but true.

"Too bad Lynne's not here," Beth said. "I think she appreciated our group the most."

"Don't you know it." Mary Kay pushed back her plate. "Do you remember when she ordered us pink T-shirts with the LSCM logo stamped right above the left breast? People kept asking us what that meant and we told them the Ladies Society for the Conservation of Marshfield." She giggled, thinking of her next-door neighbor, an octogenarian with a stern sense of propriety, who grilled her about the name. "Poor Emma Shrewsbury. She was sure the Ladies Society for the Conservation of Marshfield had been disbanded years ago after DeeDee Patterson died. For the life of her, Emma couldn't understand why she hadn't been formally invited to join."

"You should have told her what the *M* really stood for," Carol said, now on her second helping of rice salad.

"Martinis? Not if you knew Emma. She would have called in the vice squad."

"A raid by the vice squad, as if we even have a vice squad in Marshfield." Beth sighed. "Lynne would have loved that, too."

So many "would-haves" and "should-haves." Too many.

"Lynne would have loved everything about today," Carol said, feeling much, much better about everything. "She would have loved that we're together, that we're outside having a picnic and chatting."

"She would have loved us," Mary Kay said.

"She still does," Beth added, knowing this as firmly as the ground beneath her feet. "Love doesn't go anywhere when you die, you know. The person passes on, the body withers, but love, it survives. And if you have any doubts, think of what we're about to do, about how hard it's going to be telling Lynne's aunt and mother that she's died. There's only one reason and one reason alone why we're taking this on.

"Love."

Chapter Eight

Aunt Therese's hometown of Mahoken, Pennsylvania, was nothing more than a washed-up steel town rusted over and gone to seed.

At its center was a crumbling steel factory, long out of use, much of it ripped apart for scrap metal. Dollar stores, tattoo parlors, and bars—the cockroaches of economic decline—had replaced hardware stores and dress shops. Even the weather was gloomy. Clouds had moved in, threatening rain. There were only three colors, it seemed. Gray, darker gray, and despair.

On top of that, the air smelled like rotten eggs.

"Do you suppose it was this much of a pit when Lynne was sent here?" Beth asked from the passenger seat, Mary Kay having taken over the driving.

"Early 1980s? Might have been slightly better. Not much," Carol said. "Hell of a place to be a pregnant teenager on your own—that's for sure. Then again, just being a teen-age girl and pregnant is its own kind of hell."

"No kidding," Beth agreed. She tried to picture a young Lynne with her sketch pad and pastels, sitting Indian-style on the hill overlooking the steel mill, her red hair tied up in some crazy paisley bandanna as she coaxed beauty from this bleak landscape. Her pregnant belly out to there.

Would they have been friends if they knew each other then? It was hard to imagine. Beth had been such a Goody Two-shoes, graduating at the top of her class, attending her mother's proper women-only alma mater. She never even made out with a boy until freshman year. She'd gotten drunk on punch at an Amherst mixer (and puked into the bushes a half hour later). And yet, only a few states away, Lynne was pregnant by age eighteen, a runaway rebel.

No, Beth thought, chagrined by her own snobbery. She probably would have had nothing to do with her.

"Where do I go now?" Mary Kay asked when they paused at a traffic light.

"Take the next left." Beth followed the GPS on Carol's iPhone as they drove straight up and straight down roller-coaster roads through Mahoken's working-class neighborhoods. "Then another right."

Mary Kay clutched her rumbling gut, slightly carsick. "Whoever designed this traffic system must have been on crack."

"Not crack," Beth said. "Limited budgets. OK, so are we square on who's going to do the talking? Because it's not going to be me."

"I will." Carol raised her hand. "I am the lawyer, after all. Delivering bad news is my bread and butter."

"How do you think she'll take it?" Beth pointed left down another street of brick row houses. "Three strangers showing up on her doorstep with news that her niece died of cancer . . ."

"Angry. Sad. Confused. Whatever the case, I'm sure she'll be extremely upset." Mary Kay took another right, her stomach lurching.

"Here we are." Beth pointed to a house across the street. "It's that one with the Santa Claus."

Mary Kay pulled over, stepped on the emergency brake, and studied Aunt Therese's row house. Like its neighbors, it was built of brick with a concrete front porch covered in a fading green outdoor carpet. Two summer lawn chairs, their seats fraying, faced the street. Santa Claus graced the glass storm door, rosy-cheeked and merry, a contrast to the faded Halloween decorations one unit over.

"Guess there's not much to look forward to around here, huh?" Beth asked. "If you're putting up Santa before Thanksgiving."

They sat there for a while refreshing their makeup and fixing their hair, removing every tiny piece of lint from their suits until they realized they were stalling. Finally they got out, took a deep collective breath, and crossed the street.

A TV screen flickered through a part in the lace curtains. Mary Kay straightened the collar of the white shirt peeking out from Beth's wool coat. "We look like decked-out Jehovah's Witnesses." She checked Carol, who, as always, was dressed impeccably.

"Either that, or we're flight attendants on the lam," Carol said, ringing the doorbell twice.

It opened on a chain. A small pink nose, the bridge of blue glasses, and a wisp of gray hair appeared in the crack. "If you're here for my soul, I ain't interested. And Avon called last week."

The woman started to shut the door when Carol said, "Excuse me, Therese?" She repositioned herself in the doorway. "We're friends of your niece, Lynne. . . ."

"What? Wait, hold on. Hold on." Therese seemed to be fiddling with her hearing aid. "Did you say Lynne?"

"We're her friends from Connecticut, and she asked that we stop by to meet you, ma'am."

Therese said nothing. There was only the sound of her heavy breathing and the crackling of the television. "I don't know . . . ," she murmured, hesitating, stepping back from the door.

"She's frightened," Carol whispered. "You guys have any bright ideas?"

Beth snapped open her purse and produced a photo of Lynne and two older women grouped together on that very same porch. Mary Kay was astonished—where the heck did Beth get that? "Here. Lynne gave this to me," she said, sliding it through the opening.

Therese examined the photo, her hands shaking and palsied. She returned the photo to Beth, closed the door, and slipped off the chain. When she opened it again, they could see Therese was short, squat, gray-haired, and wearing a floral muumuu. "I miss Lynne," she said. "How is she?"

Dear Lord, Mary Kay thought. *Give me strength.*

"May we come inside?" Carol asked.

Therese directed them to a small living room with fern-patterned wallpaper, a brown couch covered in a crocheted blanket, a coffee table littered with magazines, and a padded rocker into which she settled herself comfortably. There was a disproportionately large flat-screen TV on mute showing an infomercial for some sort of exercise machine.

"For the love of God," Beth murmured to Mary Kay, "give Lynne some dignity and turn that thing off."

Mary Kay reached for the TV, but Therese made a clucking noise to back off. "I was just thinking of Lynne the other day," she said.

Carol perched at the edge of the couch.

"It was the strangest thing. I happened to be going through the Halloween decorations and I came across a scarecrow she made when she was staying here. I swear I've had that box for years and I've never seen it before." Therese rocked slightly. "She was always doing arts and crafts. I bought her a box of professional pencils and a sketch pad once. Had to go all the way to Allentown to get them. I hope she's still drawing."

"She's an art teacher," Beth said in a hushed tone, her voice choking up.

"Oh, I can see that. She used to run an after-school art class for the children next door. They're all grown now. . . . But where is she?" Therese swiveled to check the door.

"She's not here," Carol said, extending her hand to touch Therese's knee and then reconsidering. "That's why we've come."

"That's too bad. I'd love to see her again. I don't know if she told you, but we grew rather close, the two of us. She was such a frightened young thing when she got here. Eunice was too hard on the child, if you ask me. Like I told my sister, we all make mistakes and deep down Lynne was a good girl. She just needed loving."

"Yes," Carol said, searching for an opening and finding it difficult and strange the way Therese wouldn't look them in the eye. "The thing is, the reason why we're here, Therese, is that your niece has been ill for quite some time with cancer."

Therese went silent and kept her attention on the muted television for what felt like an eternity.

"Therese?" Beth whispered.

Therese scowled, the fat below her mouth molding into deep rivulets. "She called me, you know, around last Christmas," she said. "I had a feeling something bad had happened to her. When I found that scarecrow, it was like a premonition."

Beth leaned against the window and folded her arms. "Near the beginning of December?"

"That's right. It might have been the anniversary of the . . ." Therese stopped and cleared her throat. "Anyway, I picked up the phone and a woman said, 'Aunt Therese?' She was hoarse, like she might have had a cold. I wasn't sure. But since I have no other nieces, I said, 'Lynne, is that you?' She said, 'I just want you to know I'm OK and I want to say thanks and that no matter what happens, I love you. Merry Christmas.' And she hung up." Therese rocked, slowly. "I sat by the phone all night, hoping it would ring again, but it never did. Finally, when the sun came up, I went to bed."

Alone, Carol thought. On Christmas.

Mary Kay said, "Sounds like something Lynne would do."

"We had a bond." Therese leaned over and pulled out a

limp handkerchief from her pocket and blew her nose. "So, you're here to tell me she's gone. Is that it?"

Carol nodded, wishing there were some way to ease this woman's loneliness. "I'm so sorry."

"I assume there's going to be a funeral. I'd like to go to that, if you don't mind."

Beth winced. "I'm afraid the funeral was yesterday."

Therese quit rocking. "Yesterday?"

This, they hadn't anticipated. "We would have called you, except we didn't find out you existed until we were cleaning out Lynne's things," Mary Kay said, realizing as soon as the words left her mouth that she'd only made matters worse.

"You mean Lynne never spoke about me?" Therese asked, distressed. "After all I did for her, taking her in when no one else would? I was there when she . . . She held my hand all through it."

For some reason, Therese would not talk about the baby. Either she was protecting Lynne's reputation, even now, even after Lynne had run away, or she was ashamed.

Carol scratched a spot behind her ear, wondering if it was possible to feel any more awkward. "That doesn't mean Lynne didn't love you. Remember her Christmas phone call?"

"We didn't know her mother was alive, either," Beth offered.

Therese's eyes grew wide in shock and she picked up the remote, punching the off button. "So Eunice didn't go to the funeral either?"

Carol sighed, her shoulders suddenly aching as if they'd

been hauling burdens all morning. "No. Eunice doesn't know about Lynne."

"You people show up and tell me my niece is dead. You tell me her mother don't know. That the funeral's over. That everyone *forgot* about us, her family."

Her *family*, Beth wanted to clarify, restraining herself, was Sean and the boys. Her *family* would not have disowned her or forced her to give up her own baby.

"As soon as we learned about you and Eunice, we got on the road to tell you in person," Carol said. "Since you're closest, we stopped at your house first. Tomorrow, we hope to contact Lynne's mother. We didn't want to tell her over the phone, not after all these years."

"It was her daughter's funeral, for heaven's sake. What did people think when Lynne's own mother didn't bother to show for her own daughter's funeral?" Therese looked to each of them. "It's a scandal."

"*Scandal?* It was no scandal. People in Marshfield aren't like that," Beth asserted defensively. "The only scandal as far as I can tell is that Lynne's mother shipped her across the state to live with you and birth a baby that she wasn't allowed to hold. That's a scandal."

Carol and Mary Kay went bug-eyed.

"So that's why you came." Therese's powdery pink complexion turned almost purple. "You're here nosing around about that baby."

"We're not nosing around," Beth said. "It's Lynne's baby. She asked us to find her. And that's what we're going to do."

"It was your niece's dying wish," Mary Kay said gently. "She was searching for Julia before she died and never found her. In the letter, she suggested you might be able to help, that you might remember the name of the doctor or lawyer involved."

Therese resumed her rocking, chewing her lower lip. "She should have come to me on her own."

"I agree," Carol said, in an effort to show Therese that they were on her side. "I'm sure she would have come to you if she could."

Beth said, "She was awfully weak. And she was worried what would happen if her husband and sons found out about the baby, about you. They have no idea. Still."

This caught Therese's attention. "So she's married?"

"To a man named Sean," Beth said, sitting on the coffee table. "They had twin boys, Kyle and Kevin, now in college."

"And they don't know about me or the baby."

Mary Kay said, "They don't even know about Lynne's mother. The boys think their grandmother died when Lynne was a teenager. They'd already been through so much with her sickness that Lynne thought it would have been too hard on Sean and the boys to tell them the truth."

Therese rocked in her chair, shaking her head every once in a while as if she were carrying on a conversation in her head. The room was warm and dusty and cluttered with antiques and junk from assorted yard sales, porcelain figures of dogs and a shepherdess looking for sheep long lost. Beth felt like she was slowly suffocating.

"Well." Therese pulled herself out of the rocker with a grunt. "I don't remember much except what I got here." She waddled over to a dresser by the stairs, bent down to pull out a lower drawer, and riffled through loose papers. "Hmph. I thought I saved it, but I guess I didn't."

"Saved what?" Carol asked, hoping for a document, something official that could get the ball rolling.

"The bill from the hospital. I never paid it 'cause the doctor waived his fee, but it had his name. I thought Lynne might come around looking for it someday and I put it aside in my important files."

"Can you possibly remember?" Carol pressed.

"I can't remember exactly, but I think it started with a D. Whatever his name was, I didn't like the way he treated Lynne. She'd complain about this or that or ask what was going to happen to her baby and he'd pat her on her head and tell her not to worry, that he would take care of everything. He rubbed me wrong."

"Did you do anything about it?" Mary Kay asked, quickly adding, "Not that it was your responsibility."

"I brought it up with Eunice, but she said I should mind my own business, that he came highly recommended by her doctor out in Calais. My sister's the type that when she takes control, the rest of us say 'yes, ma'am.' That's what happens when you're the oldest."

Don't I know it, Beth thought, feeling some sympathy for what Therese went through, especially in light of her own struggles with Maddy. "I have an older sister like that who thinks she knows best. She means well, though."

"They often do." Therese nodded but made no move to return to her chair and Carol got the distinct impression that their visit had come to an end.

"We should go," Carol said.

Beth's cell rang, another excuse to leave. "Thank you so much for letting us into your home," Beth said, checking the number and heading out the door. "I'm sorry. I have to take this. It's from my mother."

"Again, I'm so sorry," Mary Kay said, grasping the woman's hand in hers.

Therese wouldn't let go. "When are you going to see Eunice?"

"If all goes according to plan, tomorrow."

"Then pass on a message from me, would you? If she doesn't want to talk about Lynne, just remind her of our trip to Dorney Park."

"Dorney Park," Mary Kay repeated. "And she'll understand what that means?"

"She'll understand. It was the day she found out she was pregnant after fifteen long years of trying. We'd all but given up hope."

Something stirred within Mary Kay. "You mean Eunice couldn't have children?"

"Not according to the doctors. That baby was a miracle, a true gift from God, and those two were like peas in the pod. When Lynne was tiny, she didn't go anywhere without holding her mother's hand. So maybe you understand why Lynne's running away and not speaking to her again was like a dagger to my sister's heart."

"I understand," Carol said from where she'd been listening on the porch. "I understand all too well."

Therese dropped Mary Kay's hand and regarded Carol with an eagle's eye. "Then let me impart a word of wisdom. Don't wait until it's too late to set things right. You don't want to get a visit from three strange women telling you your daughter died and she didn't even care enough to say good-bye. That's enough to break any mother's heart."

⁓

While Beth took the call from her mother, Carol and Mary Kay crossed the street toward the car.

"Wow," Carol said, trying to process Therese's message. "That was intense in a way I didn't anticipate. So much water under the bridge."

Mary Kay activated the automatic lock and Carol got in the back. She leaned against the window, her head heavy with thoughts.

Mary Kay slipped behind the wheel, replaying the moment on Therese's porch. Eunice had tried for fifteen years to get pregnant. Then Lynne was born and she assumed her life was complete. But look at how that had turned out. Babies were no assurance of happily ever after.

Still, she couldn't help wondering what it would be like to have a child of her own. Closing her eyes, she let herself visualize the pink plus sign on the drugstore test, the bubble of glee rising in her throat, the awe of her body's miraculous abilities. No worry or fear. Merely pure, unadulterated joy.

She could see herself laughing as Drake gathered her in his strong arms and lay her on the couch insisting that for the next nine months she not move a muscle. Knowing him, he'd insist on high-protein diets that he'd cooked with his own two hands. . . .

Beth yanked open the driver's-side door and Mary Kay snapped out of her daydream, scolding herself for engaging in a stupid, dangerous fantasy. If her therapist found out, she'd have a cow.

"Sorry about that," Beth said as she climbed into the driver's seat. "While I was on the phone, Aunt Therese was able to find out information about Lynne's old hospital. Apparently, the doctor's name was Dorfman. We looked him up in the phone book and found his number." Beth was flushed with excitement. "If you're not too wiped out, I say we stop by his house this afternoon. Therese says he doesn't live too far from here, in Scenic Valley."

Carol doubted that would get them anywhere. "It was thirty years ago and one baby among hundreds he delivered. Besides, I'd like to squeeze in a run before it gets dark."

Beth cranked the ignition. "Gee, Carol. I thought you were a risk taker."

"Are you the risk taker?" Mary Kay asked, pretending to be insulted. "How come I'm not the risk taker? I'll have you know that last week I forgot to take my calcium and went two whole days without leafy green vegetables."

"You can be the risk taker next time," Beth said. "Right now, it's my turn. I got the distinct impression from what Therese said that it was Dorfman's idea to have Lynne give up her baby right away. Maybe if she hadn't, she wouldn't have run away and everything would have been different."

Carol relented. Beth was so loyal to Lynne, so fiercely determined to set things right, it was impossible to deny her. "OK. Let's do it on one condition."

"What's that?"

"That if it's dark by the time we get to our hotel, you guys have to go for a run with me. It'll be safer and we could all do with some exercise after so much sitting."

"Gee, I'd love to," Mary Kay said, searching for an excuse. "But I'm feeling a little queasy after all this driving. I'll be fine after a toes-up, I'm sure. Anyway, someone has to hit the grocery store for tonight's dinner."

"You're pathetic, MK. How about you, Beth? Someone has to go with me. Don't make me go alone."

"Ugh." Beth made it a practice to avoid anything that smacked of athletics.

"Don't groan," Carol said. "A good three-mile run could shake out some of the frustration you're feeling. Raise your endorphins."

"I'm afraid it's going to take a lot more than a jog to get rid of this anger." She paused dramatically. "It's gonna take justice."

"And a sports bra and running shoes," Mary Kay quipped. "We'll make a pit stop at a mall on our way to the hotel to get you outfitted. My treat."

"No, Mary Kay, I couldn't allow that."

"I insist. And you're not getting out of gym class that easily, Mrs. Levinson. You'll need more than a note from Lady Justice."

Underneath Beth's scowl lurked a little smile. "You can't blame a girl for trying."

"You're right. You can't blame a girl for trying. Tease, poke fun at, ridicule mercilessly, yes." Mary Kay's violet eyes twinkled in mischief. "But blame? Never."

The Lemon Martini

※

A lemon martini is the distillation of liquid sunshine in a glass. We prefer our lemon martinis to be refreshingly tart, a combination of two parts vodka to one part limoncello, shaken with ice until beads form, then poured into a chilled glass and garnished with a sliver of lemon.

Limoncello is a liqueur made by soaking the zest of organic lemons in 100 proof vodka for weeks, if not months. The best is homemade; the worst smells like oily lemon floor polish. Be careful to choose a limoncello that tastes lightly of fresh lemons.

For us, a lemon martini conjures sparkling evenings dining alfresco on a veranda overlooking the rocky coastline of Capri as a full moon rises above the Tyrrhenian Sea. Its power to spark romance is legendary. But this magical martini is also perfect to share simply with old friends, reminiscing about sunnier days gone by and golden ones yet to come.

Chapter Nine

It took a serious pep talk to summon the courage to drop by Dr. Dorfman's house out of the blue on a Saturday afternoon. As they snaked past mansion after mansion in Scenic Valley, past circular driveways and graceful weeping willows, deep turquoise in-ground swimming pools peeking from behind wrought-iron fences, and signs warning of private security, they had to remind one another again why they were disturbing a retired physician's afternoon, brandishing lurid allegations.

"He took her baby," Beth said, clutching the wheel as Mary Kay read off the house numbers. "This man yanked Julia out of Lynne's outstretched arms and then gave her a shot to knock her out so she couldn't fight."

"Steamrolled, is what he did," Mary Kay said. "It's the next house, hon."

"And might even have profited from the adoption, which would have been completely illegal. Though, from the look of these houses, quite lucrative." Carol let out a snort of disgust as they slowed to the Dorfman mansion, where a black stretch limousine idled in the driveway.

"Maybe we should call first," Mary Kay said.

"Or contact his lawyer," Carol added.

"Nope, we have to do this now. For Lynne." Beth opened the door and got out. Mary Kay and Carol followed as Beth took charge and stormed up the walk.

"I don't know what's gotten into our Beth," Mary Kay said.

Carol said, "I'd say her best friend died."

Beth waited for the others to catch up at the door before ringing the bell. Carol positioned herself by a planter overflowing with red mums as she assessed the manicured lawn and the golf course on the opposite side of the road. The peaceful stateliness of this grand old neighborhood reminded her of her house back in Marshfield and she wondered if Beth and Mary Kay had been right, that selling it was really her decision.

It'd be a delightful place to retire and enjoy the lake and the gardens without the disruption of work. She and Jeff had been too busy to fully appreciate their location when the children were smaller and Jeff was preoccupied with establishing his practice, when they were building the future that Carol managed to destroy in one hellish night.

After what seemed like an eternity, an elegant older woman opened the front door. She was regal in a pewter chiffon gown with a lace bolero jacket, diamonds at the throat and ears, a silver clutch purse in her hand. She took a step and stopped, startled, as if she hadn't even seen them there.

"Hello?" she questioned.

Beth stuck out her hand and introduced them by full names each. "We're here to see Dr. Dorfman."

The woman batted her eyes rapidly. "I'm afraid that's not possible. We're on our way to a wedding in Philadelphia and already we're late."

Which would explain the idling limo.

"We're asking only for a few minutes of his time," Beth said boldly. "We've come from Connecticut."

Insinuating herself, Carol said, "Mrs. Dorfman, we're here about a friend of ours who died last week. She was a patient of your husband's long, long ago. This concerns her last will and testament and it's a matter of rather grave importance."

Mrs. Dorfman set her square jaw. "I'm sorry you ladies have come all this way, but you should have called first. Or at least waited until Monday."

"Who is it, Marta?" A beefy hand clutched the door, opening it wider. Dr. Dorfman—or so they assumed—was rather dashing in a full tuxedo, complete with a pewter silk cummerbund to match his wife's dress. He brushed back a wisp of hair and regarded them with a gentle, if paternalistic, gaze. Mary Kay noticed his nails were filed and buffed to a shine.

Nervously, Marta introduced them as "women from Connecticut. They *claim* they're here to speak with you about a former patient."

"Lynne Flannery," Beth said. "Though you would have known her as Lynne Swann. She was a teenage mother who gave birth in December 1980. I know, that's a ridiculously long time ago, but if you can remember anything about that birth, we'd be eternally grateful."

"I told them we were off to a wedding in Philadelphia, but . . ."

Dr. Dorfman gave her a look, indicating he would handle the situation. "Come in," he said with a stern wave toward a formal slate entry. He closed the door and folded his arms. "Marta, tell the driver I'll be there in a few minutes. This won't take long."

Marta shook her head in disapproval but obeyed, scurrying down a hall. When they heard a door slam, he said more kindly than they would have expected, "So this is about Lynne Swann, is it?"

The color rose to Beth's cheeks. "You remember her?"

"I don't remember all my patients, I'm afraid. But Lynne was a special case. Please, have a seat."

Beth sat on a chintz-covered chair while Carol and Mary Kay perched on the blue carpeted stairs, unable to believe their amazing luck. Dr. Dorfman sat on a bench made for slipping on shoes, elbows resting on his knees. A brass pendulum swung in a grandfather clock next to a marble-topped table decorated with a Chinese vase. The house smelled of perfume and furniture oil.

"She wanted to be an artist, right? Always had a sketch pad and those pastels," he said, eyes crinkling.

Mary Kay couldn't help but be impressed with his ability to recall in such vivid detail. "That's commendable. I've been a nurse for two decades and I have trouble remembering who was in my care last Tuesday."

"I try not to forget my patients, especially the young and frightened ones. Lynne was in a rough situation, not much money, few relatives to support her, and living in an unfamiliar town. That aunt of hers was no piece of cake and her mother lived clear across the state, somewhere outside Pittsburgh . . ." His voice trailed off. "Anyway, how can I help?"

Beth said, "She died of cancer last week. . . ."

"That's a shame. I'm very sorry for your loss," he said sympathetically.

"Thank you," Beth said, although she wasn't sure his quick response was truly genuine. "Anyway, in her last letter, she left us with an assignment to find the daughter she gave up for adoption thirty years ago, the baby you delivered."

He pushed back his French cuffs and checked his watch, registering not so much as an inkling of shock. "Unfortunately, there's not much I can tell you. Even if I had the records, which I don't after retiring and cleaning out my office, that was a private adoption. They're sealed."

Beth had the feeling they'd be hearing that line a lot. "We understand. We were hoping you could . . ." What were they hoping? Without records, without a full memory, what could Dr. Dorfman do for them?

Carol came to her rescue. "We're hoping you knew the name of the lawyer who contacted you from Pittsburgh and arranged the adoption." She handed him her white business card. "I'm an attorney with this firm in New York and my specialty happens to be reproductive law and family matters. I might know him, if adoptions were something he did routinely."

Dorfman examined the card. "Reproductive law. That took off after I retired."

"Yes." Carol smiled thinly. "I know you're in a rush, Dr. Dorfman, and we don't want to keep you. So, if you could think of the name . . ."

Sticking the card in his breast pocket, he scrunched up his nose and looked upward. "It's not on the tip of my tongue. Larry. Gary. Shoot, can't recall."

Carol said, "Not a clue?"

"Well, it's a good bet, if he was from as far away as Pittsburgh, that we connected through our network."

"Network?" Beth asked. It sounded nefarious.

"Nothing official. More like a grapevine of physicians and lawyers supporting the same agenda."

Mary Kay cut to the chase. "In other words, pro-life."

"I've never made any secret of my feelings on abortion. It was common knowledge among local churches and charities dealing with unwed pregnant girls that I was willing to reduce my fees or eliminate them altogether, as I did in Lynne's case, in order to save a life."

"You mean, if she gave the baby up for adoption," Carol clarified.

"That was the whole idea. Motherhood is a natural, beautiful state. Nothing to be feared. But young girls who find themselves in trouble are often too hysterical to think straight. That's why abortion is a dangerous thing, you see."

"Not exactly. Do enlighten us," Mary Kay said dimly.

"They panic, act before thinking, and then live with regrets for the rest of their lives. Whereas if they're given support and assured their baby will be placed in a loving family—and believe me, there are hundreds of deserving couples waiting for children—they slowly adjust to the situation. It's embarrassing for the girl, of course."

Beth said, "Of course."

"But I believe if we had a little more shame in this soci-

ety and less permissiveness, there'd be fewer unwanted preg-
nancies and sexually transmitted diseases."

"Hard to argue with that," Carol agreed.

It was true; what could she say? She'd been horrified by
the stories Amanda brought home from as early as middle
school, what boys were forcing girls to do at parties and in
the stairwells. What girls were *offering* to do. Talk about
long-term effects. It was denigrating and dangerous to their
self-esteem and health and, yes, the concept of shame would
go a long way, she felt, toward putting an end to it.

"Anyway, my solution has a happy ending. The baby is
born, adopted, and the girl goes on with the rest of her life,
no harm done. It's a win-win for everyone. I simply can't
understand why people can't see that."

Mary Kay crossed her legs and bit back her own, quite
contrary, opinions.

"It's the only way, Mrs. . . ." He pulled out the card and
checked the name. "Goodworthy. You know, my wife is
going to come for my head if I don't get a move on, but I
promise I'll try to tap the old noggin." He got up and opened
the heavy front door. "Meanwhile, I'm afraid I've got to go."

With clearly no room for further questions, they filed
outside to where the limo was idling, Marta presumably in
the back, annoyed by her husband's willingness to speak with
three housewives from Connecticut.

"It was so very kind of you to take time to talk with us,"
Carol said. "I do hope you'll remember the lawyer's name."

Dorfman said, "I'll do my best." Then he shut the door.
And dead-bolted it.

The women got into the car, allowed the limousine to

pass them, and did a U-turn following the Dorfmans out of the gated community.

Carol turned to check on Mary Kay, who was sitting in the rear seat, eyes closed, head back as if suffering from a pounding migraine. Laughing slightly, she cooed, "You did a good job in there, MK. Lynne would have been very proud of your restraint."

"Yes," Beth said, eyeing Mary Kay in the rearview. "You were the epitome of self-control. I was watching and your fingers didn't once flex into a stranglehold."

Mary Kay moaned. "That line about a win-win for everyone. It made me sick to my stomach, literally. No kidding, I feel like I might throw up."

"There, there." Carol patted her knee. "Put it out of your mind, dear. It's all done and you'll never have to see him again. Try to think of something pleasant."

"Like martinis," Beth suggested. "I think we all deserve one, or two. How about we have one as soon as we check in."

"Nice try." Carol pointed to the darkening horizon. "But look. Lo sets the sun. Which means you have to go running."

"About that. I just realized I have to go shopping for tonight's dinner."

"I'll go shopping," Mary Kay said. "It'll give me something to do while you two run."

Carol walked her fingers up Beth's arm. "Remember. You promised."

"I did not!" Beth made a face. Running. It was the worst!

"You sure you don't want to come with us, MK?" Carol checked again.

"Like I said, I have to do the shopping." And lie down. She didn't know how Carol and Beth handled these visits so well while she felt as though she'd been put through the wringer.

They drove toward the hotel, silent in their own thoughts, processing the day, the forlorn Aunt Therese, the rather patriarchal Dr. Dorfman, who probably knew far more than he was letting on, his philosophy on abortion.

Finally, Mary Kay sat up and said, "Is it a bad sign that I thought some of what he said made sense? That part about there being a little more shame in society and everyone having a happy ending? That kind of struck a nerve."

"You know, I was thinking the same thing. We wouldn't be in this car, the three of us together again, if Lynne had aborted her baby," Beth observed.

Mary Kay let out another groan. "Don't you hate it when everything you believe and what you thought was right turns out to be wrong?"

Carol said, "I think that's called getting older and wiser."

Carol insisted on stopping by a mall and outfitting Beth to the max with lightweight cushioned running shoes and even slimming leggings that released "caffeine-infused microcapsules" that supposedly burned off fat around the thighs.

"'Clinically shown to reduce thigh size by at least an inch.'" Carol read the label Beth had tossed into the wastepaper basket.

"Oh, come on! Are you serious?"

Carol pointed to the wording as proof. "Not only caffeine, but shea butter. All you need is a piece of toast and you've got breakfast."

Honestly, the lengths women will go to to lose weight without diet and exercise, Beth thought, yanking on the leggings and wincing as the waistband cut into her doughy middle. Then again, who was she to criticize?

It wasn't as if she didn't try to lose weight. She'd taken the advice of women's magazines to park at the far end of the parking lot and drink enough water to turn her into a human sprinkler. She dipped her fork in dressing instead of pouring it on her salad, had paid her dues on the elliptical trainer and forsworn ice cream. Nevertheless, the scale didn't budge.

Obviously, this week didn't count, what with Lynne's death and then all that cooking for the reception. That macaroni and cheese she made for dinner Tuesday night, the real kind with cheddar and Gruyère and buttered bread crumbs? Medicine. Just like the hot chocolate and cookies she took to bed for dessert. Some women popped Xanax; she popped Pepperidge Farm.

Her sister would have been appalled. According to Maddy, carbs were the big evil out in L.A., where Beth got the distinct impression all anyone ate was broiled lean chicken breast and steamed broccoli spritzed with lemon. "Nothing bigger than the size of a fist and then cut off the thumb," Maddy advised, and Maddy should know since she was a size 2. If she was a size anything.

Beth ran her hands over her thighs, packed tight and smooth like a roll of refrigerator cookies. "If these work, these are the only things I'm wearing. Like, for the rest of my life."

Carol said, "They're seventy-five bucks and last twenty washes."

"Or I could just rub Folgers on my ass and get the same effect."

"Thatta girl."

While Carol and Beth went for a run, Mary Kay spruced up their two-bedroom suite by throwing around pillows she brought from home and opening the blinds. She'd tried taking a nap, but it was too noisy with guests arriving and slamming doors so she bucked up and went out to buy groceries, Beth's shopping list in hand.

Deciphering Beth's scrawl required the skill of World War II code breakers. Was that "tomatoes" or "tonic"? The word "artichokes" resembled the drawing of an ocean cruiser. And was that "wind of pimiento" or "wedge of Parmesan"?

She searched for the cheese aisle, confused. There was something about out-of-state grocery stores that made her feel off-kilter, a foreigner in a strange land. At home, she was so used to the Stop & Shop that she could have shopped blindfolded. Here, people eyed her like she was up to no good.

Right when she found the cheese case, her cell rang. Drake.

"How's my future wife?" He lowered his voice for fun. "Miss me yet?"

"Don't you know it." She scanned the names of cheeses that Lynne used to say reminded her of characters from a fantasy novel. *Airag. Edam. Sirene.* Though *Stinking Bishop* was straight from Monty Python. "I'm shopping for cheese."

"Shopping for cheese in Pennsylvania on a Saturday night. You do know how to live the high life. And why is it again that I want to marry you?"

She found the Parmesan and compared prices with a fancier, Italian brand. "Because I'm the last single woman in Marshfield and you're stuck with me."

"I wouldn't have it any other way. How's the trip to Mecca going?"

"Well, let me tell you, Mahoken, Pennsylvania, is no Mecca." She tossed the more expensive brand in her cart, which was next to another cart where a baby sat, snug and secure in a blue cotton seat kicking his fat baby legs and showing off his two bottom teeth proudly.

She waved her fingers at the baby and he grinned even wider, sending a thin line of drool to show his pleasure.

"Did you hear me?" Drake asked.

"Sorry. Hang on just a second," she said distractedly as the baby reached for the phone, but she held it out of his reach and made cooing faces that sent him into a spasm of giggles.

"Mary Kay? What's going on over there?"

"There's the cutest baby here. You should see him, Drake. He's got two little teeth and big chubby cheeks. What a charmer."

His mother returned to the cart carrying a tub of feta. She beamed at the baby and then, as new mothers often do, quickly assessed if Mary Kay were friend or foe.

Covering the phone, Mary Kay said, "He's adorable. Eight and a half months?"

"Almost exactly. He obviously likes you," she said as he waved to catch her attention.

"It's the earrings." Mary Kay touched her dangling hoops, though it was true. She had a way with babies.

"Hey, I'm beginning to get kind of jealous," Drake joked. "A new man walks onto the scene and suddenly I'm history? What kind of way is that to treat a guy?"

"You can relax. He's out of my life now." She waved

bye-bye as the mother carted him away. "What a heart-breaker."

"What you need is one of your own," he said. "Not that I'm pressuring you or anything, but, come on, Mary Kay, you have to admit you are a natural-born mother. Look how well you raised Tiffany, and you did that on your own."

She knew it was a mistake to tell him about the baby. "I'm sure you're right, but I can't think about that now," she said, pushing onward. "Right now, all my focus is on finding Lynne's baby, not my own."

"Yeah, well, I knew Lynne too, and if she were here, she'd take my side on the issue."

If Lynne were here, Mary Kay thought, surveying a wilted bunch of basil, *I wouldn't feel so alone.*

"Don't you get it? This wouldn't be just your baby, MK. This would be *our* baby. Ours. Think about it. Think about how much love we have to give."

"Sure," she said, staring at Beth's list, trying to determine if she couldn't read the words because of her crappy handwriting or because her eyes were filled with tears.

"I'm serious," he said.

"I know."

That was the problem.

If Lynne were here.

Ah, but Lynne *was* there. She knew, and she was the only one.

And now she was gone.

Mary Kay unpacked the groceries, removing the coffee

and crackers, the various vegetables Beth had requested, remembering that night, that awful night when she called Lynne in a cold sweat. Her fever had climbed past 102 and the cramps from hip bone to hip bone and across her back indicated a raging infection.

"How do you feel about making a midnight run to the emergency room? You're the only one I know with four-wheel drive."

This was before Lynne was diagnosed, before she was so familiar with the emergency room nurses she could ask about their kids by name. "I'm on my way," she'd said, pulling on a pair of jeans. "Hold tight."

With Tiffany asleep in the back of Sean's Jeep and Mary Kay shuddering in the passenger seat, Lynne drove silently through the winter storm, gripping the wheel at two and ten, pumping the brakes slightly whenever the tires lost traction. Mary Kay would remind her of this night years later during their many trips to the hospital when Lynne was the one suffering, apologizing constantly for being such a burden.

"Some nurse I am," Mary Kay had moaned as another sharp stab rippled across her back. "You'd think I'd know the warning signs by now. I am so stupid."

"You're not stupid," Lynne said. "You're unlucky."

Pelvic inflammatory disease, the scourge of the young, sexually active woman. Mary Kay's introductory go-round had been when she was twenty-two in the tiny town of Russian Mission, Alaska, where she made the unwise choice to grit her teeth and stick it out, relying on an old cure of alternating between hot and cold baths to soothe her cramps.

But hot and cold baths couldn't stop the bacteria waging a

war within her reproductive organs. A laparoscopy confirmed Mary Kay's worst fears: scarring of the uterus and, worst of all, scarring of the fallopian tubes.

Lynne held her hand as the ob-gyn interpreted the results. Mary Kay felt as if the walls were closing in. From that point on, she would be a different woman. She'd never be able to have children.

They went home and Lynne made her a cup of tea to help ease the pain from the laparoscopy. She kept up a running chatter about Tiffany and about the marvels of modern medicine, what they could do these days to cure minor inconveniences like blocked fallopian tubes.

But all Mary Kay could think of was that internist with the blue eyes and devil-may-care attitude, bounding through life clueless and asymptomatic, like most men. Or maybe, being a doctor, he knew and hadn't bothered to tell her.

Creep.

She opened a bag of pita chips and spread them on a plate around a small dish of low-fat hummus for Carol and Beth when they returned. Folding up the bag, she collapsed on the couch and replayed the scenario again. Every possible outcome sucked. Simply sucked.

"We're back!" Beth flounced in and threw herself onto the chair, red-faced and sweaty, her brown hair in a messy bun. "That was torture."

Carol, who hadn't so much as perspired, deposited the white key card onto the table. "No, it wasn't. You loved it."

"I loved the end when you said 'last round.' That's the part I loved. As for the rest of what you put me through, I'm pretty sure it violated the Geneva Conventions."

Rallying, Mary Kay clapped her hands once. "How

about you guys hit the showers. And when you come out, I've got hors d'oeuvres and we'll discuss martinis."

"That sounds lovely. I'll cook." Beth winced as she pushed herself out of the chair and headed for the shower in the single room where she was spending the night.

"You OK, Mary Kay?" Carol stood in the doorway of the double they were sharing. "You seem kind of quiet."

"Just tired. I'll get a second wind."

Twenty minutes later, she did feel better. Beth had slipped into her pj's, her wet hair wrapped in a towel. She produced an iPod of ridiculously girlish songs, Lynne's favorites, which she plugged into mini speakers. As they listened to Cyndi Lauper's "Girls Just Want to Have Fun," Beth sautéed diced garlic in olive oil and tomatoes as a base for her famous pasta puttanesca with artichokes, kalamata olives, capers, and a touch of balsamic vinegar and crushed red pepper.

Meanwhile, Carol and Mary Kay tweaked their lemon martinis, a recipe that had taken them, no kidding, close to nine years to perfect. Not that they had perfected it. It was absurd how much time and effort they'd put into adding more limoncello, less limoncello, citrus vodka versus regular versus lemon, grated lemon rind, Cointreau, no Cointreau. You'd have thought they were working on the Manhattan Project, and that America's security—nay, world peace!— depended on mixing this martini so it was not too sweet and not too tart.

"It's a tough job," Mary Kay said, measuring out a shot of limoncello, "but someone's gotta do it."

"You guys have been working on the perfect lemon martini since when?" Beth asked, pitting olives.

"Since Cape Cod." Carol tasted their latest. Citrus vodka.

Limoncello. A squeeze of lemon juice and dash of bitters, shaken vigorously with ice. She made a face and shook her head. "Not quite."

Mary Kay dumped it out and, this go-round, left out the bitters. "Cape Cod was the first time we tried inventing our own martinis because we'd left DeeDee's cookbook at home." She rinsed the martini shaker, waiting for Carol's review of the newer version. "Well?"

Carol licked her lower lip. "I think it's almost there. You can definitely taste the lemon, though it's a tad tangy. How about running sugar around the rim?"

"We don't have any sugar."

"Yes, we do." Beth waved her spoon toward the tiny packets by the tiny coffeemaker. They ignored her.

"Then let's try zesting lemon, a touch, with a double shot of limoncello and regular vodka."

Mary Kay cracked open a new bottle of Grey Goose. "The sacrifices we make in the pursuit of perfection."

Beth wiped her hands on a towel and turned off the sauce. "Here. Let me try this."

Mary Kay shook the martini and poured out a glass of the frosted yellow liquid. In one sunny sip it all came back to her—the Cape in April, fog rolling across the Atlantic blanketing their tiny cottage in mist, Lynne with her jeans rolled up to her ankles, laughing as the waves splashed her soaking wet. Always laughing.

It was their first trip together as a group, their first without husbands or kids. A babysitter was taking care of Tiffany, and Kevin and Kyle were in Sean's care. David was with Elsie and Chat so Marc could use the weekend for writing. Jeff wasn't on call, so he could look after Amanda and Jon.

They felt incredibly guilty for caring and not caring, for daring to be free.

They rented the cottage for a long weekend, which they could do because it was the off-season, right on the beach in Wellfleet. It had a tiny fireplace and two musty bedrooms. During the day, they took long walks up and down the coast as far as they could go, arm in arm, talking about kids, jobs, books, the mothers they loved who drove them batty. And husbands.

After the sun set, they'd boiled lobsters and dined on raw oysters, a new experience for Lynne, who chased each one with a gulp of martini. Lemon martinis. Luscious, lemony, powerful martinis with a kick. That was the start of Carol and Mary Kay's quest to mix the ultimate martini, whether that be lemon, ginger, chocolate, or just plain gin. They became obsessed.

That was the weekend when they convinced Carol to return to Deloutte Watkins, her old law firm, part-time so she wouldn't feel so trapped in Marshfield. It was the weekend they told Mary Kay to break up with that egotistical anesthesiologist Connor what's-his-name because she deserved better than a man who rated her daily wardrobe on a scale of A+ (never) to C- (frequently). That was the weekend when Beth got truly, completely, ecstatically inebriated for the first time in her life. And loved every crazy minute.

That was the weekend Lynne mentioned that the flu symptoms she'd been experiencing for months weren't going away, that she felt "off," though the doctors assured her it was nothing. And they, her best friends, did too, because that's what best friends say.

It's nothing, Lynne. You're just stressed. Relax.

Relaxed, all right. Giddy on lemon martinis and oysters and the sheer joy of no-holds-barred irresponsibility, they left the cottage that night and ran through the mist to the ice-cold Atlantic Ocean. Sending themselves into hysterics, they dared one another to jump in the waves, bowling over in laughter as they reached for one another's hands in the pitch-black, salty darkness. It was nutty. They could have been sucked into the undertow and drowned. They could have died of hypothermia. But they didn't.

Beth couldn't remember when she felt so free, so lemony-light and fizzy.

Perhaps Lynne was right. Maybe it was time she let go, because you never knew, you just never knew, what the universe had in store.

Throwing back the entire drink, she plunked the glass on the hotel table, shaking her brain clear. "You know what's missing?"

"Cointreau?" Mary Kay suggested.

Carol said, "Fresh lemon juice?"

"Lynne."

Then Beth cranked the next song on Lynne's playlist—the Spice Girls' "Wannabe"—and danced, the towel falling off her head as she waved her sautéing spoon in the air, twirling around their tiny suite living room.

Mary Kay and Carol downed their martinis and joined in, dancing to Sharon Jones and Amy Winehouse and Green Day and Janis Joplin's "Piece of My Heart," Beth carefully carrying Mary Kay's flowers to the kitchen, snuffing the candles and pushing aside the coffee table, maybe once or twice jumping off and onto the couch, not caring if management called to complain.

"Whoo-hoo!" they shouted when Gloria Gaynor belted out "I Will Survive," the song that Lynne played at the start of every chemo session, the anthem that had kept her alive past the crucial five years, past when the doctors and specialists and grim statistics clinically insisted she should be dead.

They raised their fists and pounded the air, stomped their feet, for they, too, had been petrified. And like Lynne, they grew strong. They were learning how to carry on. They would survive. As long as they knew how to love, they knew they'd stay alive.

This was the song they played again and again, twirling and twirling and twirling and twirling until the pain of losing Lynne rose up and out, spinning into orbit, where it lost its force. Where it became nothing but a memory to be forgotten, leaving behind only her life and love and passions and her brilliant smile.

Twirling and twirling and twirling.

Chapter Ten

That night, Carol had the strangest dream.

She was floating on Kindlewah Lake under a gentle summer rain. Jeff was next to her, his arm across her back as they lay facedown, side by side, naked. Mary Kay and Beth sat on the opposite bank in lawn chairs, drinking martinis and chatting, and Lynne was there too. Sort of. Drifting in and out, gliding across the water, hands behind her back as if she were skating.

Carol felt like she'd been rescued from drowning and was recovering in the sun, even though it was raining. "That was strange, wasn't it?" she murmured to Jeff, his skin so warm and smooth against her body. "What was that about? Did it even happen?"

Jeff, in the voice of Dr. Dorfman, turned his head and said, "Motherhood is a natural state. Nothing to be feared."

"Hmm," Carol replied, yawning, thinking, *Whatever.*

"If there were more shame, less permissiveness . . . ,"

he drawled, suddenly humming the gypsy dance from *Carmen*.

Wait! It was more than just a song. It had *meaning*.

Amanda!

Forcing herself to consciousness, Carol extended a hand from beneath the covers and groped for her cell phone, from which Amanda's ringtone blared. She tried to answer perkily, but it was a lost cause. Her voice was like sandpaper.

"Mother?" Amanda was alarmingly youthful and awake. "Are you OK?"

"Sure, I'm OK." Carol sat up and blinked at the clock, trying to get her bearings. This wasn't her apartment in New York or her house in Connecticut. Oh, right. Pennsylvania. With these heavy, rubberized hotel curtains designed for airplane pilots and nighttime travelers, you could never tell what time of day it was. Ten thirty? No, no, no. Checkout was at eleven. There had to be some mistake.

"Mother?" Amanda said again.

"Is it ten thirty?" Carol checked with Mary Kay, who, blinded by her lavender silk eye mask, was fast asleep in the other queen bed, dead to the world.

"Ten thirty-five to be exact. I woke you, didn't I?"

"Not really. I was kind of dozing."

Amanda was doubtful. "Where are you, anyway?"

Good question. Reorienting herself, Carol said, "Pennsylvania. Someplace off I-80."

"Oh, yeah. Dad told me last night you were on a road trip with Tiffany's mom and Mrs. Levinson."

Funny how Amanda refused to call Beth and Mary Kay by their first names, a holdover from when she was in grade school. Beth would probably always be Mrs. Levinson to

Amanda, just as Lynne, her cherished elementary school art teacher, would forever be Mrs. Flannery. As the mother of Amanda's favorite babysitter, Tiffany, only Mary Kay Le-Blanc was spared. She was "Tiffany's mom," and nothing else.

Hold on. Back up. "You spoke with Dad?"

"When I got your message that you had something really important to discuss, I tried to reach you last night but you didn't answer. So I called Dad to ask him what was up."

Carol was positive her phone never rang the night before, and she'd positioned it on the kitchen counter so she could hear it while they were singing and dancing. Besides, if Amanda hadn't been able to reach her, why didn't she leave a message?

"Did Dad tell you what was up?"

"Uh-huh. Since I couldn't reach you—since I can *never* reach you—he explained about the house. He said I needed to call you so . . . here I am, calling you."

Pressure built under the bridge of Carol's nose, a sure sign of a burgeoning headache. This standoff with Amanda was eating away at her soul. If they didn't reach some sort of rapprochement soon, they were very much in jeopardy of ending up like Lynne and her mother, a cold, unyielding prospect that would leave them both miserable.

"I'm so glad you did. You know, I've been thinking a lot about us, lately. I *miss* us."

"Yup." Amanda cut her off. "So Dad said you have to sell the house."

There was a stirring in the other bed. Mary Kay was awake, eye mask on her forehead, smiling encouragingly.

"Is that OK?" Carol pressed.

"I don't know if it's *OK*. In an ideal existence, I'd have voted to keep you both on the same island, but it's not really my choice, is it?"

"In a way, it is. After all, this is your house too, your childhood home."

"I'm going to be twenty-one next spring, Mom. I'm an adult, not a child anymore."

Her heart sank, making Carol feel like a hypocrite. All those years of slogging through young motherhood, counting the days until her time was her own and wishing she could sleep through the night undisturbed, and now she was feeling sentimental. As her own mother used to say about parenthood, the hours inch by like years and the years fly by like hours.

"But what about Christmas?" she said, clutching on to the last vestige of childhood. "You love coming home to Connecticut for Christmas."

"Suddenly you care about Christmas?"

"Of course! Don't you remember the fun we used to have decorating the house and trying to string lights on the pine tree in the front yard? I swear, every year your father nearly broke his neck climbing that—"

"My father," Amanda said, "is no longer your husband. And our home is no longer our home. Don't you get it, Mom? Our family doesn't exist anymore. The Goodworthys are neither good nor worthy."

"Don't say that. A family is still a family even if the parents separate."

"Some families are, but not ours. And don't call me naïve. When Molly's parents split, we were all for it because those two were fighting constantly. Even Molly was relieved. But you guys . . . you *never* fought."

Carol resisted the urge to jump at the chance to tell Amanda that it was precisely because they *hadn't* fought that their marriage fell apart. Jeff bottled up his feelings. It was like being married to a brick wall. "Sometimes not fighting is a sign of a communication breakdown."

"Someone's been watching too much Dr. Phil," Amanda scoffed. "Anyway, Christmas is a nonissue. Like I told Dad, I'm going to France this year for Christmas. I met someone last semester in Paris and he asked me to come visit."

Carol pictured a dark-haired French scam artist in an ill-fitting suit pinching a Gauloise and trailing behind Amanda in the Louvre, a swindler who would shake her down for every last dime and leave her with a broken heart and a case of the clap. Dear. God. No.

"We've been Facebooking and just the other day he asked me what I was doing over the holidays, if I'd like to spend them with him."

"In Paris!" Carol didn't mean to scream, but she couldn't help it. "How well do you know this guy?"

"Well enough. He's the brother of a friend of my room-mate from junior year abroad."

The headache grew. "Which is to say, not at all."

Amanda was silent. "Actually, quite well. Even Dad knows him through Facebook."

Naturally, Jeff would be more involved in their daughter's life than she. Then again, it was kind of difficult to be up to speed with your daughter's comings and goings when she didn't give you the time of day. "How old is he?"

"Old enough."

"What does he do for a living?"

"We're not in court, so you can quit with the cross-examination. We're just getting together for Christmas. It's no big deal. Why do you make everything into such a big deal?"

Carol motioned to Mary Kay and mouthed, *Help me!* Mary Kay jumped up and went to the kitchen, returning, by some miracle of miracles, with Carol's favorite: a Starbucks latte, soy, three shots. "We gotta go," she whispered, pointing to the clock.

Just as well, because Carol did not have enough caffeine in her system to handle the news that her daughter would be spending Christmas with some unemployed French drifter. "Look, Amanda, they're kicking us out of the hotel, so let's discuss this later."

"There's nothing to discuss. I've got enough of my own money saved to buy myself a plane ticket. It's not your decision."

Carol inhaled a fortifying sip. "I meant the house."

"No need to talk about that, either. If Dad says you've got to sell it, then you've got to sell it. You never asked me if it was OK if you left my father. So why do you care what I think about selling the house?" And with that dramatic sign-off, she hung up.

Carol held the phone in her hand, shaking.

"You poor thing," Mary Kay said, sitting on the edge of the bed, her own cup of coffee between her knees. "That sounded rough."

"You have no idea." Carol mechanically took another sip. It had no taste. "And the kicker is, that was the longest conversation we've had in months, maybe years."

Mary Kay put down her cup and, patting Carol as she passed, went to her suitcase to find clothes. "You know the only reason she's acting out is because she loves you so much."

"You must have me mistaken for Jeff."

Mary Kay collected a bra and blouse. "She loves Jeff, sure, but it's you she identifies with. You're her hero, Carol. Remember that paper she wrote in middle school about how she wanted to be a lawyer someday? She parroted your most famous cases word for word."

"Well, she doesn't want to be a lawyer now. She wants to be an artist, like Lynne. It was Lynne Amanda turned to when I left Jeff. It was Lynne who, even in her sickness, stepped up to the plate and did what I couldn't—be her mother."

Beth appeared at the door in black pants and gray sweater, clutching her own white paper cup of coffee. "How's that soy latte working for you?"

"It's perfect. Thanks." Carol did her best to look grateful.

"She just got off the phone with Amanda." Mary Kay gave Beth a knowing look. "And now we're talking about Amanda's relationship with Lynne."

Beth sat on the bed with a bounce as Mary Kay slipped off to the bathroom to take a shower and get dressed. "That still bugs you, huh?"

"It doesn't *bug* me," Carol answered, finding it hard not to feel slightly defensive at the insinuation that she was in any way jealous of Lynne. "But it does remind me of what a failure I've been."

"Lynne didn't see it that way."

Carol tried the latte again. "She probably did."

"No, she didn't. The way she saw it, you two are so similar that you couldn't be in the same room without setting off sparks. Lynne thought of herself as a buffer, kind of like insulation."

"Insulation." Such a quirky but appropriate comparison. Leave it to Lynne.

"You know, the kind you wrap around wires so they don't touch each other and ignite."

Carol had never thought of it that way. It used to bother her that Lynne always seemed to know things about Amanda's life. Nothing major. Nothing bad. Usually complimentary. Like when a professor had chosen her as the only student to display her artwork in a show. Carol had resented the bond between her daughter and her friend, but it never occurred to Carol that Lynne might have been working behind the scenes to repair their relationship. And now it was too late to say thank you.

"I wish I'd known." Carol put her cup on the bedside table. "I just took her interest for granted."

"She wasn't doing it for the accolades," Beth said. "She was trying to keep you two connected because she knew how much you needed each other."

"Or maybe . . ." Carol had a thought. "Maybe she didn't want us to end up like her and Eunice."

Beth considered this. "Could be." She nodded. "After what Therese said yesterday, you're probably right. Sounds like Lynne and her mother were close once."

"You could say the same thing about Amanda and me."

The bathroom door opened, releasing a puff of white steam. Mary Kay stepped out in her black lace bra and matching underwear, a white towel wrapped around her hair as she brushed her teeth. "You two still talking about Amanda?"

"Partly," Beth said. "We just figured out that maybe one reason why Lynne was so eager to keep the lines of communication open between Carol and Amanda was because of her messed-up relationship with her own mother."

Mary Kay spit into the sink and ran the water. "That makes sense."

"Now that I know that, I feel like even more of a jerk," Carol said, slipping out of her T-shirt. "I should have thanked her."

Mary Kay unwrapped the towel, from which tumbled a mass of black wet curls. "It's not too late. Look at it this way, maybe that's something you and Amanda can work on together—finding a way to thank Lynne."

Carol reached into her suitcase and stopped, the answer suddenly clear. "You're right. Lynne tried to bring us together in life. What better way to honor her memory than the two of us reuniting after her death?"

It was the sort of sweet, practical advice Lynne would have given if she'd been there. And who was to say that in some way she wasn't?

⚜

That morning, Beth was in rare form.

Up since eight, she'd packed the kitchen, wiped down all the counters, and even managed to squeeze in the free hotel breakfast—artificially yellow eggs, stale toast, and sausages that didn't taste quite right. For Mary Kay and Carol, she'd pilfered a green banana, a mushy apple, and a couple of light yogurts. But the coffee didn't pass, so she got in the car and hunted down a Starbucks, thoughtfully tailoring each order to their needs before returning to the hotel and checking out to prevent them from being charged another day.

Now she had her bag in tow, ready to go. "They said the room was already paid. How did that happen?"

Carol pretended to be busy organizing her work stuff.

"Did you pay, Mary Kay?"

Mary Kay grabbed the handle of her suitcase and un-latched the door. "Not me. Must have been Carol."

Carol shrugged as if she, too, were clueless, though she wasn't. She'd paid the bill the night before, partly to save Beth the money and also as a way of mollifying the manager, who'd called twice to report that guests had filed noise complaints.

"Hmmm. A mysterious bill payer. I must get to the bottom of this." Beth dragged her suitcase out, limping.

"You OK?" Mary Kay asked. "You look a little sore."

"I am sore. I made the mistake of sitting down and reading the Sunday paper. Now I can hardly move from that running we did yesterday."

"You just need to stretch more before and afterward," Carol said, wistfully conducting a last-minute scan of the room, boring and lifeless now that Mary Kay had packed up her candles and pillows and stuck the flowers in the lobby. They'd had such a terrific night. It was almost a shame to leave. Plus, it was raining and a Sunday, a day to be home in sweats doing laundry and lollygagging on the couch reading the comics.

On rainy autumn Sundays like this, she and Jeff would make a big pot of chili, much of which they'd freeze and eat as leftovers throughout the month. This wasn't just any old chili. This was the works. Chicken, beef, pork sausage mixed with sautéed chopped onions, garlic, chili powder and cumin, mustard, high-quality tomato paste, Worcestershire sauce, two kinds of beans, black olives, red pepper flakes, and (her secret) a handful of fresh dill.

A football game would be playing in the background and Jeff, puttering around the house fixing this or that, would stop by the TV to shout at Bill Belichick while the kids did their homework in the living room or upstairs. If it were cold, too, he'd build a fire in the fireplace and she'd make both cornbread and an apple pie along with a crunchy, tart salad.

Then they'd eat early and watch *The Simpsons* or maybe a movie. Sometimes Carol read the *New York Times Magazine* in the bath and then climbed into clean sheets, snuggling up to Jeff and listening to the rain beat against the windows, the cold wind whipping across the lake. There was delicious comfort in being assured that her family was under that same roof, safe and warm, as the elements battled outside.

She never fully appreciated the quiet joy of domesticity. Before, it had always seemed so claustrophobic, which was why she'd find herself awake a few hours later, roaming the house, an inner restlessness making it impossible for her to sleep through the night.

They loaded their bags into the Highlander and Carol climbed into the back, adjusted her safety belt, her cell phone, BlackBerry, and legal pad, checked her pens. Then she booted up the computer on her lap and opened the file for the memorandum of law she was working on. Usually, after a few minutes of switching gears, she could delve right into work. Not this morning. This morning she was recovering from her martinis and Amanda's call and the dream of Jeff's skin against hers.

Mary Kay started the car and they headed out for their second day on the road.

Somewhere on I-80, about an hour into their trip, Beth put down the sock she was knitting and asked, "Aren't you curious about what Lynne's daughter looks like?"

Mary Kay and Carol were kind of stunned that they hadn't already asked themselves this question.

"She could be anyone we've come across," Beth said. "We might have walked right past her in the mall when we went shopping yesterday. She could have been at the Mc-Donald's where we changed to meet Aunt Therese."

"I hope not," Mary Kay said. "That was a pretty scuzzy Mickey D's."

Beth giggled. She was unusually chipper this morning.

"What's gotten into you?" Mary Kay asked, amused.

"I can't help it. I know I should be dragging my red wagon, but I'm so . . . giddy. Is that wrong?"

"Why would it be wrong?"

"Because Lynne's gone, and I don't know"—she shrugged—"I've stopped feeling sad. Instead, I feel kind of liberated."

"Liberated?" Mary Kay cocked her head. "Because Lynne's dead?"

"Not *because* Lynne's dead. Certainly not. It's more like . . ." Beth tried to phrase this the right way. "You know how you always say you'll do something, something big like writing a book or moving to another country, but then little problems tie you down?"

"What kind of little problems?" Carol asked from the backseat, where she was searching case law and paying only half attention.

Beth turned slightly, thinking. "Oh, like how Marc can't work on his book full-time the way he wants because we need his paycheck. We can't move because of my parents. That's what I mean by getting bogged down."

"With all due respect, in the category of worries, those don't sound so little," Mary Kay said.

"They are when you think about Lynne and how there was so much left for her to do with her life, finessing her art and, of course, finding Julia. Then she got cancer and—zip—that was that."

Mary Kay and Carol couldn't argue with Beth's logic.

"So, that's what I mean about feeling liberated. Last night, remembering how we were at the Cape, I realized there's no value in holding back. Every once in a while, you gotta let go."

Carol saved her place in the memorandum, unable to take one more soporific paragraph of arguments. "And where would you go, Mrs. Levinson?"

"Italy."

"Italy?" they chimed.

"I've never been. I've always wanted to go to Amalfi."

"Amalfi's easy enough," Mary Kay said. "Just buy a ticket and go. Where else?"

Beth reddened slightly, embarrassed to be embarrassed by an insecurity that had plagued her since high school. "It's not so much *where* I'd go as *what* I'd do. Like get a makeover. Nothing too radical," she added quickly, grabbing a hank of her hair. "Just a new haircut and some highlights so I'm not so . . . drab. Lynne was always after me to spruce myself up. She claimed it would, you know, boost my confidence." Beth punctuated this with a slight laugh.

"To feel good you've got to look good—is that it?" Carol asked, trying to keep a straight face.

"Exactly." Beth dropped her hair. "What do you think, MK?"

"I think Lynne would be pleased as punch that somehow her death finally convinced you to head off to sunny Italy and get a makeover, not necessarily in that order."

"Let's make sure that when this trip is over, you do just that, get a makeover," Carol said. "The whole kit and ka-boodle."

"The whole kit and kaboodle sounds expensive," Beth said.

Mary Kay dismissed this with a flick of the left blinker. "No sweat. It'll be our treat, our way of paying you back for driving your car all over hell's half acre."

"No, you guys have done enough already. You bought all the food and drink last night, Mary Kay, and, Carol, you got me the running gear and one of you paid for that hotel room. I'm no Blanche DuBois, relying on the kindness of strangers."

"Are you calling us strangers?" Carol asked, searching her iPhone for spas around Marshfield, thinking the coolest thing would be to invite Beth to New York and surprise her with a trip to the Frédéric Fekkai Salon on Fifth Avenue.

"I'm just saying I'm not a moocher."

Mary Kay reached over and pinched Beth's cheek. "You're not a moocher—you're a *smoocher*."

"You're a hootchie-coocher," Carol added.

Beth leaned her head against the window in defeat. "You

two are impossible." Though, secretly, she was smiling with delight.

It was a shame they couldn't do the makeover right away, but today they had to rush across this humongous expanse that was Pennsylvania in order to catch Lynne's mother at the nursing home.

They hadn't exactly been looking forward to breaking the news to Eunice before. But after hearing Therese's tragic story about how Lynne had been Eunice's miracle baby, they were dreading this meeting even more.

Beth reached into her purse and pulled out the letter that Lynne had written to her mother. "I can't tell you how tempted I am to read this. If there were a hot kettle here, I'd steam it open."

"I know. I'm dying to know what it says," Carol added.

"What if Lynne lashes out at Eunice and calls her every name in the book?"

"That doesn't sound like Lynne's style," Carol said. "And if the letter is nasty—which I doubt—we'll be there for her."

"Look, this is what we'll do," Mary Kay said. "We'll calmly introduce ourselves and tell Eunice what happened. Maybe we should mention that Lynne had always spoken about her in loving terms. . . ."

"But!" Beth interrupted. "She never—"

"I know. But sometimes a spoonful of sugar makes the medicine go down, you know? Would it hurt to say that Lynne loved her? She did, deep down."

Beth dumped her knitting in a plastic Ziploc bag and pulled the blue zipper tight. "You're right. Sometimes it's OK to lie."

Sometimes, Mary Kay thought, trying not to obsess too much over her own lying to Drake. *But rarely.*

Outside Lynne's hometown of Calais, they stopped for gas and to go to the bathroom and freshen up before heading down to the Beckwood Landing Assisted Living Center. There was no other option besides JJ's Brew 'N' Burn, a truck stop with tractor trailers lined up spewing diesel fumes.

"The last time we were at a truck stop together," Mary Kay said as she and Carol left Beth to pump the gas, "was on our way back from the Cape."

It took a beat, but Carol remembered, bursting out in laughter. "And we accidentally went into the men's room."

Mary Kay opened the heavy glass doors for two truckers. "It wasn't our fault. The men's room wasn't even marked. At least, not very well."

"What I can't get over is that you, me, and Lynne got as far as the stalls before we realized something was off. Lynne asked, 'Since when do women's rooms have urinals?' And I remember wondering if that was some liberal Massachusetts law, coed bathrooms."

"Until that guy at the sink said, 'I think you ladies meant to take a left instead of a right. Not that I'm complaining.'" Mary Kay shook her head. "If a guy had done that in a women's room, could you imagine?"

"We'd call the cops!"

While Mary Kay and Carol went to the bathroom, Beth took the opportunity to call Marc. She didn't like to interrupt him while he was writing, but all that talk about Amalfi had made her homesick.

"Well, hello!" Marc said, delighted. "And how are we feeling this fine morning?"

She glanced at the phone suspiciously. What was up with him? "Fine. Why?"

"Oh, no reason."

"I called to say I love you."

"I know."

"You do?" She eyed the pump as the numbers flipped upward: $12.46, $13.10. The price of gas was out of control.

"Yes. You said so last night over and over and over again. Marc, I love you *sooooo* much."

Oh! She cringed, completely forgetting that she'd drunk-dialed him after a few too many lemon martinis. "I'm so sorry."

"Don't be. It was adorable."

"But drunk-dialing? It spells pathetic loser."

"No, it doesn't. I haven't heard you that gleeful in weeks."

"I didn't have that much to drink, actually. It's that I went for a run with Carol and I was a little dehydrated."

"A run, you say?"

Beth could picture him sitting with his legs up on the dining-room table, the laptop open before him, drinking a cup of coffee and loving this. "That's right, wiseguy. A run. Carol took me three miles, and you know what? It wasn't that bad. Think I might do it again tonight. Also, what would you say if I colored my hair? Nothing wild, just some highlights."

"No matter what you do, you'll be beautiful to me."

Somewhere along the way someone must have handed Marc the magic guidebook for how husbands should respond to their wives.

"Listen, I'm glad you called. I just got off the phone with your sister jabbering a mile a minute about Chat's test results tomorrow."

Right. Maddy had called last night during their impromptu party, but Beth hadn't heard the phone so she'd left a message on voice mail.

"I told her that I'd go with your parents to his appointment tomorrow, but apparently that's not enough. She says she needs to talk to you ASAP."

"I'll call her as soon as I get off the phone. How is Dad, by the way? Have you heard anything?"

"All I heard was that he went out for nine holes of golf yesterday and shot two under par."

Beth smiled. That was her father, all right. No clucking hens like her mother or sister would keep him off the links on a sunny autumn day. "Trying to squeeze in what he can before the snow falls."

"You got that right. And, Beth?"

The pump turned off, but she cocked the nozzle to deposit the final drops, as she'd learned in her penny-pinching research. "Yeah?"

"Come home safely, OK? It's been disturbingly quiet without you around."

"Promise." She hung up the nozzle, got her receipt, and called her sister. "Finally!" Maddy exclaimed. "I called over and over last night. Where were you?"

"In our hotel in Pennsylvania." Beth caught her reflection in the gas pump. The long hair wrapped in a messy bun, the old turtleneck and cardigan. No makeup. With this level of frump, she was giving librarians a bad name. "I must not have heard the phone, what with the music turned up full blast."

"Music! I thought this was supposed to be some sort of dharma trip."

Maddy could get herself so worked up over nothing. "It's not a dharma trip. It's a trip to fulfill Lynne's last wishes, and Lynne wouldn't have minded if we cranked a few tunes and drank a couple of martinis in her memory."

"If you ask me, that sounds like just another girls' night on the town."

"Trust me, Mahoken's not much of a town. Is everything OK? We're about to get back on the road."

"Everything's fine. I'm just worried about Dad's appointment tomorrow. I got absolutely no sleep last night worrying that he'll get the results and he'll need some kind of procedure. I know you and I have gone over and over this, but I just don't feel right about him staying at Grace when the finest heart surgeons in the world are only a commute away."

"It'll be OK, Mad. Marc will be there. He won't let Mom or Dad make a decision without first running it by us."

"I know, but what if they need to make a life-or-death decision on the spot? What if they need to do an emergency angioplasty or open-heart surgery or a triple bypass? Mom has trouble choosing between a plaid or floral couch slipcover by herself, and no offense, but Marc's in no position to call the shots about Dad's heart. It'd be a weight off my mind if you were there tomorrow."

Beth was starting to get frustrated. These were routine tests in a reputable hospital, and Marc was perfectly capable of handling the situation. If Maddy was so concerned, then why wasn't she hopping a plane from L.A.? After forty years, Beth was getting tired of putting up with her sister's bossiness. And she was sick of putting everyone else's needs ahead of her own.

"Calm down, Maddy, and take a deep breath. I'm not going to overreact and run home. There's no reason. You know everything will be OK with Dad, and if Marc needs us, he'll call us. Besides, I'm only a few hours away if there's an emergency. But right now, this is what I need to do for my nearest and dearest friend. Go forward, not back."

There was an icy silence.

"OK, Beth. I guess you win."

A begrudging victory. Madeleine had never let her win at anything, not in their ice-skating races or Monopoly or even in school.

"Just cross your fingers that nothing bad happens, because it'll be on your watch."

And with that, Maddy hung up the phone.

Mary Kay and Carol emerged from the truck stop in their suits, looking fresh as daisies, their hair neatly pinned back, pearls in their ears. Handing Beth the keys, Mary Kay said, "You wanna drive after you get fixed up?"

Beth shook her head, her hair falling over her eyes. Maybe Maddy was right. What had she been thinking leaving Dad alone with Mom when they had these tough decisions to make? What had come over her? She shouldn't be dancing around a hotel room like some eighth grader on a class field trip.

"I'm thinking maybe I should rent a car and drive back to Connecticut," she said quietly. "Dad's getting those results tomorrow and I need to be there. I should have followed my instincts and let you two take this trip alone."

Mary Kay said, "Did you just get off the phone with Madeleine?"

Beth nodded.

Mary Kay sighed. "This is Maddy's way of working off some of her anxiety. She can't take it out on your parents, so she takes it out on you. Meanwhile, your dad's in good hands at Grace, and Marc's there. He's no slouch." She wrapped an arm around Beth's shoulder. "Everything will be fine."

"You think?"

"I don't think. I know. Now, go get yourself all dolled up and I'll call Steve Applebaum, the head of Grace's cardiac unit, and ask him if he wouldn't mind stopping by when Chat gets those results tomorrow. Steve and I go way back and he'll give your dad extra-special attention. Does that make you feel better?"

Beth nodded, feeling overwhelmed and thankful that she had a friend like Mary Kay. "It helps. It really does. You're the best, MK."

"I'm better when I'm bad."

As they headed toward their rendezvous with Eunice, Beth thought about the week after she gave birth to David, when Maddy breezed in from the West Coast bearing delicate baby clothes that had to be hand washed in cold water and then reshaped on a drying rack. She'd bought them on Rodeo Drive, a hop and a skip from the home she and her movie-producer husband shared in Beverly Hills.

Beth remembered the afternoon clearly. Elsie perched on the edge of the couch, rapt as Maddy rattled off a list of celebrities she'd met at this party and that. Ron Howard and "the Winklers," Demi Moore and Bruce Willis, and some actors they didn't know then, but would.

Beth nursed David and listened to her sister, trim and chic, her pale bleach-blond hair yanked tight into a chignon, wearing a silk pantsuit of such a perishable winter white that holding her infant nephew—the supposed reason for the impromptu visit—was out of the question. Beth seriously doubted Maddy was actually on a "first-name basis" with Julia Roberts—or "Jules" to her and everyone else in L.A.— but what could she say? The only option was to suck it up and look impressed.

Maddy took a breath and put a delicate hand to her throat, turning to Beth as if she'd just noticed her presence. "Do you have some water? Those cross-country flights are so dehydrating."

"In the kitchen." Beth thumbed over her shoulder. "Good ole Connecticut well water. Remember that?"

Elsie was about to fetch a glass when Beth saw her chance for escape from Maddy's Hollywood name dropping. "That's OK, Ma. I'll get it," she said, getting up with David still at her breast and heading into the kitchen.

With one arm, she got down two glasses and then flipped on the faucet.

That's when she saw Lynne shoveling snow off her front steps, singing "I Feel Pretty" at the top of her lungs. Having moved only a couple months before, she and Lynne hadn't had a chance to meet, really, aside from exchanging friendly waves. Just a couple of pregnant women passing each other in the night.

Beth filled the glasses and then knocked on the window. Lynne turned right and then left. Her face broke into a brilliant smile. She pointed to David in Beth's arms. "Congrats!" she yelled. "Me too." She held up two fingers. "Twins."

"Beth?" her sister called from the living room. "Mom and I were just talking about my schedule. Do you know if you and Marc can get the baby christened this weekend, or will I have to return later in the summer?"

Rolling her eyes, Beth looked back at Lynne, humming and shoveling. She put David over her shoulder, buttoned up, grabbed her coat, and went outside to introduce herself, leaving Elsie and Maddy in the living room, gossiping, while she and Lynne spent the rest of the afternoon talking and playing with their babies.

That was the beginning of her friendship with Lynne and the end of her relationship with Madeleine.

As she stepped out of JJ's in her suit, her hair tidy and lipstick neatly applied, ready to greet Eunice, it broke Beth's heart to think that, in the end, she had lost them both.

Chapter Eleven

The Beckwood Landing Assisted Living Center was a collection of interconnected white clapboard buildings set
in a wooded vale, protected from the hustle and bustle of the
workday world. Each unit sported its own lawn marked off by
railroad ties. There were flower boxes on some of the windows and pinecone wreaths on a few of the doors. The main
building anchored the center of the complex. To the left, a
low building with ramps suggested a nursing wing.

Beth parked the car in the visitors' lot and the women sat
for a while contemplating what lay in store for them beyond
its tidy exterior. It was so quiet here, so peaceful. Somewhere
inside, Lynne's mother was, perhaps, chatting with friends or
reading a book, never suspecting that by nightfall she would
be in the throes of unfathomable grief.

As an NICU nurse, Mary Kay was all too familiar with
the horrors of informing parents that their child had died.
Granted, the children were babies and the parents usually

young, but if there was anything she'd learned in her long nursing career, it was that there was no mandatory age maximum for grief. A mother is a mother from the moment her baby is first placed in her arms until eternity. It didn't matter if her child were three, thirteen, or thirty. When a child passes before the parents, it is devastating.

They got out and were heading toward the entrance when Mary Kay stopped them. "Hold on," she said, reaching for Beth's and Carol's hands. They made a small circle in the parking lot.

"We all know this is going to be heart-wrenching," she said. "But we have to keep our focus on Lynne and remember that our job is to be her representatives. We're delivering a message she was too sick to deliver herself."

"In a way, it's almost as if we're reuniting Lynne with her mom," said Beth.

"Exactly." Mary Kay gave each hand a squeeze. "We can do this because we are strong and we are together. Lynne would never have asked us if she didn't think we were capable."

And with that, they ventured forth.

The automatic doors parted and they entered a warmly lit lobby lined with original artwork. The faint strains of a Mozart concerto played over hidden speakers as they approached a mahogany reception desk. It was not what they'd been expecting when Lynne wrote that her mother was in a nursing home. Here, no detail had been spared in the preservation of dignity.

"May I help you?" A middle-aged woman in a sweater decorated with autumn leaves and a brass pin that read APRIL ANSEL, VOLUNTEER, looked up from her *Parade* magazine.

Mary Kay introduced them by name and said, "We're here to see Eunice Swann. We come on behalf of her daughter, Lynne."

April put the magazine aside, her smile both sad and welcoming. "I'm so sorry. Lynne alerted us that you'd be on your way."

Beth wondered how Lynne could alert them when she was dead. "Pardon?"

"She called us a while ago in preparation for your visit." April spoke slowly and deliberately. "She said there'd be three of you and that we should check in on her mother after you left."

Carol asked if she happened to remember what day that was when Lynne called.

"Thursday. The Thursday before last."

"That was the day Lynne died," Beth said. "Did you know that?"

"We heard. What a tragedy. Lynne was such a giving soul."

"So you knew her?" Beth asked.

"We never met in person, but she contributed generously to our foundation, and she painted that, in fact." April nodded to a watercolor by a fountain. "She had quite a gift."

Beth inspected the painting of a light green willow bending over a babbling brook. It was of Shepherd's Creek by the Marker farm, about three miles from their houses. Was it possible? Yes, she remembered the spring Lynne had painted that. Late May during one of her better remission seasons. Seeing it here, miles away from home, was like stumbling upon a signpost pointing them in the right direction.

"If you're ready," April said, coming around the desk, "I'll take you to Eunice."

In quiet procession, they headed single-file down the carpeted hall, past a library and reading room. April's footsteps padded softly, her hands folded in front of her like a nun's.

This is fitting, Carol thought, trying to be mindful of what Mary Kay said in the parking lot. Even if telling Eunice would be difficult, it was better than her learning about Lynne's death from someone who'd never met her daughter.

They arrived at the door marked MRS. E. SWANN. April said, "How about I ring the buzzer, since she knows me?"

Anything to make this easier on her, Beth thought.

April pressed the button and, after a short delay, an elderly voice said, "Yes?"

"It's April, Mrs. Swann. I have some friends here to see you."

"Friends?"

April pressed the intercom again. "Friends of your daughter, Lynne."

There was another delay and then a click. April nodded. "You can go in. I'll be right here if you need me."

Carol opened the door to a small apartment. A white galley kitchen was off a living room with windows on two sides. It was overstuffed with dark tables, Oriental rugs, and upholstered furniture left over from a larger house, from a fuller life gone by.

Mrs. Swann sat by the far window wearing a bright pink sweater, a frilly white blouse, and large faux pearls, and her hair appeared to have been newly styled. There was a book in her lap, the Bible, reminding Beth it was Sunday. Possibly,

Eunice was dressed up because she'd spent that morning in church.

"Mrs. Swann?" Mary Kay said, introducing each of them.

She waved them closer. "Come in. Have a seat."

Beth slid into a wing chair. "I hope we're not disturbing you." A meaningless statement. Another tactic to buy time.

"Just going over this morning's reading. The twentieth Sunday after Pentecost." Eunice closed the Bible. "So, you're friends of Lynne's."

"That's right." Beth gripped the arms of the wingback. Mary Kay and Carol took the couch. Though Mary Kay was supposed to do the talking, Beth suddenly felt compelled. "Lynne and I were next-door neighbors in Marshfield, Connecticut."

She'd used the past tense. Shooting a panicked look to Mary Kay and Carol, she added, "I don't know if you knew that Lynne moved to Marshfield."

Eunice folded her hands over the Bible and said nothing.

"Mrs. Swann," Mary Kay said, taking over. "Lynne asked that we give you a letter she wrote."

Beth brought the envelope from her purse and handed it to Eunice. But Eunice didn't move. Her hands remained clasped over the Bible. Awkwardly, Beth set it aside on the table, next to a framed black-and-white photo of Eunice and her husband in sunnier days.

Eunice said, "I don't understand. Why would she write me a letter?"

"She's your daughter," Carol said.

"I have no daughter," Eunice snapped, then turned to look out the window. The three women glanced at one another, trying to determine if Eunice might be suffering from mild dementia.

What to do now? The women tensed. Should they get April? Should they leave the letter there and just go?

No. They couldn't, Mary Kay decided. That would be copping out of their sacred duty. They'd come this far. They couldn't turn back. "Mrs. Swann," she said gently. "I don't quite know how to tell you this, but Lynne has been very sick for eight years with cancer."

Eunice's left pinky twitched.

"And a week ago Thursday, she finally . . . passed."

Eunice closed her eyes. The women remained still. Outside a car went by, its headlights sending a beam across the room, illuminating the tears on a mother's face.

Mary Kay took the chance and touched Eunice's knee. "I'm so sorry, Mrs. Swann. Your sister, Therese, told us how close you were when Lynne was young and Lynne spoke so highly of you. . . ."

"Lynne didn't speak highly of me." Eunice brushed away her tears with her knuckles. "She didn't speak of me at all."

That was true, of course. "She loved you very much."

"I have no daughter. My daughter left in the middle of the night and never told me where she was going. Years of sleepless nights. I waited for a phone call, a note, anything to indicate she was alive. But none came. None ever came." Turning to them, her eyes red-rimmed, cheeks damp, she said, "My daughter went off into the darkness and disappeared. My daughter has been dead for years."

"Lynne turned out fine," Beth said. "She married a man named Sean and became an art teacher and had twin boys, Kevin and Kyle. Your grandchildren."

"Grandchildren," Eunice whispered, shaking her head, as if refusing to hope. "It's been so long, so very long. You don't know how I've dreaded a visit such as this."

"I understand," Beth said. "I'm a mother, too. We're all mothers. And our hearts go out to you."

"We're here because Lynne loved you," Mary Kay said, leaning close. "Therese said you should think of Dorney Park and the day you found out you were pregnant."

Eunice rubbed her brow. "How would Therese have remembered that? Dorney Park. I couldn't go on any of the rides."

"Please read the letter," Carol said, getting up and handing her the envelope for another try.

Turning again to the window, she said, "One of you do it. I can't."

Carol opened the envelope, removed the folded, white, lined paper, and read a bit. "Why don't you do the honors," she said, handing it to Beth. "Lynne would want that."

Holding the paper firmly between her hands, Beth cleared her throat:

Dear Mom,

> *If you've received this then my friends have done as I've requested. Please thank them because I know that what brought them to you was their love for me. Their task was not easy. Nor is it easy, I expect, for you to hear that I have passed on to hopefully a better place without pain or sickness, where I can be with Grandma and Grandpa and dear friends who've gone before. Pray that I might find the peace I seek.*

Mom, I love you.

You are my mother.

I have always loved you and will forever love you. You were the one who stayed up with me when I was sick as a little girl and even now, as a sick big girl, there have been nights when I have cried for your gentle touch, your comforting hug. Somehow, I felt you were there, so it's OK. Let's not feel bad today. Let's feel good because at last we are putting our bitterness behind us and reuniting.

Do you remember when you used to take me to the park for our Winnie-the-Pooh tea parties? I think of that often. Just you, me, and Pooh and tea and cookies on a blanket in the sun. These are things I think of: the two of us holding hands in church. You letting me roll out dough for my own pie. (Did you have a special tin?) That day when Josie Kauffman and Tammy Jacobson were so mean I ran home crying from school and you took me in your lap and stroked my hair and told me someday I would have real girlfriends, and I would forget the Josies and Tammys of the world.

Well, Mom, I did find those friends and here they are because you believed in me and, therefore, I believed in myself. You were a great mother. How do I know? Because the gifts you gave emboldened me in my darkest hours— you taught me to be strong and to never lose faith. You taught me to be a loving mother, too, and maybe, God willing, you will come to know your twin grandsons Kevin and Kyle. Kevin, especially, is the spitting image of Daddy.

My only regret is that I did not get to know Julia. But now I see this, too, is OK, because I sense that she was loved by a warm family and enjoyed a much more stable childhood than I was equipped to offer her then. What you did, you did for the right reasons, and I am fine with that. I'm sorry if my leaving caused you anguish. I never meant to hurt you. (Though, I know I did.)

If you find it in your heart to do so, please tell my good friends what you know about Julia. It is my last request to them, that they find her. Also, that they tell you in person of my death.

That word is not so hard to write. It is freeing, not frightening. Someday, Mom, you and I will be together again and then we will hold hands and spread out a blanket in the warm sun and laugh and catch up. Maybe even Pooh will be there too.

Until then—
Love always, Your Daughter
Lynne

Beth folded the letter and set it on the Bible on Eunice's lap.

Eunice ran her arthritic fingertips over its edges, smoothing them. "I loved her," she said. "I loved her as much as any mother could love a child. She was my angel. I used to rock her on my lap at night and roll her hair in rag curls and sew her dresses. I made her paper dolls. She was my darling. And now this is all I have left of her. This is all that's left of my only child. Words."

Mary Kay took Carol's hand.

"Lynne never realized how proud I was of her. Even after

the baby." Eunice straightened the pink cuff folded over her white blouse. "All I wanted was for her to have a normal life. She deserved that."

Mary Kay said, "Do you know what happened to . . . ?"

Eunice wasn't listening. "I never wanted her to be a mother at such a young age, to be saddled with that responsibility. I wanted her to be able to truly enjoy motherhood when she was ready."

"She did enjoy motherhood," Beth said. "She was the best mother ever and her children made her incredibly happy."

"Lynne got it into her head that I was ashamed of her. Nothing could be further from the truth," Eunice went on. "I was frightened and acted hastily, bossily, which I tend to do when I'm scared. I went to our priest, who suggested a lawyer, Douglass Andersson. Mr. Andersson suggested I send Lynne away to spare her humiliation. So, I called Therese and we found Dr. Dorfman and it was done. Mr. Andersson arranged everything." Eunice bowed her head, ashamed. "Lynne hated me for what I did. Hated me. But why she had to run away and never come back—that I'll never understand."

What was it about mother/daughter relationships that made them so complicated? Mary Kay asked herself, not for the first time. Was it because women feel too much? Or that they expect too much? Look at Eunice and Lynne. Years lost over a stupid misunderstanding. Grandbabies never held. Christmases never celebrated. And now Lynne was dead and nothing would be the same. Ever. Memories could not be recaptured.

Mary Kay went over to kneel in front of Eunice. "Lynne didn't hate you—she emulated you. Like Beth said, she was a hands-on mother. She helped the boys build tree houses and took them camping. . . ."

"And she made your cupcakes!" Beth just remembered. "They had frosting an inch thick. She used to say they came from her mother's recipe."

"Yes, those are my buttercream." Eunice put a hand to a gold pin on her sweater, near her heart, pleasantly surprised. "That recipe was handed down from my own mother. Oh, my. The things you never think will matter . . ."

"Are the things that do." Mary Kay stroked the woman's hands. "Your daughter remembered those small gifts and she passed them on to her sons. Her only regret was that she couldn't pass them on to her own daughter. Do you suppose there's a way we can fix that?"

Eunice thought about this. When she spoke, her voice was thick and dull. "I don't know exactly what happened to Julia, but I know this much: She stayed nearby. That's what Mr. Andersson assured me. Go ask him. He knows where Julia is. His son took over the firm, but it's still on Main Street, right by the courthouse."

Mary Kay rose, sensing that Eunice might want to be alone. "It's too bad you and Lynne had a falling-out, Mrs. Swann."

Eunice smiled weakly as she slid the letter into the Bible. "Lynne wrote me this because she never stopped loving me, just as I never stopped loving her." She cleared her throat. "Do you have a daughter, dear?"

"I do," Mary Kay said. "Her name is Tiffany. She was my

niece and I adopted her when her parents died in a car crash, but I love her as my own."

"Then you're lucky. Sons are a godsend, but a daughter stays with you through thick and thin, fire and rain, life and even death." She placed her hand over the gold pin over her heart. "Here."

Dessert Martinis

⁓

The end, as we like to say, is often a fine beginning.

So it is with our two favorite dessert martinis: ginger-pear and chocolate-raspberry.

Ginger, long heralded for its digestive properties, gets a boost from the French-made Domaine de Canton, a heavenly aperitif made from the highest quality Cognac and young Vietnamese ginger that infuses its mesmerizing essence with fiery taste. While the Domaine de Canton recipe for a ginger martini—two parts vodka to two parts Domaine de Canton—is quite good, we like to lighten it by adding one part pear nectar. A lemon twist is a nice touch.

Chocolate-raspberry, however, is pure decadence. There is nothing light about it.

First, dip the rims of martini glasses in melted bittersweet chocolate. Freeze. At the bottom of a martini shaker muddle a few fresh raspberries, add raspberry vodka and Godiva chocolate liqueur, along with a splash of Chambord—a French black-raspberry liqueur that is to die for. Shake vigorously with ice. Pour into the chocolate-dipped glasses and garnish with two fresh raspberries. Warning: Don't let the chocolate and fruit deceive you. This packs a punch.

So delicious, you might be tempted to skip dinner altogether.

Chapter Twelve

The women burst from Beckwood's stifling heat into the refreshingly cool evening air.

Beth felt light-headed, like she might faint. "I don't know how you nurses do it, Mary Kay, breaking bad news to families day after day."

"Bad news is what we try to avoid."

"Even so." Beth unlocked the car and climbed in, eager to get away—far, far away. She felt guilty about not staying longer. They should have at least accompanied Eunice to dinner, but she insisted on being alone and April gently suggested that Eunice should be given space. She assured them that her doctor had been alerted, as had the staff, to check on Eunice frequently and offer support.

The situation was so awful. So sad and lonely and . . . hopeless. Beth couldn't conceive of twenty-four hours of not speaking to her mother, much less thirty years. Sure, sometimes their closeness was suffocating. It was impossible for

Elsie to resist weighing in if Beth so much as rearranged the furniture, and it would be nice to pack on a few pounds over the holidays without her mother discreetly pushing the grapefruit.

But Elsie was so much a part of her life that when she and Chat left for a two-week cruise, Beth found herself automatically picking up the phone to call them, forgetting they were incommunicado. It was the longest two weeks of her life. She missed not being able to brag about David and hear Elsie gasp in admiration or ask how to get her hydrangeas to bloom in pink instead of blue. She felt almost disembodied.

It made sense now, why Lynne was so reserved when every spring Elsie swooped in with a trunk of annuals so she and Beth could spend a glorious warm afternoon digging, weeding, and planting. It hadn't occurred to her until meeting Eunice and reading that letter that Elsie's presence must have made Lynne long for her own mother.

"What do you think will happen to Eunice?" Beth asked as they pulled out of the Beckwood parking lot. "Her husband's dead. Her daughter, too. She doesn't have any children. Who will be there for her?"

"Seems like Beckwood's been preparing for this," Mary Kay said, heading across the parking lot. "Eunice might have talked herself into believing that her daughter was dead as a coping mechanism, but obviously Lynne maintained close contact with the staff. They knew she was alive and knew she was dying, too. You heard April say they had professionals on call to help Eunice deal with the shock."

"It wasn't shock." Carol, who'd been quiet in the backseat lost in thought, suddenly piped up. "I've had a glimpse of what it's like to be estranged from your child, and even if you're separated physically, that doesn't mean you're apart spiritually. I would know if Amanda were dead, perish the thought. I could feel it in my bones."

Beth turned around in her seat. "And you think Eunice felt that too?"

"I think Eunice knew a lot more than she let on. I bet she suspected that we—or someone—was coming to tell her Lynne had died."

Which would explain the pearls and frills, Beth thought, and possibly the Bible in her lap. Not because it was Sunday, but because by the time they arrived, Eunice was ready to mourn.

They didn't have far to travel to get to their hotel, twenty miles at most. A pittance compared to the four hundred miles or so they'd clocked so far. But they were tired and it was dinnertime, so the last thing they wanted to do was get back on the road.

"There's a Douglass Andersson and Sons law office in downtown Calais," Beth said, checking Carol's iPhone.

"That's got to be them," Mary Kay said. "We'll stop by tomorrow."

"We should go bright and early in case Dorfman gets the swift idea of giving Andersson a heads-up," Carol said. After the doctor's pat lecture about what was right and wrong for women, she didn't put it past him to call the lawyer who'd orchestrated the adoption.

"And then, if we get some info, we can start searching

for Julia," Mary Kay said excitedly. "That would be a welcome change after two days of playing the grim reaper."

Beth said nothing.

"What do you think, Beth?" Mary Kay asked.

"I don't know, MK. I'm tired."

"We're almost at our hotel."

"Not that kind of tired. I'm tired of these confrontations." She didn't mean to complain, but she wasn't like Mary Kay and Carol, who were used to dealing with strangers in sticky situations day in, day out. She preferred to keep to herself and read. You couldn't make a book cry or make it angry. Books didn't have hearts that could be broken. Books were friends and she missed their silent company. "Besides, my father's getting his test results back tomorrow morning. I really need to be available."

"I hear you," Mary Kay said. "Why don't you take the morning off?"

"Besides, this is a job for a couple of professional bitches," Carol said. "Not an amateur like you."

Mary Kay said, "Seriously."

"OK." Beth breathed a great big sigh of relief. Already she felt better.

A Radisson loomed ahead on a knoll off the highway, lit up green like the Empire State Building on St. Patrick's Day. The parking lot was packed with cars end to end. "Yowza!" Mary Kay exclaimed, turning into the driveway. "What gives?"

"Guess this is the place to be on Sunday in Calais, PA," Beth said, noticing the KARAOKE TONITE! sign with grave disappointment. So much for going to bed early. "Maybe we should stay someplace else."

"My credit card's already been charged," Carol said. "It's not like this area is brimming with options—unless your idea of an upgrade is a Motel 6 down the interstate."

"We'll leave the karaoke on for ya." Mary Kay parked and headed inside, where another sign exclaimed WELCOME PENN. SOCIETY OF CHEMICAL ENGINEERS.

"Nothing says party hearty," she said as they wheeled their bags to check in, "like mathematicians on a bender."

The lobby reverberated with a booming bass beat, and every once in a while the bar door would open and a chemical engineer would emerge, making a beeline for the bathroom across the hall.

"And when do the festivities end?" Carol asked as she signed her slip. "It's been a long day and we're knackered." Not to mention that Jeff was supposed to call at six sharp to discuss the house. She hardly needed Bon Jovi's "Livin' on a Prayer" to add to her stress.

"Normally, around two. But since it's a convention and most of the guests are in-house, in all reality, three." The clerk handed them their plastic keys.

Mary Kay, who'd checked out the karaoke scene, returned with a report. "After eight, ladies get in free. Whaddya say, girls? Can't beat 'em, join 'em?" She wiggled her eyebrows suggestively.

Carol said, "There's not enough alcohol on the planet."

Had there not been a virtual frat party rumbling below, their rooms would have been perfectly adequate, large, with outdoor balconies. Tonight, Beth and Mary Kay shared a room with two queen beds while Carol got the adjoining king so she could finish a law memo due Monday.

"Work, work, work for me," Carol singsonged as she dragged her cases down the hall. "I'm afraid that means no martinis, either."

"Come over for dinner, at least," Beth said. "Mary Kay heard there's a sushi bar not far from here. We'll do takeout."

It was hard to resist sushi. Clean, fresh food. (Though Carol had to wonder what grade of tuna made its way to this neck of the woods.) She paused at her room, tempted, though she really needed to be alone when Jeff called.

"Maybe I better order in from room service so I don't get distracted. A crappy chicken Caesar salad and Diet Coke should be fine." Discipline had always been her ally.

Beth shrugged. "Suit yourself. We'll order a little extra, just in case you change your mind."

"You don't have to go to all that trouble, but thank you," Carol said sweetly. "Well, good night."

"Good night."

Beth went into her room next door and found Mary Kay sitting on the edge of the white Jacuzzi. "Is this skeevy, or what?" She played with a button by her foot. "I keep thinking of all the drunken chemical engineers over the years who scrumped in this thing."

"Ewww." Beth laid her suitcase on the counter and began her search for a telephone book. "Carol's not joining us for dinner. Is it me, or do you get the feeling she wants to be by herself?"

"Definitely got that vibe." Mary Kay opened the Igloo cooler, surveying the contents to make ginger martinis. They needed pear nectar, which she did not have, darn it. Maybe she could find some in the lounge. "Don't take it personally. Lynne's fight with her mother is hitting Carol close to home. You heard what she said about having a glimpse into being a parent estranged from her child, about being able to sense if Amanda were dead. This has got to be killing her."

"I didn't see the point of disagreeing when she said that. But sensing your child's death seems to me something we'd like to believe, even if, scientifically, it doesn't hold water."

"In the words of the immortal John Lennon, whatever gets you through the night." Mary Kay pulled out the vodka. "On top of that, she's talking to Jeff tonight about selling the house. You know how that's bumming her out."

Beth had the phone to her ear, on hold waiting to place their sushi order. "Doesn't she have to get the OK from Amanda first?"

"She did. That's partially what got Carol so upset this morning." Mary Kay dug out her pretty glasses. "Amanda was really hard on her, laying the guilt thicker than marmalade."

"She said no way."

"Worse. She said yes."

"Amanda wants them to sell the house?" Beth was incredulous. "After her tantrum last year about them giving up her childhood home?"

"That's when it was a home, when Amanda thought of her parents as being together. But her parents aren't together anymore." Mary Kay grabbed a key card in her search for some pear nectar downstairs. "So, it's not a home anymore. It's just a plain old house. And those are a dime a dozen."

Carol pushed her bags against the wall and flopped onto the bed, staring at the blank white ceiling.

She hadn't been able to stop thinking about Amanda since they'd left Eunice. She pulled out her phone and searched for Amanda's name. Her cell number popped up, she pressed Send, and, like clockwork, Amanda's voice mail came on.

"Hi," Carol said, deciding to let the words come instead of carefully scripting them as she usually did. "I know you don't want to talk to me, but we have to. We have to talk about Lynne. There's something you need to know. Call me, please."

Tossing the phone aside, she took a shower, slipping into her pink cotton pj's and white terry-cloth robe. Then she called up the memo she'd been working on and flipped to a new white page on her legal tablet to take notes and doodle, which for mysterious reasons helped her brain function when she got stuck. Like she was now.

It was gratifying to immerse herself in work, to focus on something besides family breakdowns and death. Work had always been her salvation, the one consistency that she could count on when things got scary.

OK, think, Carol. The memo pertained to her lawsuit on behalf of a college student suing a sperm bank so it would release the identity of her biological father. The girl had a deep desire to know who she was and where she came from and there was nothing wrong with that. After all, what's more basic than understanding our origins? Carol asked herself, doodling.

Despite her concentration on what was a fairly interesting case, Carol's thoughts drifted from the girl to Lynne's daughter. Here they were, expending so much effort trying to find Julia and never once did they think about tracking down the father. It didn't make sense that Lynne didn't want them to even try.

The clock on her computer got closer to six. She carefully placed her cell on the desk and folded her hands, waiting. Somewhere across Pennsylvania, across New York, and in Marshfield, Connecticut, Jeff was probably doing the same. Except he'd be in his study, the most recent medical journal open to something distressingly technical.

At five fifty the phone rang and her heart skipped a beat. He was early, which meant he was probably as eager to talk to her as she was to him. "Jeff?" she said hopefully.

There was a pause. "Actually, it's Scott."

Oh. Shit. Carol knew it was wrong to feel disappointed, but she couldn't help it. "I'm waiting for a call from Jeff about the house. Sorry."

She checked her phone. She had five minutes.

"I've been waiting for your call, but I didn't want to bother you in case you were in something deep. I couldn't take the suspense. How's it going?"

"Pretty well," she lied, writing her name in perfect cursive, a holdover from when she was bored in law school. "I mean, if your definition of 'well' is telling a mother that the child she hasn't spoken to since 1981 is dead and she'll never have a chance to hold her or see her again."

"Wow. That's a tall order. I know Lynne and you were close, but to obligate you to break the news to her mom seems above and beyond the call of friendship, I have to say."

Carol bristled slightly at the implication. "She didn't *obligate* us to do anything, Scott. We're her friends. This is what friends do."

"But clearly you're upset about it, and that has me worried. You know, social workers and chaplains who have to inform families their loved ones have died often go through a formal counseling process. CISM, it's called. Critical Incident Stress Management. I had a case once, where . . ."

Scott often slipped into technical jargon, a trait that hadn't really bothered her until now.

"That's not all that's got me down." She wished Scott knew Lynne and knew Amanda so he could relate. "It's also Amanda. The way she's not talking to me and refusing to take my calls reminds me of how Lynne stopped talking to Eunice."

"The aunt, you mean."

"No, Eunice is Lynne's mother," she said, slightly exasperated. "Therese is the aunt."

"The names are so similar it's hard to keep them straight. Go on."

"Well, Lynne and her mother stopped speaking when Lynne was slightly younger than Amanda. What if that's what happens to Amanda and me? What if I end up alone in a nursing home and three friends of Amanda's come to tell me she's dead? I can't imagine anything worse."

"Those are two entirely different situations, Carol. See, this is what I mean about post-traumatic stress and you not being your usual logical self. If you were in your normal state of mind, you'd recognize that Amanda's simply going through some sort of obnoxious phase."

Carol quit doodling. "My daughter is not obnoxious."

"Let me rephrase. Adolescent is what I meant."

"Beth says we clash because Amanda and I are so much alike."

"That's what they always say when parents and kids don't get along, isn't it? They used to say it about my father and me when the bottom line was the old man was just an S.O.B." Scott laughed slightly. "I'm sure that as a nurse Beth fashions herself to be an observer of human nature, but the fact of the matter is that Amanda was a teenager when you left Jeff and this is what teenagers do when their parents get divorced. They act out."

Carol said, "Beth's not a nurse. She's a librarian. Mary Kay's the nurse."

"Right. I knew that." Then, sensing her growing irritation, he said, "You're very tired and understandably so, especially with this conversation about the house hanging over your head. I'll let you take this call from Jeff and maybe we can talk tomorrow when you've had a chance to recuperate."

Frankly, Carol was relieved to have him off the line. "You're right. Like they say, tomorrow is another day." Then again, it was doubtful Scott had ever seen *Gone with the Wind*. If he had, he would have detested Scarlett O'Hara.

No sooner had she said good-bye to Scott than the phone rang at 6:01. This time, Carol checked the number, saw it was Jeff, and said, "Hi."

"Hey, is this . . . Carol?" he asked, unsure.

"Of course it is. It's my cell."

"I wasn't sure. You sound different."

"Tired." She told him about Therese and Eunice. "It's been draining, to say the least."

"Sure, sure. I should have guessed. How insensitive of me."

"No, it's OK. I didn't mean to guilt-trip you. It's just . . ."

"Just what?"

She repeated almost exactly word for word what she'd said to Scott. "I'm afraid of ending up like Eunice. It's because I've been such a lousy mother."

"Don't do this to yourself, Carol," he muttered, understanding where she was coming from right away. "You know Amanda. She was always a drama queen, even as a tiny kid. You were a terrific mother. The problem is, you two are cast from the same mold."

"You mean, we're too much alike." She sniffed and patted a Kleenex to her nose, thinking about Beth. And Scott.

"Yeah. You're both hardworking and ambitious. Always going someplace, never staying still. Never time to talk. You and Amanda give one hundred and ten percent. Whether it's the law or school. Your dedication is one of the qualities I most admired."

Admired. Past tense. Carol sniffed again.

"Remember that spring when you collected tadpoles and set up the aquarium so Jonathan could see how they turned into frogs?" Jeff said. "You didn't just leave it at that. You got out books from the library on amphibians and made a huge poster of the stages between eggs and full-formed frogs. That was the beginning of Jon's interest in environmental science, you know, those stupid frogs."

"We had to let them go in the park." She thought of Jonathan and her, hand in hand, waving good-bye to each frog he named. Lumpy. Bumpy. Croaky and Chirp.

"And remember the chrysalis you found?" he said.

She hadn't thought of that chrysalis in years. She'd come

across it in the field behind their house and stuck it in a mason jar with holes punched in the lid to see what would happen. For weeks it was just a lump on a twig. But one warm July night while the kids were at a sleepover and she and Jeff were sharing a rare moment alone sipping chardonnay on the back deck, something stirred inside the clear cocoon.

Carol sat in Jeff's lap as they watched in awe as the butterfly extended first one limp wing and then another before inflating both and becoming fully magnificent. After it flew off, Jeff kissed Carol's fingers and led her upstairs to the bedroom, the fireflies twinkling outside their window.

"The monarch night," Carol sighed, remembering the sensation of his incredibly taut body moving with hers, responding to a call as natural and magnificent as the butterfly's flight.

"One of the best nights of my life. Next to the night we got married, of course."

"Of course." She pulled her robe tighter, her heart actually aching liked she'd read in books. She hadn't known such a phenomenon was physically possible.

"Hey! Guess what." Jeff shifted to an upbeat attitude. "You won't believe what we're getting tonight."

She decided not to overanalyze his use of the word "we."

"Snow! I can't think about first snows without thinking about when the kids were small."

Carol laughed. "Amanda and Jonathan, co-conspirators in their flannels, insisting they sleep in the same room with an AM radio tuned to the news so they could be the first in the house to hear the official cancellations. And then their utter disappointment when, in the ultimate betrayal, the snow refused to stick. Cruel world!"

"Speaking of which," he said, "Amanda tells me the two of you have discussed the house."

Carol gripped her doodling pen, disappointed their stroll down memory lane had reached an end so soon. "We spoke this morning. Did you know she's thinking of spending Christmas in Paris with some man she hardly knows? A friend of a roommate's brother or something."

"She's almost twenty-one."

"I know, but . . ."

"But let it go. She's old enough, Carol. Face it. Your chicks have left the nest."

No! Bring back that magic time of little sticky hands and soft hugs, sweet kisses, tadpoles and butterflies on balmy summer evenings. "I can't believe our children are grown," she said. "I miss those years." Then, though this contradicted everything she thought she knew about herself, about how she hadn't been cut out for motherhood, she added, "I'm glad I had the chance to stay home with them."

"Me too. We were very fortunate."

She nodded. "Very."

"So, I guess it's decided then."

What? What were they talking about? "You mean the house?" She hoped Jeff couldn't hear the panic in her voice.

"The kids are OK with it. Which means the only people holding back from selling are you and me, ironically."

"Yes," Carol said quietly. "Ironically."

"By the way, I've put aside a few things that the Realtor said we should remove for showings, like your grandmother's antique fish plate and the photos of our family skiing vacation in Vermont."

Another golden memory. Another twist of the knife.

The two of them snuggling by the fire as a light snow fell outside their window, Jeff running his hands under her sweater, kissing her neck, her shoulder, and then more, both of them stifling moans of pleasure so as not to wake Amanda and Jon in the next room.

Did he mention this, the monarch night, the first snowfalls on purpose? Or was she just being supersensitive?

"Carol?"

"Hmm?"

"I said I thought maybe you might want to pick those up on your way home if you happen to be stopping off at Marshfield before you go back to New York."

"OK. Sure," she said, a little dazed. What was she supposed to pick up again?

"Or I can pack them up and ship them to you, if that makes more sense."

"No, I can stop by."

"There's some china involved."

"No, honestly. I don't mind at all."

"Really? Could be awkward on the train."

Carol wanted to throttle him. First he reminds her how wonderful it was when they were married; then he refuses to be in the same room with her. What was he up to?

He waited a second and said, "Carol?"

"Yes?" she asked, hopefully.

"I'll need your signature on the Realtor form. Once that's done, I expect we'll have an official offer by the end of this week and then we can formally, completely, start our new lives."

They hung up and that was that. Carol blinked at the computer screen. Forget the stupid memorandum.

Shutting down her computer, she grabbed her key card and padded to Mary Kay and Beth's room. "I just got off the phone with Jeff."

Mary Kay quit shaking the silver martini shaker. "And?"

"And we might have an offer on the house as early as this week."

Mary Kay lifted the top off the shaker, poured a ginger martini to the rim, and handed it to her. Carol knocked it back in one gulp. Like a cowboy slugging whiskey.

"Hit me again," she said, holding out her empty glass.

"Don't you have to work?" Beth asked.

"Fuck work." Carol took the shaker and poured herself a glass. "Work can kiss my ass."

⁄∂

"The amazing thing about ginger martinis is they feel almost healthy for you. No, really. I'm serious." Carol exhaled a plume of smoke over her shoulder, so it wouldn't pollute Mary Kay and Beth, who stood next to each other on the other side of the balcony, clutching their half-drunk martinis, keeping watch.

She hadn't had a cigarette since learning about Lynne's suicide and it felt great. Fabulous!

"How about some sushi?" Mary Kay suggested. "And then you can go to bed."

"Bed? Hah!" Carol took another hit of the cigarette and tossed it over the balcony so it landed in a bush by the parking lot. She emptied the last of her glass and regarded it fuzzily. "Who wants another round?"

Beth opened the sliding-glass door to their room, hoping

to entice Carol to put some food in her stomach and drink something besides alcohol. Right now, though, she was on a tear.

"What's in this again?" Carol asked, making a beeline for the martini shaker.

"Vodka, ginger brandy, pear nectar, and a squeeze of lime."

"It's delicious."

Mary Kay eyed Carol warily as she sloppily poured in the ingredients, pausing at one moment to take a big swig of vodka straight out of the bottle. "Just checking to see if it is fresh," she said, wiping her mouth on her pj's. "Forget this ginger, pear watchamacallit. Straight vodka is A–OK by me."

"You wanna talk about it, hon?"

"Talk about what?" She tried capping the bottle, but the top fell off, forcing her to bend down and pick it up with a groan.

"Jeff. The house. Amanda."

"It's done. The house is practically sold. And then we'll all live unhappily ever after." She peered into the martini shaker and scowled. "No ice." She checked the ice bucket, where a layer of water was all that remained. "No ice there, either." Placing a hand on her hip, she said, "Now what are we going to do?"

"Sushi?" Beth offered.

"No. Hold on. They have ice machines here. I know because this is a *hotel*. And in hotels they have free ice. It's a perk!" She hiccupped slightly.

Mary Kay said, "Oh, don't bother about that, Carol. There's a cold Diet Coke in the cooler."

She went over to the Igloo, but Carol grabbed the bucket.

"You two stay here and I'll be right back in a jiffy." And she toddled off in nothing but her slippered feet and pink pj's.

The door closed and Beth let out a breath. "Whoa. I have never seen her like this."

Mary Kay handed Beth her sushi. "It's exactly like when she decided to leave him. And we called that emergency meeting. Did we have ginger martinis then, too?"

Mary Kay ripped open a packet of soy sauce and dumped it over the dollop of wasabi. "I think so. Ginger's supposed to promote healing and Carol could have used a dose of that. Lynne, too. Didn't work, unfortunately."

"But at least Carol kept it together." Beth thought back to that night, Carol still in her navy business suit from the school board meeting, coolly grasping the stem of her martini glass as she drank one after another with mechanical efficiency.

They had done their best to dissuade her from leaving, reminding Carol of all she and Jeff shared—twenty years of marriage, the kids, the house, their memories. Finally, Lynne threw down the trump card.

"What I would give for twenty more years with Sean. You have no idea how lucky you are, Carol, to have that luxury. I didn't appreciate what I had either, until cancer made me stare down death. Now I thank God for every blessed day."

"Exactly," Carol had replied, starting in on her fourth martini. "Your cancer was my wake-up call, Lynne. If I don't start living for myself, today, then soon it might be too late."

It was crass. Beth was pissed off at Carol for being so self-centered.

"That's not where joy comes from though," Lynne shot back. "Joy is in the little things. One afternoon, when I was too tired to move an inch, I just lay on the couch and watched a hummingbird buzzing at the feeder and it made me so happy. That's what I mean by every moment is a gift."

Carol had shrugged and kept on drinking, harping on how she had more support from her friends than her husband. Later, Lynne and Beth went home while Carol slept over at Mary Kay's. And the next morning, she cleaned out her essentials and had them sent to Deloutte Watkins, where for the rest of the week she crashed on her office couch.

By the weekend, she'd moved into a small apartment Deloutte kept for clients and witnesses visiting from out of state. Beth and Mary Kay sent her another shipment from the Connecticut house—stuff they'd gathered while Jeff was at work—and that was it.

Carol didn't set foot in Marshfield again. Until Lynne's funeral.

"If only she and Jeff could sit down and have an honest discussion instead of suppressing their anger and wants," Mary Kay said, dipping her *uni* into the wasabi. "I'm sure if she owned up to how she still loves him, all would be forgiven. Look at her—she's not the ice queen anymore. She's *hurting*."

Beth sucked the end of her chopstick. Mary Kay was right. If Carol and Jeff had been able to communicate their emotions from the get-go, there wouldn't have been a divorce to begin with. "She's self-destructive." Then, remembering how she'd drunk-dialed Marc the night before, Beth said, "You don't think Carol will do something crazy and call Jeff while she's like this, do you?"

"She might." Mary Kay wrapped up her sushi. "Would that be a bad thing?"

"Are you kidding? She'd never speak to Jeff again. She'd be too mortified. That would be the end of them once and for all."

Mary Kay left to throw the sushi containers outside so they wouldn't smell up the room. When she returned, she said, "Carol's not at the ice machine. I just passed it and there's no one there."

"She has been gone an awfully long time."

They looked at each other. Uh-oh.

"Maybe she went to her room and passed out," Beth said, getting up and dumping her sushi tray in the wastebasket.

"Not likely," Mary Kay said, picking up Carol's key card, which had been lying on the desk.

"Maybe she took her spare."

"Or maybe not."

"Jeff!" Beth said. "She's calling Jeff."

They went to Carol's door and knocked loudly. "Carol. You in there, Carol?" Had Carol been sober, she would have been appalled by their ruckus. "Come on, Carol, wake up!"

A man passing by carrying a brown paper bag and a pizza box said, "You wouldn't by any chance be looking for a blond woman in her Dr. Dentons?"

Beth said, "You've seen her?"

He grinned and pointed toward the karaoke bar. "The life of the party."

Shit! Without waiting for further details, they dashed to the emergency exit, taking the stairs two at a time. "She's in her pj's," Beth said, running so fast she nearly slipped on the bottom step. "What is she thinking?"

Mary Kay said, "Obviously, she's not thinking."

They arrived at the lobby floor and pushed open the emergency exit doors, quick-stepping down the hall toward the music that grew louder as they got closer to the bar. Bursting into the lounge, they squinted as their eyes adjusted to the darkness, searching for Carol.

It didn't take long to find her. For there, on top of a table at the center of the hotel lounge, surrounded by a group of chemical engineers, Carol Goodworthy was in her pajamas belting out "Harper Valley PTA."

It was shocking.

It was also kind of funny.

She was surprisingly entertaining. Not because Carol was slapping her thighs and gyrating her hips to the applause of ogling engineers, but because she was actually doing an admirable job, singing all the words on cue and not missing a beat.

They let her finish, to resounding applause. Carol bowed and said, "I'll be here all week." Then, catching sight of her friends, she waved like a lunatic and got down from the table, as steady as a rock. "It's after eight. Ladies free. Remember what you said? If you can't beat 'em, join 'em."

A group of men in the bar urged Mary Kay and Beth to join the party. "Don't be a spoilsport," one said. "What'll you have?"

"A pink cosmopolitan," Carol answered for her. "For her, too." She pointed at Beth.

Beth opened her mouth to object. She'd already had one martini and it was time for bed. *Oh, screw it,* she thought. *When in Rome* . . . "Thanks," she said. "A cosmo on the rocks would be nice."

"How about 'I Love Rock 'n' Roll' next?" Carol suggested, flipping through the monitor.

"Carol . . . ," Mary Kay began, trying to do the right thing. "Don't you think . . ."

"No. I'm tired of thinking, MK. Lynne was right. We need to have more fun in our lives and I plan on doing exactly that, starting tonight."

Without further argument, Carol climbed back on the table and started snapping her fingers to the opening strains of "I Love Rock 'n' Roll." If Lynne were here, she'd tell them to let Carol be, that this was exactly what the doctor called for.

"Come on, you two." She held out her hand, pulling up Beth, then Mary Kay, who were promptly handed microphones.

"OK," Carol directed. "The trick to this is you've got to become the chanteuse. Channel your best Chrissie Hynde."

"Joan Jett," Beth corrected. "And the Blackhearts."

Carol slapped the air. "Whatever. I always get those two confused. Brunettes. Eighties music."

The cosmos were delivered and the women clinked their glasses, taking huge swigs as the words started rolling across the screen.

At first they were really lousy. Beth was too careful to articulate each lyric and Mary Kay was off-key. But then Carol let out a couple of trademark Joan Jett cougar calls, much to the thunderous appreciation of the chemical engineers, and the women got the hang of it.

Let go, Beth thought, strumming her air guitar as she flung her head in circles until her hair fell out of its clip. "I'm a librarian!" she shouted. "And I'm here to rock 'n' roll!"

"Get the librarian a shot! Get 'em all shots!" someone demanded. "Schnapps."

Probably, schnapps was not the brightest of ideas. Then again, neither was Mary Kay's decision to pole dance without a pole while crooning "Lady Marmalade" or their attempts to jump out the letters to "Y.M.C.A." on the tabletop. It was a miracle they didn't break something, like their necks. Or that the police weren't called.

But mostly it was a miracle that their grief could be washed away in a greasy hotel bar by the unholiest of Madonnas.

Chapter Thirteen

"Like a Virgin'?" Drake loved the story of Carol Goodworthy letting loose, even though he'd met her only once. He had no idea what a big deal it was that the past chairwoman of the Marshfield School Board closed down the Calais Radisson lounge, seducing strange men with her impersonation of Madonna. "How did she top that?"

"She couldn't." Outside their balcony overlooking the parking lot, Mary Kay took a sip of peppermint tea in the gray dawn as tractor trailers rumbled past on highway 80. She watched a groggy engineer unlock his car, throw in his bag, and drive off. "Then Beth and I put her to bed in our room so there'd be someone with her all night in case she got sick."

"And did she get sick?"

"No, she slept like a baby. Me, on the other hand, not so much."

"Overserved, were we?"

"Actually, I didn't drink all that much. One ginger martini in our hotel room and then part of a cosmo downstairs. I don't know why I feel so lousy this morning." She decided it was better not to tell him about the schnapps. "I'm thinking maybe sushi from the boonies isn't such a hot idea."

"Either that," he said with a devilish tone, "or you're pregnant."

Mary Kay let out a snort. If he only knew. "Yeah, right."

"Well, I wasn't going to say anything, but I did happen to notice you left your birth-control pills in the bathroom."

The blood drained from her face as the churning in her stomach returned. Drake had found her pills. She was cooked. "Yeah, I know. I realized that yesterday morning."

"If this is your way of roping me into a shotgun marriage, the old trick seems hardly necessary. As you recall, I *did* propose."

She twisted the ruby on her finger. "I'm wearing your ring now."

"That's a start. Now, repeat after me: 'Drake, I would love to marry you.'"

"Drake, I would . . ." This was it. She had to ask him while she was too hungover to know better. "Drake, what if I *couldn't* get pregnant?"

There was an ominous silence. "What are you talking about?"

"I mean"—she peeked into the room where Carol and Beth were still asleep, half snoring—"what if we get married and we find out I can't have children?"

"Don't worry about it, MK. I'm not marrying your uterus. I'm marrying you. If it turns out that after a few years of trying we can't have kids, then we'll deal with it."

Mary Kay clutched her middle. "Deal with it like how?"

"You're a nurse. You know better than anyone what kind of reproductive technology's out there."

But what would happen when he found out that she'd known all along? In vitro fertilization—the most common treatment for women in her situation—was a long, arduous process of doctors' appointments and fertility drugs. That Drake would learn Mary Kay's blocked fallopian tubes had been diagnosed years before they met was inevitable.

Her deception had woven a tangled web, indeed. "Yeah, you're right. I'm getting all worked up over nothing."

"So, it's a yes? I can tell our friends we're going to do the deed?"

Another twinge. "Wait until I get back tomorrow. Just do me that favor, OK? Meantime, Carol and I are meeting the lawyer who arranged for Julia's adoption. This could get us the names we need. I should concentrate on that."

"Fair enough. I have to go to work anyway. Can't wait until you get home."

Mary Kay's stomach turned again. "Me too."

An hour later, everyone was up, showered, packed, and ready to go. The plan was for Beth to drive Carol and Mary Kay to the Andersson law office while she waited for Marc to call with Chat's test results. That would be stressful enough without adding a lawyer to the mix.

Carol, slightly shaky, gripped her tea in the backseat. Beth and Mary Kay might have had a blast the night before, but she was embarrassed beyond belief. Periodically, blurred images, like drunken Polaroids, reminded her of what a fool she'd been. Shots? Honestly?

"In my pj's," she murmured. "In front of strangers."

"Look on the bright side," Mary Kay said. "They *were* strangers and you'll never see them again."

"Nor will they forget you, either," Beth added.

Carol slid down and groaned. "Getting plastered and singing karaoke. What got into me?"

Mary Kay turned and said, "Jeff?"

"Jeff?" Carol took another sip. "He has nothing to do with me getting drunk."

"I know it's none of my business," Mary Kay said tentatively, "but it's pretty evident to me . . ."

"And to me," Beth said.

"That you still love him."

"What?" Carol said this so loudly she hurt her own head and had to press her temples to stop the pounding.

"In fact," Mary Kay continued, "I'm willing to go so far as to say that you never stopped loving him and, possibly, he feels the same way."

Carol didn't have the energy to mount an objection. "Even if that's true—and I can't speak for him—it's too late. We've been divorced for a year."

"If Lynne were here," Beth said, "she'd point out it's never too late as long as you're alive."

"She said something similar the night I left Jeff and went to your house, MK," Carol said. "I should have listened to her instead of going off half-cocked like a spoiled brat."

Beth and Mary Kay kept their peace, thereby tacitly confirming she was right.

"So, you think I was a spoiled brat?"

Mary Kay said, "I think you were stretched wire thin and that Jeff and you were both so busy with your careers and the demands of two teenagers that you quit communicating."

"That's putting it graciously."

"Whatever happened, happened," Beth said. "It's water under the proverbial bridge. The question is, what are you going to do to set things right between you two?"

"Nothing. Jeff has already made plans to meet up with a friend of his who's volunteering for Doctors Without Borders. The house is on the market. That window of opportunity is closed."

"Just tell him you still love him," Mary Kay said. "Throw it out there and see what happens."

"Yeah," Beth said. "What do you have to lose?"

"My dignity."

Mary Kay said, "Oh, honey, you trashed that last night."

Carol grinned. "That was kind of fun, wasn't it?"

Mary Kay couldn't disagree. "It was. Though, I'm not sure it was entirely necessary for me to swagger like a stripper when I did 'Lady Marmalade.'"

"You were great. You stole the show! Too bad Drake wasn't there. Speaking of which," Carol said, slowly rising out of her slump, "have we made any decisions on that ring?"

Beth slowed to take the exit to downtown Calais. "Can't help but notice you haven't taken it off once. Can we assume this means yes?"

Mary Kay said, "What it means is . . ."

From her purse, Carol's iPhone blared. She dug it out and read the number. "My, my, my."

And here Mary Kay was just about to tell them what she'd decided, Beth thought, bummed.

Carol put the phone on speaker and said, "Why, hello, Dr. Dorfman."

Dorfman! He actually called. Mary Kay poked Beth. If this brought them closer to finding Julia, then Mary Kay's decision could wait.

"Hello?" he said, sounding slightly skeptical. "I'm trying to reach a Ms. Goodworthy."

"This is she. And I'm here with my friends Mary Kay LeBlanc and Beth Levinson, whom you met when you were headed out to the wedding. I hope you don't mind if I put you on speaker so all of us can hear at the same time."

"I don't mind." He paused. "At least, I don't think I mind."

"Thank you for calling us," Carol said. "It's very kind after we delayed you Saturday afternoon. How was the wedding?"

"Very nice. Very nice. My nephew spent a fortune," he said absently. "I would have called sooner but the law office wasn't open until this morning."

She knew he'd try to get to them first, dammit. "Would this be the Douglass Andersson law office in Calais?"

"You . . . So you've contacted them?"

"We were thinking of heading over there this morning." A tiny fib, since they'd just turned onto Calais's Main Street.

"I'm glad I caught you, then." He seemed pleased. "Because I'd hate for you to make an unnecessary trip. I spoke to the younger Andersson and I regret to report that his father, the one who arranged for the adoption, is not well. *Non compos mentis,* one might say."

Another setback, Mary Kay thought.

"It is a pity, but there you have it," he said. "Without the older Andersson in the picture, there's no institutional memory. I asked his son, Doug Junior, and he knows nothing of the adoption except that he knew Lynne vaguely from high school. Very cheerful girl, he recalled, though he said they ran in different crowds. He was quite upset by the news."

Mary Kay's heart began to sink. Dorfman was a closed book and the lawyer was senile. That left them heading for a dead end.

But Carol was not so willing to wave the white flag. "There must be interoffice files. I know at my law firm we don't destroy anything, and everything that's ten years old is converted to digital."

"That's interesting. We did discuss the possibility of there being files, but there's really no point in sorting through all of the firm's muck to find them."

"Really?" Carol said. "Why?"

"To be perfectly blunt, your friend is deceased." He cleared his throat. "And while finding her daughter may have been her dying wish, it's not really practical, is it?"

Mary Kay coughed at his callousness. *Say what?*

"Practicality," Carol replied crisply, "is the least of our concerns right now, Dr. Dorfman."

"Now, don't get upset. I realize she was your friend and that you ladies have expended considerable time and effort completing this task for her, but unearthing information of this nature could have traumatic consequences for this child."

Carol rolled her eyes. "This *child* is thirty years old, Dr. Dorfman."

"Nevertheless, Pennsylvania specifically prohibits releasing names of adopting parents and their adopted children."

"But if we could get those records," Beth ventured,

barging into their conversation. "If they were perhaps leaked to us . . ."

"They'd be of no use," Dorfman said.

"And why is that?" Carol was growing tired of going around in circles.

"Because in Pennsylvania back in 1980, the infant's name would have been blacked out on sealed adoption forms and substituted with her adopted name. There would be no record, either, of the biological mother ever having given birth. In other words, according to our commonwealth, the baby Julia Swann never existed."

Beth vaguely remembered this from Lynne's letter, though it was no less stunning. How could a person simply be . . . *erased*?

"Not in public records, but the original names would be identified in private law office records, yes?" Carol corrected.

"Ms. Goodworthy," he said firmly, "the birth mother is dead. The family has moved on. Take it from a wise old physician, it's in everyone's best interest to let well enough alone."

Beth was astonished. What about Lynne? What about the letter? They couldn't give up just like that. From Mary Kay's startled expression, obviously she felt the same way too.

"But finding Julia was so important to Lynne," Beth pleaded. "In her letter, she said making sure her daughter knew that Lynne loved her was the only way she could rest in eternal peace."

Dorfman was strangely silent for so long Mary Kay and Carol wondered if they'd lost their connection. "Dr. Dorfman?" Carol asked. "Are you there?"

"I am." He paused again. "I get the impression that you

ladies are determined and there's nothing I can say or do to prevent you from going to Andersson's office even if it is a complete waste of time. That said, perhaps I can offer you a tip."

They didn't dare breathe.

"If you happen to be passing by Wilkes-Barre on your way back to Connecticut, you might want to check out the Crescent Hollow area. There's a scenic overlook of the Susquehanna at Council Cup near there. Supposedly, on a clear day you can see thirty miles and the foliage is spectacular and, conveniently, it'll be on your way home."

Mary Kay made a face at Carol, who was just as confused as she and Beth were. "I'm sorry," she said. "I'm not following. You said you were offering us a tip?"

"Exactly. I think you'll understand if you happen to come across the names of the adopting parents. And if you don't find those names? Then you can take solace in knowing that you left no stone unturned."

"Thank you," Carol said, though she wasn't exactly sure what for. "Thank you very much, Dr. Dorfman."

He hung up and she decided knowledge really was power. Dorfman had it and they didn't and for that reason, they—and Lynne's hopes—were at the mercy of others.

❦

While Carol and Mary Kay disappeared into the redbrick Andersson law office to try their luck with Doug Andersson, Beth sat in the car and called Marc. Her father's appointment was at eight and already it was past ten and there'd been no word. She was getting nervous.

"No big deal," Marc said. "Your dad's doctor got called down to the emergency room so the appointment was pushed back. Anyway, I spoke to the receptionist a few minutes ago and she said he's on his way so I'm headed to the cafeteria to find your parents. They couldn't take waiting around in his office with a bunch of elderly heart patients. It was depressing."

"I'm sorry," she said, feeling guilty that he'd sacrificed a whole morning to manage her responsibilities. "I should be there."

"Would you stop with that? Hey, what else was I going to do, make a few cold calls? You know how I'd rather do anything but sell insurance."

Marc had no business being in this business. "Still, you're a sweetheart for doing this."

"I'm a sweetheart, period. And your dad's a buddy of mine, so I'm glad to help. Seriously, Beth, go do what you have to do and quit worrying. I'll call you as soon as I know anything."

With plenty of time to kill, she got out of the car, locked it, and headed off to explore the town in search of a cup of coffee and maybe a bookstore.

It was refreshing to take a walk, considering she hadn't had much exercise since her run with Carol two days before. And Calais wasn't that dingy, just your usual small town with a couple of banks, a post office, a former Woolworth's that now sold gently used clothing, a small shabby grocery store, and a corner newsstand.

Beth went inside, poured herself a cup of thick, burnt coffee, and debated whether to get a homemade blueberry muffin wrapped in plastic, the debate ending when her stomach growled in reply. At the cash register, she asked the clerk where she could find a bookstore.

"A bookstore?" The clerk acted as if she'd asked directions to the nearest crack house. "There's a Borders about eight miles from here in the mall, I think."

Eight miles was too far, since Beth really didn't want to get back in the car if she didn't have to. "There's nothing downtown?" All she had in her purse was *Middlemarch*, too dense for her dizzy head.

"You could go there." He pointed to a low gray stone building set slightly back from the street next to the post office. "The public library."

The library! Her haven. Her oasis. Happily, Beth crossed the street and sat on the library front steps. While she finished her stale muffin and caffeine sludge, she checked her phone to see if Marc or Mary Kay had called. Then she went inside.

The library was small, about the size of her beloved one back in Marshfield. It was also about as old, with dark wood running halfway up the walls, green shaded lamps, and two outdated computers on oak desks where patrons sat perusing job openings, killing time.

She introduced herself to the woman sitting behind Returns and Renewals—Annie Marx, head librarian just like her. After briefly talking shop about budgets and staffing and fund-raising, she headed to New Fiction to see what a place like Calais could afford when it came to recently released hardcovers. Turned out, not much.

"So I've got to ask," Annie said as Beth was inspecting the latest James Patterson. "What brings you all the way from Connecticut to Calais?"

"A long story." But since Annie didn't seem to be in any hurry and since no one was tapping their toes at Returns and Renewals, Beth gave her the abridged version. Having also lost a friend to cancer, Annie was sincerely sympathetic.

"I am so sick of women in the prime of their lives getting struck down by this disease," she said, shaking her head. "It gets freakier when they're your age, too. Did she go to CRHS?"

"What's CRHS?"

"The local high school. If she grew up in Calais, she probably did."

"Then she probably did unless there's a Catholic school nearby."

"Our Lady of Lourdes. That's where I went." Annie pushed back her chair. "Let's find out."

Beth replaced James Patterson and went with Annie to the stacks in Reference, where navy spines of old yearbooks aligned in a neat row. "Nineteen seventy-eight, seventy-nine, eighty . . . Got it." She slid out the Calais Regional High School *Bugle* and flipped to the back. "You said her name was Swann?"

"Like the bird, only with two *n*'s." Beth tried peering over the top of the book as Annie scanned the page of *s*'s.

Flipping it around, Annie said, "Is this her?" She pointed to a black-and-white photo of a freckled face with ridiculous Molly Ringwald bangs.

Lynne beamed up at them, her smiling eyes looking off into the distance as if the future promised nothing but endless adventures ahead. "Yes," she said as Annie laid the book in her arms. "That's Lynne." Her fingers traced the bangs, the pointed collar of the shirt, the tidy pullover sweater.

So young and fresh. So innocent.

"I better get back to the desk," Annie whispered. "There's a bench against the wall if you want to sit down and go through it."

Beth couldn't take her eyes off the photo. Lynne was nothing like the hippie chick she'd imagined. Quite the contrary. With the wool sweater and haircut, she'd been kind of preppy. She searched the back for Lynne's list of organizations. Yearbook. Glee Club. Art Society. *That figured.* Drama.

Then Beth started at the front, inspecting each page. She passed the teachers and administration and support staff and ignored the endless photos of the CRHS Hurricanes football team and its roster of stars. It came as no surprise that Calais, Pennsylvania, would be a town that loved its Friday night football.

Finally, she found a photo of Lynne dressed up as Lady Macbeth for the fall senior play, her hair yanked into a tight bun and makeup so overdone that she could have been acting in kabuki rather than Shakespeare. Behind her, Macbeth himself, slightly shorter, placed a protective hand around her waist.

The caption read LADY MACBETH (LYNNE SWANN) AND MACBETH (DOUG ANDERSSON) CONTEMPLATE THEIR EVIL DEEDS.

Beth read it again. And again.

Doug Andersson. But it couldn't be the same. Didn't Dr. Dorfman say he ran with a different crowd? Beth turned to the back and, under the *a*'s, found Doug Andersson, equally preppy in his button-down shirt and vest, his hair parted on the side. Debate. Tennis. Yearbook. Drama. What a geek.

She quickly flipped through to the group photo of the yearbook staff. Doug and Lynne again. Side by side. Beth inspected every inch of that book and counted no fewer than four more photos of Lynne—Lynne walking to class, Lynne sitting on the grass in front of the school, eating lunch in the cafeteria, at the prom.

And in each one, Doug Andersson was by her side, grinning at her with puppy-dog adoration.

Beth slapped the book shut and marched over to Returns and Renewals. Annie said, "You find out anything more?"

"I need to ask you a huge favor, librarian to librarian," Beth whispered. "I know this is a reference book, but would you please let me take it outside of the building so I can show it to my friends?"

"Oooh." Annie cocked her head, doubtful. "There's a photocopier in the corner. I'm afraid I can't let you leave with this. You know the rules of reference."

"Please." Beth clasped her hands together. "I swear that by noon it'll be back on this desk. Photocopies won't have the same effect." She didn't want to get Annie in trouble, but this was a matter of life or death. Almost literally. "This book could help us find my friend's daughter."

Annie sighed. "Only because you're a fellow librarian." She nodded. "But please don't forget to bring it back. Not like they're issuing any more 1980 *Bugle*s."

Beth practically flew out the door, clutching the yearbook to her chest like a treasure, as if it were more valuable than the Holy Grail.

The bell to the Andersson law office tinkled as Mary Kay and Carol let themselves into a small lobby with weathered red carpet and framed maps of various local points of interest. It smelled of musty journals, as law offices should, and dampness from the creek that ran behind Main Street. It was very quaint with its old-fashioned charm.

"May I help you?" A frazzled woman looked up from a desk piled high with manila folders. Also quaint, Carol thought, considering how every last letter, memo, and file was digitally converted at Deloutte Watkins. It was like stumbling into a law office circa 1954, right down to the tarnished brass nameplate: JEANINE DeCARLO.

"Hello, Jeanine. I'm Carol Goodworthy, an attorney with Deloutte Watkins in New York City." Carol handed her a card. "And this is my, um, associate, Mary Kay LeBlanc."

"Pleased to meet you," Mary Kay said, extending her hand.

"I wonder if we might have a brief word with Douglass Andersson Junior."

Jeanine pinched the card between her fingers as she rotated on her chair. "And this is regarding? . . ." she asked, eyes wide with suspicion.

Carol said, "It's confidential."

"I see." Jeanine carefully punched #1 on her desk phone. "There's a"—she glanced at the card—"Carol Goodworthy from a firm called Deloutte Watkins in New York City here to see you. She says it's confidential. Uh-huh. Uh-huh. OK, I'll tell her." Jeanine returned Carol's card. "Unfortunately, you've caught Mr. Andersson at a bad time and he can't see you today. But if you make an appointment for next week, I'm sure he can fit you in."

"Jeanine," Carol said gently, "this won't take long. Please."

"There's nothing I can do, Ms. Goodworthy. When the boss says he can't be disturbed, the boss can't be disturbed."

"Look, I have no intention of going all the way back to New York and then returning in a week. So, how about you look the other way while I poke my head into his office. You can pretend I snuck in."

Jeanine said, "I think your friend beat you to the punch." She nodded to her left, where Mary Kay was sauntering into Douglass Andersson Jr.'s office like she owned the place.

"Thank you," Carol mouthed, joining Mary Kay and closing the door behind them.

Douglass Andersson wore his dark hair, graying at the temples, in a stylized helmet and his shirtsleeves rolled to the elbows. The firm grip of his handshake was manly, business-like. He smiled broadly, as if not only had he been expecting them but had been eagerly anticipating their visit all morning.

"Guess you gals done flushed me out," he said, hitching up his pants. "I thought I could hide and get some work finished, but Mary Kay just walked right in and introduced herself." He winked to show they were pals nonetheless.

Mary Kay said, "I'm sorry. Carol was talking to your receptionist and I just started wandering, peeking in doors. Should we leave?"

"That depends. How long are we talking, here?"

"Five minutes, tops," Carol said. "Trust me, I know how annoying it is to be interrupted in the middle of the day."

He motioned for them to have a seat. Carol took in the plaques on the wall. Pitt Law School. Member, Pennsylvania Bar Association. President, Pennsylvania Young Lawyers As-sociation. A citation from the Rotarians. Another from the

Special Olympics. Two from the Democratic Party and one highly valued, front-and-center plaque proclaiming adoration of the local steelworkers.

There was also a formal family photo taken on the wrap-around porch of a stately Victorian home: a blond woman holding a toddler in an adorable striped shirt and shorts. Three other boys, ranging from college age to preteen, flanked her protectively, the de rigueur golden Lab at their feet. Douglass Andersson towered behind them, one hand on the shoulder of his wife, the other on the shoulder of his firstborn. *Pater familias.*

"So I assume you're here about Lynne Swann's baby," he said bluntly, rocking back in his chair.

"You got it. Dr. Dorfman called this morning and mentioned you'd spoken," Carol said. "But we wanted to hear what you had to say, considering you're the lawyer and he's just . . . a doctor."

"I'm a doctor, too. So are you. Doctors of jurisprudence."

She laughed like this was a new one. "I never thought of that before." She had. Every lawyer has. "About Lynne's file . . ."

He rocked forward and linked his hands earnestly. "Let me cut to the chase, Carol. The law doesn't permit release of her file, and to be perfectly frank, records that old . . . I wouldn't even know where to begin the search. We had a flood in our basement a few years back that wiped out most of our older papers."

Carol offered another suggestion. "Perhaps, if you have a way of contacting the adoptive parents, you could give them a call for us. We have a letter for Lynne's daughter and that's all we need to do, deliver the letter. You wouldn't be violating your code of ethics since you're acting on behalf of your father, who was their lawyer."

He rubbed his chin. "I can't make any promises, but why don't you give me the letter and I'll try."

Carol thought, *No dice.* "Stupidly, I left the letter with our friend who's not with us. I'd have to make a return trip. However, if I knew for certain that you'd spoken to the parents . . ."

"Like I said. The adoption file—if we had one stored in the basement—is lost. The best I can do is keep your letter on record and should the adoptive parents happen to contact us, though I can't for the life of me reason why they would, I'll willingly share what Lynne wrote."

That would never do, especially since Doug was right— the chances of the parents contacting his law office were slim.

Mary Kay crossed her legs and tried a different tack. "Dr. Dorfman says you went to school with Lynne."

"I dimly remember her. In all fairness, it was a big regional high school. More than seven hundred kids in our class." He frowned. "Shame what happened. If my wife got sick and died, well, you might say I don't know how I'd go on. She's my everything. Not to mention what it'd do to our boys."

Carol gestured to the photo. "Is that your family?"

"They're two years older now." He rubbed a smudge off the glass. "I should probably get a new one."

"Thinking back," Mary Kay said, "is there anyone who might have hung out with Lynne senior year you might know? A good friend? A boyfriend?"

He shook his head. "I'm sorry to be shooting blanks here, but I didn't even know Lynne Swann well enough to say hello. Her friends were into drama and art. I was into tennis and debating. Our paths just simply wouldn't have crossed." He got up and went to the door. "I wish I could be more help. What you two are doing is yeoman's work. But my hands are tied and, you know, we're talking about thirty years gone by."

He opened it and smiled. "Five minutes."

Carol and Mary Kay thanked him for his time—even if it led them right into a wall.

"How'd it go?" Jeanine asked as Doug Andersson closed his office door behind them.

"Disappointing," Carol said. "To say the least."

"There was a woman in here a few minutes ago looking for you. She was very excited, but then she got a call she had to take outside."

Must have been Beth. They went out and found her leaning against the bumper of the Highlander deep in conversation. When they got closer, she covered the mouthpiece on her cell and said, "I have big news," and handed them an old high school yearbook. Into the phone she said, "Hold on, Marc. I'll call you right back."

"How's your dad?" Mary Kay asked.

"He's OK, considering." She shrugged off her worry. "We have some big decisions to make, I think, but according to Marc the doctors are very optimistic. Anyway, look at this." She opened the yearbook, showing them what she'd found while in the Calais Public Library. Carol and Mary Kay were stunned.

Not to mention pissed.

"He lied to us." Mary Kay tapped the photo of Doug and Lynne at the prom in matching powder blue formal wear. "Out-and-out lied."

Beth said, "Don't tell me he denied dating her."

"He denied ever speaking to her," Carol said, adding that his exact words were that he wouldn't have known her to say hello.

"What a jerk," Beth said, indignant.

"There's only one reason why he would lie about something as innocent as whether they dated in high school," Mary Kay said. "Because he's the father and he's covering his rear."

"Right," Carol agreed. "What I don't get is why Lynne wouldn't have just told us he was the father. That would have saved us so much aggravation."

"Because she's protecting him," Beth said sadly. "Because maybe she might have loved him once upon a time and she doesn't want us coming in and ruining his life."

"Wow." Mary Kay slung her purse over her shoulder and clasped her hands. "Now what do we do? Abide by Lynne's wishes and pretend he's not the father or show him the yearbook?"

"We do what will help us find Julia," Carol said. "We show him the yearbook."

This time, they didn't even bother asking Jeanine if he was in. They knew the answer. As Beth went back to her phone call with Marc, Mary Kay and Carol marched past Jeanine's desk and opened the door to Doug's office.

He was sitting there, hands in his lap, staring out the window. Some pressing workload indeed, Carol thought.

"Mr. Andersson?" she said.

He swiveled his chair so his back was to them and said rather testily, "I thought our five minutes were up."

Carol dropped the yearbook onto his desk. "I thought you didn't know Lynne to say hello."

He kept his back to them.

"Let's see. Here you are in the 1980 high school year-book as Macbeth and Lynne as Lady Macbeth," she said, though Andersson refused to look. "All those practices and you never recognized her, huh?"

She flipped to another photo. "And here are you two on the yearbook staff. And here you are hanging out on the school lawn, knee to knee."

"What's your point?" he said angrily.

Carol closed the book. "The reason why Eunice Swann hired your father to arrange the adoption of her grandchild was not happenstance. Your father had a personal interest, didn't he?"

"I think you're making some pretty wild assumptions based on a couple of yearbook photos." But he didn't deny it.

"If you were so close, as it appears here." She opened the book again. "How about you give me the name of one other guy in your high school who might have been the father of her baby so we can look him up."

"I can't possibly think back that far."

Carol let Mary Kay take over as she randomly found a page and read off names. "Could the father be Bill Danish?" Mary Kay asked. "Thomas Detcko? Vinnie D'Mazilla? Or maybe it was . . ."

"OK, OK." He rotated toward them, his head down. "What do you want from me?"

"I want you to tell us who adopted Lynne's baby," Carol said. "That's all we ask."

"And I told you that I'd love to help, but I can't."

"Why not?" Mary Kay asked. "Didn't you love Lynne?

Don't you care that the only thing she wanted before she died was to find her daughter?"

"Of course, I did . . . I do. But in a small, conservative town where reputation is everything, I cannot take the risk of people finding out that I fathered a child out of wedlock." He clenched his jaw. There. He'd said it.

Mary Kay gestured to the framed photo. "I assume 'local people' includes your lovely wife. Surely she has no idea of your love child."

"You wouldn't."

"You're right," Carol said, two hands on the desk and leaning forward. "We wouldn't. For Lynne's sake."

"What do you mean," he asked, "you wouldn't tell my wife for Lynne's sake?"

"In her letter to us, Lynne never mentioned your name," Carol said as Douglass listened intently. "She didn't leave you out to hurt you, but to protect you. It would have been far easier to tell us to hunt down that S.O.B. Doug Andersson and force you to find her baby. Hell, she could have done that herself."

He bowed his head again, his bluff called, his cards poorly played. "OK, here's what happened. Actually, Lynne and I have been in contact."

Carol sighed deeply. Finally, they were getting some-where.

"We reconnected a few years ago through Facebook. You have no idea what effect it had on me when she wrote that she was dying. Lynne was always so . . . full of life. So vivacious." He smiled to himself. "I asked her to marry me when she told me she was pregnant, but she didn't want to be stuck here in Calais. She wanted to get out of this mudhole. I could have given her the world if she'd let me. Nice house over on the Hill District. Security. But there was no stopping her. No matter how hard I tried, there was no way I could get her to stay."

Carol said, "Do you mean to tell me that during all your Facebook reconnecting, Lynne never asked you what happened to the baby you two conceived?"

He shook his head. "I never said that."

"Then she did."

"Yes."

Carol was close to becoming exasperated. This was worse than some of her tougher cross-examinations. "And how did you respond?"

"That I couldn't release the information for the same reasons I gave you." He rubbed the bridge of his nose, unable to meet their gazes. "I had no idea she was this close to death. The last I heard from her was a week ago last Thursday when she said she was feeling a lot better and was planning to spend the day outside."

"A week ago last Thursday," Mary Kay said, "was the day Lynne killed herself."

"I didn't know that until I got a call from Dorfman saying that she'd died. I went online and looked up her obituary. . . ." He covered his face with his hands, his shoulders heaving. "I'd hoped he was mistaken."

They let him cry. For a while, those were the only sounds in the office, Douglass Andersson catching his breath, the springs in his chair squeaking as his body convulsed in sobs.

After a long while, he looked up and asked them to tell him everything.

Carol related the story of Lynne's suicide and tried to recall her letter to the Society word for word as best she could. "We have no interest in ruining your life or your marriage, Doug. All we want is a way to find Julia."

He rested his elbows on his desk and closed his eyes as if he were praying. When he was done, he leaned over, unlocked a bottom drawer, and handed them a thin blue file. "Here. I checked its contents when Dorfman called, and it should have all the information you need."

A zip of energy shot through Carol's arm as she took the file from his outstretched hand. This was too good to be true. "You don't want us to make copies?"

"I don't ever want to see it again. Take it away from here. Burn it if you want." Then he swiveled his chair away from them and went back to looking out the window, his shoulders drooped. "Anyway, that chapter is closed and behind me now. The future is all that matters."

Carol took a last glance at his family photo, of his innocent children smiling under the protective gaze of their father, and decided that maybe he was right.

Chapter Fourteen

They drove the five blocks back to the library since they had the feeling their Highlander was no longer welcome in the Andersson law office's parking lot. Along the way, they filled in Beth about the details, how Doug Andersson had refused to release the file until the very end, relenting when they promised not to tell anyone.

"May I just say this is why public libraries kick ass," Beth said. "Try finding online what I found in the high school yearbook. You couldn't. This is why the local library must be saved."

Mary Kay and Carol parked the car and while Beth went into the library to return the yearbook to Annie, they got some bad coffee across the street.

"I think this hangover's finally going away," Carol said, popping an Advil to make sure.

"Mine isn't," Mary Kay said. "Hear me now and believe me later, I am never drinking again."

Carol laughed. "Famous last words."

Unable to take the suspense any longer, they met Beth on the steps and opened the forbidden file.

The paper on top was the adoption decree:

IN THE ORPHAN'S COURT OF NORTHAMPTON COUNTY, PENNSYLVA-NIA in re Adoption of Julia Eunice Swann, a Minor.

DECREE

The Court hereby decrees that the said Julia Eunice Swann shall be in law the adopted child of Donald Miller and his wife, Grace Szymankowski Miller, and shall have all the rights of a child and heir of said petitioners, and be subject to the duties of such child, and is hereinafter named and known as Alice Marie Miller.

Walter J. Schneider, P.J.

COMMONWEALTH OF PENNSYLVANIA COUNTY OF NORTHAMPTON.

Carol turned over the page to the petition attached. "And here's Lynne's signature forfeiting all rights." She pointed to a scrawl.

Beth and Mary Kay each took a gander. "That's her signature?" Beth asked.

"Keep in mind she'd just given birth," Mary Kay said. "And she was drugged."

"What we've got here is sealed forever, you know. Our possession of it is definitely illegal," Carol said. "Beth, if you hadn't come across that yearbook, we would not be reading this now."

Mary Kay checked the file and removed a yellowing memo. "This could be their address."

It read: DONALD AND GRACE MILLER, 18 PINETREE LANE, POCONO LAKE, PENNSYLVANIA.

Carol scrolled through the White Pages listing for Millers on her phone. "That was thirty years ago. Chances are slim they're still there."

"Most people don't keep their house more than seven," said Beth.

"We can track them down—if not by ourselves, then I'll hire one of Deloutte Watkins's private investigators," said Carol. "Do you know how many Donald Millers are in Pennsylvania? Hundreds." Carol scrolled through page after page, discouraged. "Not a good sign when you run a name and the response comes up 'Whoa! Over 100 Found.'"

"Any on Pinetree Lane, Pocono Lake, Pennsylvania?" Beth asked.

"Nope. Nor any in that area, as far as I can tell. I think we're screwed, ladies. For all we know, Donald and Grace might have died or moved to Florida."

"Usually, it's the other way around." Mary Kay jabbed Carol in the ribs. "Hey, didn't Dorfman say something about checking out Crescent Hollow if we find their names?"

"Geesh. I must be more hungover than I thought. That completely slipped my mind." She typed the Millers' name and Crescent Hollow, Pennsylvania, into Google.

"Bingo!" Carol held up the phone to show them the address. "Dorfman came through."

"We found them," Beth exclaimed. "Julia's parents. I never thought we would."

"Me neither," Mary Kay agreed.

But Carol couldn't share their enthusiasm. How would the Millers react to three strange women showing up at their door with a letter from the dead mother of their beloved daughter?

"You know, we really haven't thought this through enough," she said. "We have to be very careful. It was hard enough for Eunice and Therese. Imagine what it'll be like for Julia."

"I've thought about that," Beth said as they crossed the library lawn and headed toward the car. "I think Lynne did too. That's why she wrote the letter."

"While she was at it, she should have written Doug," Mary Kay said, "instead of telling him the day she killed herself that she felt a whole lot better and was going to spend the day outside."

Beth placed a hand on her arm. "What?"

"Doug told us he and Lynne were communicating through Facebook," Mary Kay said. "Her last words were probably to him—right under Farmville."

Lynne's last words hadn't been to her or Mary Kay or Carol or, probably, even Sean, Beth thought. They'd been to Douglass Andersson, a stranger from a life they'd had no idea she'd ever lived.

It was so strange to think that Lynne had never so much as hinted about her hidden past. In the course of fifteen or so years, even after the lubrication of fairly potent martinis, she never let it slip that she'd been forced to give up her baby. Or, more recently, that she'd reconnected with her first love online.

She'd said *nothing*.

It was the kind of crazy circumstance Beth had found only in books. And not very good books, at that.

All of which left her somewhat miffed. Weren't best friends supposed to share *everything*? "There was so much going on with her. I had no idea."

"None of us did," Mary Kay said as they piled into the car. "Makes me wonder how much of the real Lynne we knew."

"What matters is that she's sharing her life with us now," Carol said. "Hey, not even Sean knows what we know, not her sons or her mother, not her doctor or colleagues at work. In the end, it was us she chose. *Us*."

It was small, bittersweet comfort. But it was all Beth had.

⌒

The drive to Crescent Hollow would normally have taken a good four and a half hours. But Mary Kay floored it east, across I-80, weaving in and out of tractor trailers, sending Beth into fits, gripping the door handles and bracing her feet against the dashboard.

"Have a heart, MK. I'd like to live to see my grandchildren."

"Don't worry. I've got it all under control." Mary Kay scanned for lurking state troopers and, deeming it safe, depressed the accelerator to 85.

There was a particular urgency in her need to get this

over with and get home. It wasn't just that they'd been on the road since Saturday morning and the Highlander was getting rank after three days of crisscrossing this big block of real estate called Pennsylvania. It was that her last conversation with Drake had left her in a state of high anxiety. When he mentioned he'd found the birth-control pills, when he asked if he could start telling people the good news, she realized he was getting his hopes up, and that was when she started to panic.

"Who's up for a new martini?" Carol asked.

Mary Kay blanched and gripped the wheel, her knuckles white.

Beth put down *Middlemarch,* her umpteenth attempt. "Now? We're driving."

"I don't mean to drink. I mean to create. My memo's in so I've got nothing to do. I'm bored stiff."

Beth said, "There was one I came across the other day, a sherry martini."

Carol scoffed. "No, that's for church ladies. You know what I want to try that we haven't? A Manhattan martini. Rye, vermouth, bitters, and a Maraschino cherry."

"My father would have liked that," Beth said. "He liked Manhattans, before the doctors put him on the wagon. Hey, you know what we need to do? Invent a martini to commemorate this trip."

Carol clapped. "Now you're talking. Let me start by saying it should be strong, like we are."

"And light," Beth added. "Maybe some champagne or fruit."

"Not dry, though," Carol said. "Because this weekend has been anything but dry."

They decided it should also be slightly sweet and piquant, in honor of Lynne. Strong, sweet, fruity, and bubbly. If they could only have thrown in a touch of determination.

"What do you think, MK?" Beth asked. "You're awfully quiet."

"Just keeping an eye on the road ahead, hon, and where it's gonna take us now."

They didn't talk much for the rest of the drive. Carol napped in the rear while Beth put aside *Middlemarch* and chatted with her mother and Madeleine and then her mother again, hashing and rehashing every minuscule detail of Chat's tests. Finally, the three of them managed to arrange a conference call that took the good part of an hour.

The results showed blockage in two arteries, in addition to fluid within the lung walls indicating congestive heart failure. The cardiologist at Grace suggested stents to relieve Chat of chest pains, though they would not necessarily repair the damage done from years of indulging on thick juicy rib eyes at client lunches and Sundays spent vegetating in front of Patriots games on his fifty-inch widescreen TV.

The alternative was a bypass, a risky procedure in Chat's case. Needless to say, Maddy was all for at least exploring the option in New York.

"Bill Clinton and David Letterman didn't wait around to die," Madeleine said. "They were whisked into Columbia-Presbyterian and treated immediately. Doesn't Dad deserve the same? Why should he receive lesser care?"

Elsie didn't know what to do. Her preference would have

been to make no decision at all. "I wish I could turn back the clock," she mused, "to when we didn't have to worry about stents or bypasses. Your father used to be so strong. Do you remember when he used to pull the dinghy across Kindle-wah Lake while swimming the backstroke? With you two girls in it?"

Madeleine let out a groan. "I know this is hard for you, Mom, but unfortunately we can't turn back the clock. Dad's reached a certain age where he can't do what he used to."

Coming on top of Lynne's sickness and suicide, Beth was getting fed up with mortality. When she was younger, she never thought about death and illness. Sure, she and Marc would get old someday. *Someday* far, far away. But she hadn't stopped to think about how close that day was and that Marc, like her father, could lose his vitality or that she, like Lynne, would wake up to find that a routine bout with the flu was something more. She couldn't fathom being in her mother's position, having to make these life-and-death decisions for the man who'd once been the family breadwinner.

Procrastination was a trap, she decided. It was how people ended up in the hospital, how they got so old without ever having fulfilled even one promise of youth.

"Beth?" Elsie said. "Which would you choose?"

"I would like to choose not to choose." Those were Lynne's words when her doctor laid out three options to treat her cancer, all of which carried unpleasant side effects.

Maddy said, "I know what you mean, Beth. And Mom's right. It seems like yesterday when Dad was pulling us across the lake. His shoulders were these massive boulders and I remember thinking there was no one stronger on earth than my father."

"Me too," Beth chimed in, glad that Maddy had dropped the bossy, know-it-all, older-sister routine for once. "By the way, Maddy has a valid argument about New York hospitals. Grace doesn't even begin to compare to Columbia-Presbyterian. Of course Dad should have his bypass there."

"Thanks," Maddy said, sounding surprised. "That's very big of you, Beth. I'd also like to add that I've been doing some soul searching as well and I have to agree there are plenty of advantages to keeping Dad close to home. Beth's right when she says he'll recover quicker if he's in familiar surroundings, and, Mom, I know it'll be easier on you."

It was so much more pleasant not to fight about this, Beth thought. It was a wonder they weren't so cordial more often. Like Lynne used to say, "It's hard enough fighting *for* your life, without spending your life fighting."

"So what's the answer?" Beth asked.

"I don't know," Elsie said dreamily. "I think the only answer is to live life to the fullest while you can and collect memories like fools collect money. Because in the end, that's all you have—happy memories. If you're fortunate."

If the view off Scenic Cup was as awe-inspiring as Dr. Dorfman claimed, the women wouldn't find out that day. The storm had caught up with them, filling the Susquehanna riverbed with fog that inched up the sides of the mountains and rolled onto the roads. Darkness was falling and they had just reached Crescent Hollow.

What they could make out in the dim light and rain seemed to be another tidy Pennsylvania town brimming with pride. Immaculate vinyl-sided or brick houses lined the wide streets. The small yards had been raked free of leaves, and driveways had been freshly blacktopped for winter. Even in this weather, Old Glory hung limply from most doorways.

"Small-town America," Beth said with satisfaction. "Vintage Sherwood Anderson. Except Sherwood Anderson was Ohio, not Pennsylvania."

"Same difference," Carol said as she tried to negotiate the GPS. "You need to hook a left, MK, and the Millers should be three doors down at the end of a dead-end road." They turned onto a quiet street, leaving the noise of traffic behind.

"What a lovely neighborhood," Beth noted with delight. "And with the dead-end road, so safe."

She'd been making observations like this ever since they'd entered the greater Crescent Hollow area. "Such a nice place for Lynne's daughter to grow up."

Mary Kay slowed the Highlander to 8 Bound Book Road. While the Cape Cod–style home would never make the cover of *Town & Country,* it was adorable and sweet, with ginger-bread overhangs and a brick chimney covered with climbing ivy. Rain rolled off the eaves, and a white picket fence, a throwback to another era, bordered a thick green lawn with large dripping oaks, between which swung a hammock. A backyard boasted gardens, a silver cedar swing set, and a brick patio. Where the lawn ended, the woods began.

The plantings of juniper bushes and azaleas, rhododendrons and mums, obviously had been tended with loving care. Even the mailbox had its charms. Red cardinals flying over a winter field.

"Oh, Lynne!" Beth said, delighted. "You should see Julia's home. You would love, love, love it."

Mary Kay pulled over and Beth jumped out of the car, into the pouring rain, not bothering to so much as pull up the hood of her raincoat.

Carol shrugged. "That's it, then."

"We're committed." Mary Kay depressed the button on her umbrella. The long journey was about to come to an end. She hoped.

Beth had rung the doorbell, practically hopping up and down, as Mary Kay and Carol made their way up the walk. "I hear someone. Julia's father."

"*Alice's* father," Carol emphasized. "Her name is Alice."

Beth made a mental note to remember that.

Before they could plan their strategy, however, the door swung open and there stood a little portly man in jean bib overalls. Hardworking farming stock, Mary Kay thought. Honest.

He greeted them with the warm cheer of a doting grandfather. "You poor gals standing out in the rain. Come in, come in."

They gathered in the small tiled foyer, wet and dripping, encouraged by the reception. A bouquet of cut flowers rested on the hall table, another under a mirror. Yes, this did bode well. Very well indeed.

"Heck of an evening to be out like this," he said. "Your car break down?"

"Not exactly." Beth brushed rainwater off her cheeks. "Are you, by any chance . . . Donald Miller?"

"I am. And you?"

She inhaled deeply, unable to restrain herself. "Julia . . . I mean, are you Alice's father?"

Mary Kay cringed.

Carol said, "Maybe we should explain first, Beth."

"Is Alice OK?" he asked earnestly. "I haven't heard from her in . . . Gosh. Days." He ran a hand through his white hair. "Normally, we talk every night, but her husband took her for a getaway for a few days, you know, so she could recover after her mother's funeral last week."

Mother's funeral last week? This didn't make sense. Did Alice know about Lynne?

"Something is wrong, isn't it?" Donald had dropped his arm, his shoulders going limp. "What? What is it?"

"Nothing, nothing." Carol stepped forward. "We don't know anything about Alice. We've come here for a completely different reason concerning your daughter. Maybe we should all sit down."

Baffled, Donald led them to a small formal parlor with a fireplace, a couch, and two recliners, one of which he obviously preferred because the arms were worn and it was littered with newspapers. A reading lamp overhead was on bright and a book was overturned on a nearby table. There was another vase of cut flowers by the bay window.

He took the chair while Mary Kay and Carol took the couch, as they had at Aunt Therese's and Eunice's. Beth sat separately, absorbing the news about Julia's mother. *Had Julia really been at Lynne's funeral?*

Carol led the charge. "Mr. Miller, we are friends of Alice's biological mother, Lynne Swann. Actually, Lynne Swann Flannery."

He rested his large farmer's hands in his lap. "Well, I'll be."

"And I'm afraid we don't come under the best of circumstances. As you may or may not know, Lynne died two weeks ago after an eight-year battle with cancer."

He furrowed his brows, puzzled. "How the heck would I know that? I haven't thought of that name for thirty years, not since we adopted Alice. If you hadn't said 'biological mother,' I wouldn't have had the foggiest idea who Lynne Swann was."

Now it was Beth who was confused. So Julia hadn't gone to Lynne's funeral after all. Then . . .

"So when you mentioned the funeral for Alice's mother," Mary Kay said, "you were talking about . . ."

"I was talking about my wife, of course, Grace. *She* was Alice's mother."

"Of course," Carol parroted, diplomatically.

It was too little, too late. Without meaning to, they'd gotten off on the wrong foot and Donald was working himself into a mild lather. "Alice never had another mother. Never. She and Grace were attached at the hip. Why, Alice even looks like Grace."

Beth turned her attention to a collection of framed photos, nearly all of which featured the same cherubic strawberry blond girl, from a baby posing with a fuzzy white blanket and pink bow in her hair to a kindergartner with her lunchbox and fist raised on her first day of school to a young woman in a wedding photo, Alice's long cream satin train wrapped around her feet, her auburn hair adorned with matching roses, Donald on one side, Grace on the other.

Alice wasn't the spitting image of Grace. She was the spitting image of Lynne.

It was like seeing Lynne when they first met as young mothers with babies, when she was shoveling snow and singing show tunes. It was like coming across her photo in the high school yearbook earlier that day. There was the same faint patch of freckles across the nose, the mischievous green eyes and daring smile at her lips.

A lump formed in Beth's throat as she remembered the wedding dress in Lynne's closet and the pair of earrings she'd set aside just for her daughter. They would have gone perfectly with Alice's complexion.

So lost was she in memories, she didn't notice the tension filling the room like a poisonous cloud.

Donald had been insulted, understandably, Carol thought, wishing she could retract the last ten minutes. They should have mentioned they were friends of Alice's biological mother and then quickly segued into asking about his wife and her funeral and his feelings. That way, he might have been more receptive to their visit, instead of taking it as some sort of an affront.

"Mr. Miller," Mary Kay said, "we didn't mean to imply that your wife wasn't Alice's mother."

"She was buried only last Wednesday. Have you no sense?" His jowls trembled and his eyes watered. "With all due respect, the last thing I need are three strangers coming for Alice, too."

Was that what he thought, that they were here to win over Alice? "Oh, no," Beth piped up. "That's not our intention at all. We had no idea your wife died. We're here only to fulfill our friend's last wish."

"Which is?" His hands had moved from his lap and were gripping the arms of the chair.

"To find Julia." She mentally kicked herself. "I mean, *Alice*."

"Alice," he said again. "And what could you possibly want with her, seeing that your friend's passed on?"

The women were suddenly at a loss for words. Obviously, their purpose had been to hand Alice the letter from Lynne and then leave. But they couldn't give the letter to Donald, not with the fire in the fireplace right behind him ready to devour the envelope. They couldn't take the chance.

"Lynne spent the last few years looking for your daughter," Beth said again. "And after she died, she left a note asking us to take up the search. We have a letter for Alice, too, that Lynne wanted us to give to her."

"For what purpose? To tell a heartbroken daughter that the mother who gave birth to her was dead too?" His words were civil, but the sharpness in his tone was piercing. "That's a darned self-serving goal, if you ask me. Might make you feel good, but did you ever stop to consider what getting a letter like that would do to Alice?"

Not deeply enough. "It wasn't our place," Beth said weakly. "We are just doing what was asked of us."

"So I keep hearing. But that doesn't make it right." He flexed his beefy hands. "People ask lots of things from other people. But that doesn't mean they're *right* just because they ask. No disrespect to your friend, but it was wrong of her to ask you to find Alice. She had no business and, quite frankly, neither do you."

Carol rested her cheek against the cool palm of her hand. There was some merit to his words. "What, exactly, are you afraid of, Mr. Miller?"

He scowled. "I'm not afraid of anything. What I am is disgusted that after all these years you and your friends think you can show up on my doorstep one night and intrude on my family. When your friend gave up Alice for adoption, she forfeited her parental rights. She signed off. She agreed to walk away."

Carol said, "And what if I told you she did that under duress, that Lynne was drugged and manipulated into signing those papers?"

"Then I'd have to ask what took her so long to have a change of heart. Alice is thirty. It's a bit far gone to be coming in and taking my little girl."

"We're not taking your little girl," Mary Kay began, but it was no use.

"Please," he said, directing them to the front door. "Try to understand. I buried Grace on Wednesday, my wife of forty-eight years. Wednesday."

Beth nodded in sympathy. After all, she'd just buried someone dear to her heart, herself. Clutching the purse that held Lynne's precious letter, she bustled to the doorway, Mary Kay and Carol on her heels muttering apologies.

This had been their one opportunity to find Julia. After all that work and perseverance, after driving over hundreds of miles to locate Julia's adoptive parents, in the end they had blown it.

They had failed Lynne. They had let her down.

And now they were out of hope.

The Bad Boy Martinis

~∽∽~

If the classic martini is elegance in a glass, our two favorite alternatives, the Blue Margarita and the Manhattan Martini, are her bad-boy cousins.

Blue Margarita gets its kick from tequila, a bandit's liquor distilled from the agave plant and rumored, depending on the brand and method of manufacture, to have hallucinogenic properties. Too often lost in the sugary blanket of artificially flavored margarita mixes, we like to combine a high-quality tequila with a splash of Cointreau, an ounce of fresh lime juice, and a drop or two of Blue Curaçao for color. Proportions depend entirely on your taste. Serve in a chilled glass with a lime twist. Perhaps, a salt-rimmed glass?

Elusive rye whiskey is the often-overlooked ingredient in concocting the perfect Manhattan. Some establishments cheat by using Canadian whiskey, but rye is the preferred base. To this add several drops of Angostura bitters, a mysterious brew of herbs and roots once promoted to cure a variety of ailments from bad skin to flatulence. To the rye and *bitters add equal parts dry and sweet vermouth. Shake with ice and pour over Maraschino cherries.*

Why Maraschino cherries? Because every bad boy needs a sweet and innocent accompaniment.

And often, vice versa.

Chapter Fifteen

"How could I have been so dumb? Dumb. Dumb. Dumb." Mary Kay gripped the steering wheel as she negotiated a winding uphill road in a downpour with zero visibility.

"It's not your fault, MK," Beth said. "You saw him. He was besotted with grief."

But Mary Kay was inconsolable. If only she'd handled Miller with more tact, if she hadn't made that ignorant comment about Grace's funeral, if she'd simply held her cursed tongue for once instead of blabbing. It might have worked out OK.

There were so many ifs.

If Lynne had been alive. *If* she hadn't killed herself, *if* she had held on a few weeks longer, and *if* she'd asked them to help search for Julia while she was alive, she and Alice could have been reunited.

If.

Mary Kay was so bloody sick of ifs.

Now, exhausted, they headed to a hotel near Wilkes-Barre to recoup. This was no night for more travel, not with the pelting rain and darkness and the disheartening realization that their mission had come to an abrupt, useless end.

Beth in the backseat put on her headphones and listened to classical music and tried to sleep—anything to drown out her own thoughts. *"I have become comfortably numb,"* Pink Floyd once sang. She longed to be comfortably numb.

Mary Kay squinted, trying to see through the fog. "Put yourself in Miller's shoes," she said to Carol, who was searching for hotels on her iPhone. "Less than one week after your wife dies, three strange women show up on your doorstep looking for the only child you have. You'd be irrational too."

"He wasn't that irrational," Carol said as the car swerved. Mary Kay must have been exhausted from hauling ass across the state. "Mary Kay, you've done more than your share of driving. Let me take over the wheel."

"Don't be silly. You haven't driven in years."

It was true. After two years of living car-free in New York, Carol's skills were probably a little rusty, to say the least.

"Bullshit. I still know how to drive. Look, you're weaving and distracted. You're going to get us all killed."

Carol had a point. They pulled over and switched seats. Carol clicked her seat belt, adjusted the seat and mirrors, flicked on her blinker, and got back on the two-lane road. It wasn't so bad, driving again. Piece of cake.

"The question is, what do we do now?" Mary Kay reclined her seat and closed her eyes. "What the heck do we do now?"

"Go home, I guess. Put the letter in safekeeping in case

we ever make contact with Alice. Otherwise, it's back to our regularly scheduled programming." The wheels slipped a bit and she gasped.

Mary Kay sat up. "You OK?"

"Some hydroplaning. I have to get used to driving in the rain again. That's all."

"It's no big deal for me to . . ."

"No. I'll just slow down." She pumped the brakes and took a turn down the wooded serpentine road in what, according to her GPS, promised to be a shortcut to I-84 that would bypass the hassle of going through Wilkes-Barre. "We did what we could, Mary Kay. It was an impossible mission from the get-go, especially with Lynne already dead."

"I wish she hadn't done it," Mary Kay said.

Carol was temporarily blinded. A car coming around the bend sent a wave of water onto their windshield, coating it with invisibility. "Damn him," she cursed, her heart beating fast as she fiddled with the wipers, accidentally turning them off. "What did you say?" she asked when they were back on track.

"I was saying I wish Lynne had held on a little longer instead of throwing in the towel. I understand why she did what she did. I wouldn't have wanted to live with that pain, either."

"Ditto."

"But she might have had a few good weeks, even a few good months, left in her. There's no telling what might have happened in that—" She gripped the door handle and closed her eyes. "Oh, God. Is there any way you can drive straighter?"

Carol chuckled. "Sorry, MK. I'll do what I can, but this road is switchback, first this way, then that, up and down."

Mary Kay covered her mouth.

"Are you all right?" A flash of oncoming headlights revealed her friend's complexion, white and waxy. "Oh, my God. You're *not* all right. You're sick."

"Shh." Mary Kay gestured to Beth, dozing in the backseat. "It's nothing." She lowered the window for some fresh air. "Nothing more than the combination of car sickness and stress."

"Stress from this trip?"

"That and"—Mary Kay took another calming breath—"this marriage proposal."

"That's not the way most women in love react to a marriage proposal." Carol kept one eye on the road, and one eye on her seatmate. "I have to say, this thing with you and Drake has us all confused. If you're getting sick over this decision, then you need to talk about it."

Mary Kay stuck her head out the window. "There's nothing to talk about. I just need to get out of this car."

"I don't think the car's the problem. Is there something wrong with Drake we don't know about? Is he a closet control freak? A closet abuser? A closet . . . anything?"

"No. He's perfect. He's the most perfect man, ever. He's funny and warm and just great to be around. I love him. Next to you guys, he's my best friend."

Carol threw up her hands and slapped the wheel. "Then what is it?"

"He wants a family." Mary Kay lowered the window more and inhaled. "And I can't give him one."

"What do you mean you can't have a family? How do you know?"

Mary Kay told her the saga, starting with her two infections and the laparoscopy that confirmed her fears.

Carol pieced the timeline together. "So Lynne knew?"

"She was the only one and I swore her to secrecy."

"Why didn't you tell us?" Carol couldn't help but be slightly hurt. She'd always thought of them as a tight circle of four friends, the Society.

"I'm not completely sure why I didn't tell you." Mary Kay took another breath. "In retrospect, there might have been a fair amount of denial. And I didn't know you guys that well back then. The only reason I ended up calling Lynne that night was because it was a blizzard and she had four-wheel drive."

"You do realize, this is what I do for a living, right?" Carol said. "Reproduction law is my thing. Every day I help infertile couples find the right surrogates."

"I can't see myself using a surrogate mother."

"I doubt you'll have to. Blocked fallopian tubes are fairly common and easily treatable. In vitro fertilization is the first option, of course. But you know that already. What does Drake have to say about this?"

Mary Kay turned toward her. "That's just it. He doesn't know."

"He doesn't . . . what?"

"He doesn't know what I just told you." Another breath of fresh air. "He's fully convinced I'll have no problem getting pregnant. When we first started dating, he came across an old packet of birth-control pills and made a comment. You might say I didn't exactly leap to correct him."

"You were taking the Pill to avoid an ectopic pregnancy?" Carol asked.

"Right. I stopped them a few years ago when I turned forty, since they put you at an increased risk of stroke after thirty-five. I'm glad I did, too, because I lost about ten pounds."

"But why didn't you tell him the truth?"

"So he wouldn't leave me for a younger, more fertile woman. I know, it's bad." She studied her hands in her lap, ashamed. "I'm like the teenage girl who agrees to sex so she doesn't lose her boyfriend, except, in our case, the stakes were higher."

"I'll say." Carol tapped the brakes. "That would explain your tummy ache. I bet you have an ulcer." Though the symptoms were exactly like Lynne's in the beginning—and they'd passed those off as the flu or stress, too.

"It's gotten worse since Drake found my birth-control pills this weekend and knows I haven't been taking them." Another wave of car sickness. "The kicker is, now that I know what a stand-up guy he is, I'm pretty sure he would have stuck with me if I'd been honest about all this in the beginning. But now I've messed up everything. Who wants to marry a colossal liar?"

And with that, she wiggled off the engagement ring. Carol hit a pothole and the ring went flying out of Mary Kay's hand. "Oh, crap."

Mary Kay bent down to find it.

Beth, rousing in the backseat, sat up and, over Mary Kay's bent back, spied the oncoming disaster. "Look out!" she screamed, gesturing to the deer lumbering toward them.

Mary Kay threw her arm across Carol as Carol slammed so hard on the brakes she lurched forward and seized up the safety belt, but it was too late. The front end of the car hit the galloping brown body, its hooves flying in the headlights, big black eyes wide in panic. The thwack was so hard, the car shook.

"Shit!" Beth exhaled as the deer limped off. "Did you kill it?"

Carol, her hand over her wildly beating heart, was too breathless from shock to answer. "Is it dead?" she whispered hoarsely.

Mary Kay rolled down the window and peered into the night. They could hear it thrashing in the underbrush, struggling, getting up, and falling down. Injured.

"No, honey. It's worse. It's alive."

The state trooper crested the hill and, spying the Highlander with its Connecticut tags, lights on and idling by the side of the road, did a U-turn, angling his cruiser behind Beth, who nervously waited in the driver's seat while Mary Kay and Carol were in the woods seeing if they could find the deer.

He dawdled for what seemed like an unnecessarily long time to run her plates before getting out and approaching the Highlander. He swept his flashlight over the backseat, illuminating the suitcases, Carol's laptop, and the Igloo full of martini mixings. The beam lingered there, curious.

"Were you the one who called about the deer?" He appeared at her window, stocky and short, a brass D. EVANSTON name tag pinned to his left pocket. Beth found it interesting that he wore wire frames, like her husband, and decided he couldn't be all bad.

"Yup."

"May I see your license and registration?"

With a quivering hand, she turned over the tidy Dartmouth-green plastic packet marked BREWSTER INSURANCE: A FRIEND IN NEED IS A FRIEND IN DEED. Marc had taught her it was best to have your papers organized and ready.

The trooper left, returning a few minutes later sporting a kinder and gentler attitude. "So, you came to Pennsylvania to bag you a deer, huh?"

"Uh-huh," Beth said, not getting the hunting joke. "It ran right into us."

His boots crunched on the gravel as he proceeded to inspect the front end. Beth joined him to assess the damage and was shocked to find that not only was the bumper of her pristine Highlander caved in, but that stuck to the license plate were tufts of brown fur.

"Oh!" she cried, horrified. As someone who stopped traffic to avoid hitting even the smallest animal, Beth found it unthinkable that Carol had taken out a large mammal with her car. "We tried to avoid it. We really did."

"We?"

"Yes, my girlfriends are in the woods where the deer is. She's a nurse."

The trooper said, "The deer's a nurse, huh?" He was trying to make her feel better, but it wasn't working.

"No, my friend Mary Kay. She's seeing if she can help it."

The trooper nodded to himself. "Wait here," he said, then scrabbled down the embankment.

Beth ran back to the car, where she turned on the heat and snuggled into Carol's good camel coat. The night air was awfully cold in this damp, remote place. At least the rain had stopped. Two cars passed, slowing down, rubbernecking.

Finally, Mary Kay and Carol emerged from the woods, Carol giving Mary Kay a hand up the steep part. They were covered in wet leaves and twigs and looked very somber. The trooper followed and went to his cruiser.

"What's going on?" Beth asked.

Carol sat in the back. "He has to shoot it."

"Can't they bandage it or something?"

"It's in pain and suffering, Beth," Mary Kay said. "It's not fair to let living things suffer. Putting him down is the humane thing to do."

Mary Kay was referring to the deer, but Beth couldn't help thinking about Lynne. Beth had tried to deal the best she could with Lynne's suicide, helping out with the funeral and throwing the reception, even putting her own parents' needs aside so she could fulfill Lynne's last wishes.

But this deer thing was the last straw.

Suddenly, she was *mad*. Mad about how her car had been ruined, mad about how an innocent animal had been needlessly injured because Carol and Mary Kay hadn't been paying attention. She was even mad at Donald Miller for saying they had no business trying to find Julia.

Mostly, though, she was mad at Lynne for going to a place where Beth could not follow, for writing the suicide notes alone, for not telling her about Julia.

For not saying good-bye.

"I'm sick and tired of all this talk about needing to mercifully put people down because they're in pain and suffering," she said. "Whatever happened to fighting to live?"

"We're not talking about putting *people* down," Mary Kay said gently. "We're talking about an injured wild animal."

Beth wiped her dripping nose on the sleeve of Carol's coat. "That's what I mean."

"I don't blame you for being upset, Beth," Carol said. "This is all my fault. If I'd been paying more attention to the road, this wouldn't have happened."

"What were you two talking about, anyway, that had you so distracted?" Beth made eye contact with Carol in the rearview.

"Lynne," Mary Kay lied. "We were talking about Lynne."

Carol replayed what Mary Kay had done in the woods trying to save the deer, bending to get close to its head, murmuring soothing sounds. Its large eyes, frightened, gradually closed; its breathing subsided from panicked breaths to a calmer rhythm. Carol had knelt, quietly transfixed.

She had never thought about it before, but she knew then, in the woods, that Lynne's suicide was particularly hard for Mary Kay. Mary Kay had invested years chauffeuring Lynne back and forth to New Haven, taking notes during her oncology appointments, researching her chemotherapy options, encouraging her with positive thinking. And yet, Lynne had died. She had *chosen* to die. She had given up.

And Mary Kay, knowing full well that Lynne was contemplating suicide, let her.

"There he goes," Beth said, watching the trooper plunge into the darkness, shotgun in hand. "I can't listen." She punched on the radio, cranking it to full volume. The song playing was "Hotel California," an Eagles number they'd heard so often during their trip, Mary Kay had christened it the Pennsylvania state anthem.

Beth stuck her fingers in her ears. Mary Kay broke out in the chorus and Carol joined her, belting the lyrics at the top of their lungs. They sang and sang and didn't think. Just when Beth crooned, *"You can never leave!"* there was an unexpected banging. All three women jumped.

"Holy Toledo," the trooper said after Beth cautiously lowered her window. "I've been standing out there for ten minutes. What the hell were you women doing, yodeling your heads off in there?"

Yodeling? Carol tried not to take offense. They were hardly yodeling.

Beth said, "We were trying to drown out the shots of your gun. Is it over?"

"Beats me. Went down there and the deer got up, ran off. Looked A-OK from where I was standing. Probably, it was just in shock when you two found it."

Carol squeezed Mary Kay's shoulder.

Beth exhaled in relief. "Awesome."

The trooper got back in the cruiser and waited for them to pull onto the road. They drove off, shaken by the accident and relieved the ending was relatively happy, though none of them would be the same as they were before the deer rushed headlong into their car.

That had upset everything.

∽

The hotel off the interstate was nothing special, a simple business joint, though with its well-lit lobby and warm cookies waiting for them at the check-in desk, it felt like a five-star resort.

"It's warm and dry," Beth said, shaking out her umbrella. "And it's not on four wheels."

Carol lifted her nose. "Chlorine. There's a pool."

"I say we meet there in our suits for martinis and what-ever I can order from the room-service menu." Mary Kay applied her signature to the reservations with a sweep of her pen.

"Let me get the ingredients for the martinis, and I insist on springing for the rooms," Carol said. "After trashing the front end of your brand-new car, it's the least I can do. OK?"

And so it was separate rooms for each of them. Carol's treat.

Beth set up a luggage rack and opened her suitcase, find-ing her black-skirted swimsuit rolled to the side. It was one of those Lands' End suits where you could mix and match tops and bottoms depending on your shape—circle, triangle, and rectangle. She stepped out of her clothes and yanked on the suit, reluctantly assessing her image in the mirror and discovering that, for once, she was at peace with what she saw. This body of hers wasn't about to grace the cover of *Vogue* anytime soon, thankfully. But it was a fine body. Just fine.

She ran her hands over her sturdy thighs, barely con-cealed by the kicky pleated skirt, over the slight pouch of her stomach and around what was left of her waist. So what that her thighs were big, that her stomach protruded somewhat. She was healthy and alive. Such a thing we take for granted, being alive. Such an amazing gift. She would have to be more appreciative, she decided. No more groaning at the mirror or avoiding fluorescent lighting.

From now on, she was going to dress with panache like Lynne used to. Colors. Silks. Patterns! She was going to cel-ebrate her womanly form and get on her knees and thank

God for another day in it. On that note, she grabbed her key card and walked out the door, not even bothering to disguise herself in a towel.

Across the hall, Mary Kay, already in her suit and flowered sarong, surveyed the room-service menu. Man, was she starved. She picked up the phone and ordered everything that looked good: chicken wings and a quesadilla, guacamole, a few club sandwiches—no french fries, though. And tons and tons of fresh-cut fruit. Extra pineapple.

"Is that all?" the receptionist asked.

"Is that *all*?" In Mary Kay's opinion, that had been quite a lot. "It's only for three people."

The receptionist didn't say anything after that.

Several doors down, Carol couldn't stop thinking about Mary Kay's dilemma. In light of all they'd learned this weekend, it seemed absurd for two deserving people to lose out on a life together because Mary Kay had suffered some momentary lapse in judgment. It was unfair that Mary Kay had to pay twice for a random infection that could have ravaged any woman.

Drake might be understandably hurt when Mary Kay told him the truth, not because she couldn't get pregnant, but because she'd lied. Premarital counseling might be in order, something Carol wished she'd done with Jeff to improve their communication problems. But surely Drake and Mary Kay could overcome this, couldn't they?

Or was she thinking about her and Jeff?

After changing into her swimsuit, a navy boy-cut bikini with white piping, she turned on her cell phone to call Scott and tell him that she'd hit a deer. What she didn't expect to find was a voice mail from Amanda.

Hi, Mom, I got your message from last night that we needed to talk about Lynne. What's up? Leave a message because I'll be in and out all evening. Project due. Click.

Carol replayed the voice mail and grinned at the familiar efficient delivery, the sense of business. *It's me,* she realized, remembering what Lynne said about them not getting along because they were so similar.

That was exactly how she'd sounded at age twenty—always on the go, clipped, as if she couldn't be bothered to speak in full sentences. A roommate in college once observed that when Carol was on the phone she sounded pissed for no reason and Carol had been dumbfounded. She didn't *feel* pissed. She was just . . . *busy.*

We're a trio of lousy communicators, Jeff, Amanda, and I, she thought. Jeff was as bad as she was. When he wasn't treating his patients, he was thinking about them. And Carol was habitually catering to her roster of clients, many of whom, as eager prospective parents, were pretty demanding. She listened at work, but when it came to her personal life she never afforded those she loved most the same close attention. Not really.

Except this weekend. This weekend she had listened and shared because she'd been squeezed into a car with two of her oldest friends and had no choice. And it had been nice. It was *meaningful.*

She pressed Call Back and got Amanda's voice mail greeting.

"Thanks for calling me back," she said. "I should have been clearer in my message. I wanted you to know that

Lynne used to tell me things that were going on in your life, and I know she told you what was going on in my life, and I realize now that it was because she wanted us to stay connected. And I thought . . ."

Carol paused, careful. "I thought we should honor her in some way. Got any ideas? You're so creative. I know you can think of something.

"Oh, another thing. I drank a few too many ginger martinis and danced on tables in front of a bunch of chemical engineers last night. Thought you might appreciate that."

She turned off the phone and nodded. If that didn't blow open the lines of communication, nothing would.

A half hour later, Carol waited in the pool room with the ingredients she'd picked up at a store across the parking lot—tequila, Cointreau, lime juice, and Blue Curaçao, the makings for a blue martini, the drink that had started it all.

"Awww," Beth said, stepping into the pool room. "You remembered. How sweet."

"I thought on our last day together we should do something to commemorate our first meeting of the Society—don't you think?" Carol held up the bottle of lime juice apologetically. "It was all I could find at the last minute. Sorry."

"It'll do in a pinch," Beth said, pulling out a white deck chair and having a seat as Carol mixed DeeDee Patterson's special recipe for blue tequila martinis, measuring out the lime juice and the tequila in equal portions. That brought back memories.

Tequila had been the only booze in Mary Kay's house that night if you didn't count the Cointreau and Curaçao, leftovers from her Mexican-themed New Year's party months before. Then again, they hadn't come to the PTA meeting at her house to party. It just worked out that way.

The PTA meeting itself was the usual Michelle Richardson dog-and-pony show. Since it was the opening gathering of the school year, Michelle was busy assigning members to run the holiday craft fair and debating whether they should sell wrapping paper or candles to raise money for their spring project. Beth and Lynne were new members, so they sat side by side, quietly counting the minutes until they could split, praying that Michelle wouldn't ask them to oversee the annual food drive.

Finally, conversation turned to the PTA spring project. Several mothers were in favor of bringing in puppeteers to run a workshop on puppet making. One group felt that since there was no music instruction in Marshfield worth a fig, the PTA should buy recorders and teach children how to play "Three Blind Mice." Others were all for buying encyclopedias for the school library.

It wasn't until someone mentioned funding a gifted program that the wind shifted. Women who'd been delightfully congenial while discussing puppets immediately, upon hearing the word "gifted," extended their claws in defense of their offspring. Beth was horrified to learn that not only were children in her son's kindergarten learning their letters, but they were reading *chapter* books!

Her son, David, bless his heart, was still drawing his *d*'s and *b*'s backward, and though she and Marc were avid readers, their attempts to teach him how to parse out words had been disasters. Either David yawned and pretended to fall asleep or he drew over the Beginning Reader pages with angry orange crayon. In light of what she knew now about his peers, Beth wondered if he were possibly verbally retarded.

Meanwhile, across the room, Mary Kay was fretting over her own inadequacies as a single mother. Yes, Tiffany was studying piano and ballet, but these mothers had husbands who took their children on camping trips and coached indoor soccer. They championed the importance of "family dinners"—father, mother, sister, and brother gathered around the table, sharing their day—while every night it was just her and Tiffany eating their grilled cheese sandwiches and talking about stupid stuff like the Spice Girls.

With absolutely no male role model, Mary Kay started to sense the limitations to her parenting. No matter how much she loved and volunteered, Tiffany would always have only half of what she deserved.

Having exhausted ways to compare their kids, thankfully the meeting ended. Beth and Lynne stayed to help Mary Kay clean up the coffee cups and cookie crumbs while Carol, as PTA secretary, polished her notes. In the kitchen, Beth had just thrown out the coffee grounds when Mary Kay said, "What would you do if your son didn't have a father?"

Beth was so caught off guard, she didn't know how to respond.

Lynne, stacking cups in the dishwasher, said, "Are you worried about Tiffany?" As the art teacher, Lynne had taught Mary Kay's daughter for several years and found her to be cheerful, bright, and firmly well-grounded. "Because you shouldn't. That girl is awesome."

"I can't help it." Mary Kay tossed away a wad of pink paper napkins. "Everyone was talking about what their husbands are doing for their kids, what good fathers they are, how they're teaching them to ski or . . ."

The swinging door flew open and Carol breezed in, a pencil behind her ear. "That's a bunch of BS, Mary Kay. They might say their husbands are perfect, but take it from me, the wife of the local pediatrician, no family in this town is perfect. I could tell you stories—if Jeff would let me."

"I know what you mean, Mary Kay." Beth pushed down the trash. "I was just thinking about my son, David, who's often lost in his own world. He didn't start talking until he was about three, and to this day he can't pronounce his *r*'s. After listening to these other mothers talk, I'm thinking of having him tested."

"But you have someone to lean on. I'm all alone in this." Mary Kay told them how her sister and brother-in-law had died in a crash four years before and how without any living relatives nearby she was learning how to be a mother on the fly.

"I had no idea you had no family around," Carol said, giving Mary Kay a big hug and finding the muscles in her back were knotted harder than steel. "You know what you need?"

"A husband?"

"A martini."

Beth laughed and Mary Kay said, "No, I'm fine."

"I'm not," Carol said, dropping her notes on the kitchen table. "All that talk about whose kid was taking Suzuki violin and how much they planned to spend on summer camp has me on edge too." Carol started opening cabinet doors, searching for liquor. "Come on. Don't tell me you're a teetotaler."

Indeed not, though all Mary Kay had on hand were the margarita makings, but no margarita mix. However, she also had a cookbook containing martini recipes that she'd found among her sister's collection, *Best Recipes from the Ladies Society for the Conservation of Marshfield, 1966*. It had belonged to the original owner of the house, DeeDee Patterson, who'd jotted quirky notes in the margins detailing the effects each martini produced.

Next to "Blue Martini," DeeDee had written: *Turns strangers into friends and, therefore, turns failures into triumphs. Good icebreaker for tough crowds.*

"Let's do this one," Mary Kay said, pointing to DeeDee's scrawl. "We have most of the ingredients, except for the fresh limes." Opening the refrigerator and peering in the back, she said, "Aha! Rose's lime juice."

"I've never had a martini before," Lynne said, curious as Mary Kay handed her the startling blue drink.

"I don't know if this counts as a martini, but it's close enough."

Beth had had the pleasure of a few martinis in her time, but none like this. This was cool and tangy and powerful all in one punch. Lynne said it reminded her of her honeymoon with Sean in Mexico and Carol said it was like a margarita, only without the annoying dilution of a mix.

Mary Kay lifted her glass and toasted to "friendship and failure."

"We're not *failures*," Carol countered. "We're women who walk to the beat of a different drummer."

"Ringo?" Lynne joked, her nose instantly pink from the tequila.

What happened after that was mostly a blur. Beth remembered that they'd made sandwiches and stayed so late that Marc called, wondering where they were. When he found out they'd been drinking, he insisted on picking them up, smiling to himself as Lynne and Beth giggled that they had just formed the Ladies Society for the Conservation of Martinis—a title they found in their tipsiness to be sidesplittingly hysterical.

That was the beginning.

Now, fourteen years later and miles away from Marshfield, Beth was so grateful that Carol had thought to remind her of what they'd once been.

Shaking the mixture vigorously, Carol poured out three glasses, garnishing each with a tiny paper umbrella.

"They're beautiful," Beth said.

Carol handed her one. "*We're* beautiful."

Mary Kay burst into the pool room, a wild red-and-gold sarong wrapped around her waist. It perfectly matched the gold rings on her toes and her thin bangle bracelets. She was about to apologize for being late when she took one look at the blue martinis and blanched. "How did you know?"

"Wasn't that thoughtful of her?" Beth said. "Our first martini together."

"Not exactly." Mary Kay twisted the knot of her sarong. "I'm not sure we should drink those anymore."

Carol's lips had barely touched the rim of the glass. "Why?"

"That was Lynne's last drink. The one she used to chase the morphine."

Beth felt a shiver ripple up her spine. "Huh? You told me she drank martinis, but not *these* martinis."

"When Drake and I went to her house that morning, on the kitchen counter were a bunch of bottles. Tequila. Cointreau. Curaçao. I didn't know what was going on. Then Drake checked the back porch and"—Mary Kay replayed the awful scene in her mind—"there she was, a half-drunk blue martini on the glass table next to her. The police told me later the oral morphine is so bitter that she would have needed something super strong to cut the taste."

Carol rested the drink on the table, mortified. "I had no idea."

Beth said, "I never knew she drank the morphine, though that makes sense since she told me she couldn't swallow the pills anymore, what with the scar tissue in her throat." She went silent, regretting her choice of words. "I'm sorry. That was pretty morbid."

"No, it's not. We have to discuss these things to get them out in the open." Mary Kay got up, unleashed the sarong, and took a few steps into the pool, her hourglass figure emphasized by her orchid-colored low-cut wrap tank and bandeau top. "That morning when Drake found her, I kept thinking how that had been our first martini and that we'd have to send the recipe into retirement because we'd never be able to drink it again."

"It was her favorite," Beth said. "Even after she tried a vodka martini and those delicious cosmopolitans and the raspberry-chocolate, she always came back to this."

Carol noticed offhandedly that Mary Kay hadn't replaced her engagement ring after she'd dropped it in the car. Joining Mary Kay in the water, she said, "Trust me, I had no idea. I was just being sentimental."

Beth sat by as Mary Kay and Carol worked their legs and

arms in the pool, each lost in her own thoughts. It was a shame their party had been ruined. They should be celebrating their efforts to find Lynne's daughter and toasting to the hope that Julia would someday come into their lives. They'd done what Lynne asked, and if Lynne were here, she'd be lifting her glass too.

This was not what Lynne had in mind when she wrote that they should drink a different martini every night on the trip. Not at all.

"You know what?" Beth went back to her untouched drink. "If Lynne were here, she'd want us to drink this. *L'chaim*." Not bothering to wait for their reaction, she took a big sip of the martini and let the distinctive tequila taste slide down her throat.

Palm trees swaying in balmy Caribbean breezes. Steel drums softly tinkling in the air. Toes in the sand and walking hand in hand by turquoise waters. This was the essence of a blue martini. Not death, but the best of life.

She let the potion wash away her guilt and anger and flood her with happy memories of their martini nights. She remembered a sudden frost when, at midnight, the women tipsily tiptoed through Lynne's and Beth's gardens—and the gardens of their unsuspecting neighbors—covering their perishable tomatoes with pillowcases and towels for protection. An entire neighborhood of vegetables was saved, thanks to them.

She thought of the blizzard that left them snowbound at Mary Kay's house, gathered around the fire in her spare nightgowns and robes after a power outage had cut the lights. Playing Scrabble. Drinking hot chocolate and giggling like they were schoolgirls. And those spring evenings among the roses, rejoicing in the rebirth of life. A summer solstice at the lake. Splashing in the waves on the Cape.

She thought of them coming together and trying to save Lynne for as long as they could.

Beth realized why Lynne chose to die by this, of all their martinis. It was her signal to the Society that, in the end, she was with them. And that they were with her.

Mary Kay and Carol emerged dripping from the water. "How is it?" Carol asked.

"Here," Beth said, handing a martini to each.

First Carol, then Mary Kay took apprehensive sips, followed by less apprehensive ones. "I'd forgotten how delicious this is," Carol said, holding her glass slightly away from her, admiring the shimmering blue. "Like lying on a hammock."

"Or at night on the beach after a day in the sun, your shoulders brown in a white sundress next to the man of your dreams." Mary Kay put hers down.

"It was Lynne's way of saying good-bye to us, so we'd know not to be sad for her." Beth lifted her chin. "It was her decision and she was at peace with that."

Carol put her arms around Beth and Mary Kay and hugged them both. They were standing there like that when there was a knock on the door of the pool room and a woman in a black uniform entered, wheeling in a cart piled high with plates of fresh fruit—pineapples, strawberries, grapes, and cut apples—along with a dish of guacamole, chips and salsa, chicken wings, and several sandwiches.

"Did you order all this, MK?" Carol broke away and wiped her eyes.

Reaching for a piece of pineapple, Mary Kay said, "Yeah. I might have gone overboard."

While Carol signed the check, Beth dug out her iPod and tiny speakers, searching for the Beach Boys and Bob Marley, to complete the atmosphere.

"Looks like you guys are having fun," the waitress said, tucking away her bill and pen.

"We are," Beth said.

"We're toasting to a dear friend of ours." Carol clicked the pen and handed her the black case.

"Somewhere in heaven, she's dancing on a Caribbean beach under a glorious full moon," Beth said. She knew this in her bones.

Lynne is OK.

The waitress left, turning down the lights as she went. Mary Kay lit a few candles she'd brought and Beth assembled her playlist as Carol mixed another batch of blue margarita martinis, splashing in more tequila, extra Cointreau. They hoped no one else showed. Maybe, since it was a Monday night, they'd have the place to themselves.

Then they got in the water and floated on their backs, their bare feet touching as they formed a three-petaled flower. "One Love," Lynne's favorite Bob Marley song, filled the air.

"You know what?" Beth said. "We're not failures."

"Failures?" Mary Kay said. "What made you say that? Because we didn't find Julia?"

"We came close," Carol said. "Closer than anyone."

"No, it's not that. The blue martinis brought back memories of the night you toasted to friendship and failures."

"Because that's what DeeDee's entry said. The blue martini turns strangers into friends and makes triumphs out of failures," Mary Kay said. "I was just fooling around after a meeting where I felt like such a loser mother."

Beth swam over to the edge of the pool and took another sip of her drink. "You forgot the 'therefore.' The exact line was 'Turns strangers into friends and, therefore, failures into triumphs.' That 'therefore' makes all the difference." A glass in each hand, she frog-kicked out to the middle of the pool and handed them to Mary Kay and Carol. "We triumphed *because* we are friends—get it?"

Carol said slowly, "Maybe. Though I'm pretty sure DeeDee was talking about how to save a dull cocktail party."

Mary Kay laughed and Beth playfully tweaked her button nose.

"Look at it this way," Mary Kay said. "If we hadn't become friends, I'd have raised Tiffany without any advice or help or babysitting from you guys. You became my family and you saved my ass."

Carol kissed her on the cheek. "You're my family too. I ran to you when my marriage fell apart and now, when I wonder if I made a mistake, I'm back again like bad breath."

Mary Kay slid an arm over her bare wet shoulders. "Glad to hear you say that, Carol. We're here for you, still. You know that, right?"

Carol nodded.

"Think of Lynne," Beth said. "She wrote in her letter if it hadn't been for us, she never would have been able to deal with cancer as bravely as she did. Mary Kay drove her back and forth to her appointments and I tried to keep her house neat and keep her fed. But I never did learn what you did for her, Carol, besides buying the Swedish divan."

Before Carol could shut her up, Mary Kay said, "She paid for all her outstanding medical bills."

Carol blushed. "Not *all* of them. Only the ones that her insurance didn't cover."

Beth was flabbergasted. "You're kidding! That must have been huge. Thousands of dollars."

"It was what it was," Carol said dismissively. "It's not worth getting into."

Nonsense. It was further proof that without their support, each of their lives would have been harder and lonelier. A mound of medical bills was the last hassle Lynne should have had to face in her dying days.

Beth gazed into the blue at the bottom of her glass, realizing there wasn't that much she could do about scraping up the money for David's tuition or repairing her father's heart, just as, despite her most valiant efforts, she hadn't been able to cure Lynne.

But no matter what happened, she fully trusted that Mary Kay and Carol would be there for her if things got tough. Lynne, too, in a way.

For death might take a woman in the prime of her life, might rob two sons of their mother and a husband of a wife, but it could never sever a friendship.

Friends were forever. They were the ultimate triumph over failure.

DeeDee was right.

Chapter Sixteen

The wind and rain from the night before left an awful mess on Don Miller's yard. Snapped twigs and leaves littered his driveway, defeating a weekend of raking and bagging. Winter was on its way, he thought grimly as he unlocked the front door and prepared himself for a blast of arctic air.

He sniffed. Snow. His heart broke.

It would be his first winter without Grace in forty-eight years. Forty-eight years of standing by the window, watching the first fluttery white flakes fall and melt on the ground. Forty-eight years of making fires and winterizing the house together, of putting up storm windows and taping the cracks. He'd worried how she'd be able to handle the climbing and lifting after he was gone, never imagining she'd be the first to go. It didn't make sense. Grace religiously walked three miles a day and counted out her omega-3 capsules. He had an irregular heartbeat and saw a doctor once in a blue moon.

He turned up his collar and trudged down the driveway to get the morning paper. But when he reached into his mailbox, his hand landed on something else. A long envelope addressed: *To My Lovely Baby Girl, Julia.*

He stood there a long time in the cold, turning that letter over and over in his hand, debating whether to rip it open and read it before chucking it in the trash. At last, he folded it and tucked it into the inside pocket of his coat. Then he went inside to read the morning paper and drink his coffee, alone.

⌐⍭⌐

Beth rummaged through her purse and Carol adjusted herself in the backseat, preparing for the three-hour drive home. They might be able to make it to Marshfield by noon, thereby giving her all day to sort through the stuff Jeff had left in the house, if Mary Kay could get a move on.

Carol lifted the lid of her soy latte and blew on the coffee. "Where is she?"

"Mary Kay? I don't know." Beth removed her wallet, phone, pens. "She came to my room earlier, asking for the keys to my car so she could get some Pepto-Bismol. Apparently, last night's orgy of appetizers didn't sit well." Beth flattened a receipt and tossed it aside. "What do you think's going on with her?"

"Nerves." Carol took a bite of her blueberry scone. "Tonight she tells Drake she can't marry him."

Beth quit rummaging and looked up. "Are you serious? I thought she changed her mind."

"She took off her engagement ring right before the accident and then didn't put it back on."

"That's too bad." Beth went back to searching. "I wish she'd tell us what's wrong. Maybe we could help."

Carol changed the subject. "What *are* you looking for?"

"You're not going to believe it. Lynne's letter. I think I lost it in the car."

"The one to Julia?" Carol checked under the seat. "When did you see it last?"

"I *thought* I saw it last night when we went to the Millers'. It was right there on top of my wallet so I could find it easily. But this morning it was gone. I just hope it didn't fall out when we were leaving his house." She bit a nail. "With the rain last night it'll be ruined."

They should have made a photocopy, a thought that had crossed Carol's mind when she was in New York. Like all wise ideas, she'd promptly forgotten it.

The back hatch flew open and Mary Kay stuffed in her cooler and bag. "Sorry. I had an errand to run and then I came back and took a shower. Thanks for letting me borrow your car, Beth."

Beth cheerfully offered Mary Kay the other coffee and remaining scone. "No problem. Did you find what you needed?"

"Uh-huh." She gestured to the mess on the front seat. "What's this about?"

"I was looking for Lynne's letter to Julia. I had it just . . ."

"I put it in Don Miller's mailbox this morning. That's why I needed the car." Mary Kay held up her hand in playful defensiveness. "Don't kill me. I just thought he should have it since that's the only way it'll find its way to Alice."

It was a risk, but the women agreed. The letter wouldn't

further Lynne's cause by gathering dust with her wedding dress and pearls.

Carol's cell rang in the depths of her bag as Beth merged onto I-84. *Jeff,* she hoped before immediately chiding herself for being so foolish. She should be hoping for Scott's call, and yet, she'd barely thought about him all weekend.

Nope, Amanda. Finally, she had caught her daughter's attention. Though Mary Kay and Beth would have been fine with her taking the call, she let it go to voice mail, where Amanda left a message.

Hi, Mom. What you said about Lynne trying to keep us talking, is that for real? That really got to me. She was such a cool person and I'm so going to miss her. You're right. We should do something to honor her memory. Maybe I could do a painting for the elementary school.

So, hey, what's this about you getting drunk on martinis and dancing on top of tables? Has my mother gone crazy?

I've got class in a few minutes and no cells allowed. Sorry I missed you.

Call me.

When was the last time Amanda had asked her to call? Not since the divorce, certainly.

Twenty minutes after nine, when she was fairly confident Amanda would be in class, Carol called her back and, sure enough, was sent to voice mail again.

"I can't believe we keep missing each other," Carol said.

"The painting for the elementary school is a brilliant idea. Lynne would love it. I'm not crazy. Every woman's got to let loose now and then, don't you think?

"By the way, I'll be at the house this evening to go over some knickknacks your father put aside in preparation for selling the house. If you want anything, now's the time to say so. I know you're busy, but I'd hate to throw away something of yours with sentimental value like your American Girl dolls."

Amanda couldn't part with her American Girl dolls, Carol thought, ending her message and wondering about the ethics of keeping sweet plastic Felicity Merriman hostage for her daughter's affection.

One hour later, Amanda called again. And again Carol didn't answer.

My dolls? No way! Save them for me, would you? And their dresses. Though, on second thought, I'd like a chance to pick through all my things myself. My schedule's pretty clear tomorrow, so I might take the train up. Don't throw out anything before then! Gotta run. Class in ten minutes!

Hey, thanks for keeping me in mind. I know Dad would have chucked those dolls.

Fifteen minutes later, Carol called back.

"Great. I'll remind Dad to leave the spare key under the planter for you. Don't worry if you can't take everything back. We'll ship it." Then: "Love you."

They had crossed the border of New York when Amanda left the message Carol had been waiting for.

*Love you, too, Mom. Sorry I've been such a snot lately.
I miss you. Think we can get together next week for
something, maybe planning Lynne's memorial?*

*There's this place on Sixth Street that you've got to
try. Best brunch ever.*

Carol called back right away. "The place on Sixth Street
it is. And you're not a snot. I am. We'll talk. Love you
back."

She hung up and Beth whipped around. "OK, this is
driving me nuts. She calls and you don't answer. Then you
call her right back and she doesn't answer. Back and forth.
Back and forth. What's going on?"

"We're having a voice mail conversation. One without
dramatic pauses or sighs. I'm not getting angry and she's not
taking offense." Carol smiled. "It fits our style."

Beth was doubtful. "How long do you think you can
keep this up?"

"I don't know. I'm just grateful we've come this far."

They headed down Freedom Plains Road across New York
State, past mowed fields and wooded lots, houses and farms,
until they reached Marshfield. It was a little after three in the
afternoon and their trip had finally come to an end with
some, but not total, success.

"I can't believe it's over." Beth dropped the keys into her
lap after pulling into Mary Kay's driveway. "We started only
four days ago and it seems like an eternity. I don't feel like
the same person."

"Maybe you're not the same person," Mary Kay teased. "Maybe you're Marilyn Monroe."

"You know what I mean. Think of what we've done. We've knocked on the doors of strangers and learned secrets about Lynne that not even her husband knows. We even met the man who adopted her baby."

"We met the love of her life," Carol said, "or so Douglass would have us believe."

"Hit a deer, don't forget," Mary Kay added.

"And danced on tables in front of chemical engineers." Carol bowed. "One of my finer moments, if I do say so myself."

"And drank a mess of martinis," Mary Kay said. "Tons."

"But we didn't find Julia." Beth fiddled with the keys. "Our most important task and we fell short. I can't get over it."

Mary Kay opened the door. "Don't take it so hard, Beth. Like Oprah says, it's the journey, not the destination." The rest of them followed suit, getting out and stretching their stiff muscles.

They helped Mary Kay carry her stuff to the porch. Mary Kay opened the door and the three of them stood there, not knowing exactly how to say good-bye. "I'd invite you in for martinis but, to be honest, I think I'm going on the wagon for a while. I need a whole new program of exercise and fruit, lots of sleep and meditation."

"Exercise, yes," Carol said. "I could do with a cleansing too. Hey, that's what we should rename ourselves, the Ladies Society for the Conservation of Our Aging Bodies."

Beth gave her a playful smack. "Don't you dare. Look, I, for one, loved our martinis and when I get a chance I'm going to do something we should have done a long time ago: update the original *Ladies Society for the Conservation of Marshfield* cookbook with all our recipes. DeeDee Patterson's 1966 edition is way outdated."

"But all we revised were the martinis," Carol said. "What about the hors d'oeuvres and soups and salads and main dishes, not to mention desserts?"

"You think anyone cares about those? All people care about are the drinks. And, on that note"—she leaned over and gave Mary Kay a hug—"is it champagne or tears tonight when you get together with Drake?"

"Tears, I'm afraid." Mary Kay put on a brave smile and squeezed her back.

Carol put her arms around the other women and the three of them stood there, rocking silently, saying good-bye.

Breaking away, Carol wiped her damp cheeks and said, "Let's make a deal. This winter, after the holidays, you two come down to New York and stay with me. By then, I'll probably have a new, larger apartment and we can take in a few shows, go shopping, update the cookbook, that sort of thing. Agreed?"

And though Beth and Mary Kay had each been silently hoping Carol would have moved back to Marshfield by then, they agreed.

"As long as you promise that next summer when the roses are in bloom," Mary Kay said, "you come home for a long weekend of drifting around the lake and hanging out in the pool."

"Sounds divine."

So, with more tears and hugs, they parted, waving good-bye and promising to keep in touch every day. Beth drove Carol to her old house, which was so dark and buttoned up tight she almost didn't want to get out of the car.

"Come on," Beth said, sensing her apprehension. "I'll go in with you."

"I probably won't even see Jeff," Carol said, checking under the planter and finding the spare house key in its old hiding position. "We'll pass like ships in the night."

Beth lingered on the steps as Carol stuck the key in the lock. "You want me to pick you up and drive you to the train station? I don't mind."

"No, thank you. Go see your father. I know you're dying to."

It was true. Even so, Beth said, "You sure?"

"I'm sure. You should be with your parents. You guys have a lot to discuss." Carol pushed open the heavy door, revealing the slate foyer lined with boxes of memorabilia, china, knickknacks, and framed photos and, yes, those American Girl dolls. This was going to take hours. "Oh, geesh."

"You'll be here until tomorrow," Beth said hopefully.

"I don't think so. Jeff's so efficient there must be a system to this mess that I'll figure out soon enough." Though Carol wondered how she was supposed to get this done in time to catch the eight p.m. train home.

"Well, call me if you need me. You know my cell." Beth gave her a quick hug.

Carol stood on the doorstep as Beth climbed back into the Highlander and pulled away from the curb with a short beep good-bye. She watched until it took a left and disappeared around the corner and she was back to being alone.

⌒

Beth turned down their shared driveway and stared at Lynne's empty house. She'd intended to grab her suitcase and head inside to call Marc and check on her parents but instead found herself wandering over to Lynne's side door, cupping her hands against the glass and peering in. There was the kitchen with the same red-and-white gingham curtains, the red rooster cookie jar and electric teapot.

But there was no Lynne.

She tried the knob. Locked. Lynne had never locked up during the day. Never.

Beth didn't know what else she expected. Of course, Lynne was gone. It was almost two weeks since she died and, eventually, the weeks would turn into months and the months would turn into years. Grass would grow over her grave and snow would blanket it in the winter.

Sean would erase Lynne's voice from the answering machine; he'd change his listing in the phone book from Sean and Lynne to just Sean. He might start seeing another woman—Lynne would have wanted that. Odds were likely that he'd sell the house and move permanently to their weekend cabin. And then another family would move in, people who'd never met Lynne, who never knew she existed.

Beth tried the knob again and turned away.

If this was how it was going to be from here on out, then maybe she and Marc should leave town too. Sadly, she let herself into her own kitchen and threw her keys on the counter. What would she do without Lynne? She could not live next door to that empty house.

It was time to move on.

After dumping her suitcase on a kitchen chair, she washed her hands and headed upstairs, almost missing the blinking red light on the telephone answering machine. That was strange. Most people, if they couldn't reach her at home, would call her cell.

She pressed the button and listened. Two messages. The first was from Marc in a slightly anxious tone asking her to call him, that he had tried her cell and hadn't had any luck. "It's important, Beth. Call me as soon as you get this."

It wasn't like Marc to be excitable. Ever.

The next was from her mother. At least, she thought it was her mother. It was hard to tell with the blubbering voice halting and hiccupping from the machine. The best she could make out was "Grace Hospital" and "he's going into surgery now."

Beth fumbled for the phone and dialed Marc's number. He answered on the first ring. "You're home?" was all he said.

"Just got in. I must have missed your call."

"Stay put. I'm coming to get you." He was walking. She could tell by his rapid breathing, which only made her breathing rapid too.

"What's wrong?" Though she knew. "Is it Dad?"

"He's had another heart attack. He's in surgery now and they're doing all they can." She heard the sound of a car door slamming. Marc was on his way. "But you should be pre-pared. It doesn't look good."

"Stay put," she said, snatching up the keys. "I'll get there faster if I drive myself."

Chapter Seventeen

O h, God. It was finally happening, everything she'd
feared since her father suffered his first heart attack five
years before was coming true.

Beth peeled off the backing from the ICU visitor pass
and slapped the sticker above her left breast and pushed open
the double doors to the white linoleum hallway, where the
clinical smells of disinfectant and chlorine mingled with the
all-too-human odors of urine and blood. She passed a gurney
on which a gray-haired woman was being wheeled, uncon-
scious, to destination unknown.

She dreaded hospitals and couldn't stand the idea of her
father being poked and prodded like a hunk of flesh.

What a relief to see Marc coming straight for her down
the hall, smiling broadly in an effort, she knew, to assure her
that everything was going to be all right. Even though, in
her bones, she knew everything was not all right. Everything
was very, very wrong.

Wordlessly, he gathered her into his arms and let her cry against his shoulder, rubbing her back in soothing circles. "It's OK, Beth," he murmured. "We got to him in time and these doctors know what they're doing. They know him. You gotta have faith."

After a while, they broke apart and Marc smoothed the tears off her cheeks. "That's my brave girl."

"Hah!" Beth blinked and sniffed. "Brave, nothing. I'm scared shitless."

"Your father doesn't think so. To him you are his smart, resourceful, beautiful daughter and I wholeheartedly agree." He smiled.

Beth didn't want to start crying again, so she brought up her sister. "Does Madeleine know?"

Marc ushered them through another set of swinging double doors to the heart of intensive care. "Your mother's been talking to her. Lots of should-haves and if-onlys."

So much for their brief sisterly rapprochement.

They turned a corner and found Elsie idling outside the waiting room, a crumpled ball of tissues in one hand, a half-empty cup of water in the other. She was surprisingly composed.

"I'm so glad you're here." Elsie put down her cup and tissue and took both of Beth's hands in hers, beaming kindness. She looked old, but capable. "Don't worry, honey. Your father's going to be fine. He's still got a lot of that Brewster strength in him."

"And what he doesn't have in strength," Beth said, hoping to comfort her mother, too, "he has in spirit."

"That's the attitude." Elsie winked. "I'll pass that on to Madeleine the next time she calls, which should be in"—

she checked her watch—"five minutes. She's so concerned."

"Is she angry about us not taking him to New York?"

"No, no. Of course not. She understands time was of the essence. We can thank our lucky stars Grace was only five minutes away."

"I mean . . . earlier. If we'd taken Maddy's advice about the tests."

"Oh, sweetie. Your father and I are touched by how much you and Maddy look after us. Most men should be so fortunate to have two grown daughters bickering over which hospital is the best for their father. But we're not incapacitated, you know. Dad chose Grace because that's what he wanted."

Elsie brushed a strand of hair off Beth's forehead. "Don't look so hurt. He took your opinion into consideration. Maddy's, too. Then he stayed here."

Beth wished Maddy were there to see how strong their mother was. "You're amazing, Mom."

"I'll go get us some coffee," Marc said, wisely sensing that this was a moment for the Brewster women to be alone.

The mother and daughter watched him stroll toward the cafeteria. "You made an excellent choice with that one," Elsie said. "If it hadn't been for him, your father would be . . ." Elsie's gaze wandered. "Gone."

"*Gone?* As in . . . dead?"

"Marc stopped by this afternoon with some mail from the office and a James Bond video to keep your father entertained while he was recovering from the tests. Took one look at him and told me to call nine-one-one immediately."

How had he known?

Marc returned, balancing two cups of coffee, some yogurt, and a banana. "There's not much there that's edible. But this should keep you going." Elsie only wanted the coffee and to stay out of the waiting room, which she found depressing and noisy, what with the TV on full blast.

So Marc got her a chair and a *People* magazine. Then he sat beside her and took her hand in his, the two of them talking and not talking. Beth found a chair at the end of the hall and dragged it over so she was on her mother's other side.

Hours later, that's how the heart surgeon found them, quietly holding one another's hands, when he came down the hall, pulled off his mask, and delivered the news.

❧

Carol removed a pair of soft, worn jeans from her weekend bag, along with her familiar dark green Middlebury sweatshirt. In the downstairs powder room that she had redone herself in a French Country motif with tea-stained walls and blue accent tiles, she pulled her hair into a ponytail and washed her face. It was only five o'clock. Jeff normally didn't make it home until seven, maybe seven thirty, so she had plenty of time to snoop.

Girlfriends left clues to mark their presence the way dogs piddle on fire hydrants. First, Carol checked the powder room medicine cabinet, searching for the stray tampon or bottle of sandalwood perfume. Nothing but the usual. A spare unopened toothbrush for guests. Advil. Band-Aids. An old prescription for skin rashes left over from when Jonathan got shingles. She stepped on the lever to open the wastepaper basket and dumped it. As a doctor, Jeff should know better than to keep expired medicine.

After the downstairs bathroom revealed no treasures, she couldn't help tiptoeing upstairs to see what evidence might be hidden in the master bath. At the top of the stairs, Amanda's room was to the left. Carol flipped on the light and gripped the doorjamb, remembering happier days when she and Jeff took Amanda at age twelve down to the local hardware store so she could pick out her own paint colors. Orchid and lime green on alternating walls.

Somehow they managed to keep straight faces as Amanda had chosen the paints in not pearl or eggshell, but high gloss. She'd seen it in *Seventeen* magazine and as soon as she was out of earshot, Carol and Jeff had collapsed in laughter, though the joke was on them. *They* were the ones who had to spend a weekend prepping and painting orchid and lime green walls.

It was all worth it, though, because Amanda was delighted when Jeff led her into the room, his hands over her eyes. She squealed and threw herself on her new full-size bed, bouncing up and down, gushing about the pillows Carol had sewn, the polka-dotted lampshade and complementary throw rug, the mosquito netting Jeff had hung from the ceiling and the tiny little fairy lights outlining her windows. "I'm never leaving. I love, love, love it!" she declared, hugging both of them at once.

Jeff had put another arm around Carol and kissed her on the cheek and she noticed the splatter of bright green paint in his hair, right above his ear. She'd been so proud that the man she'd chosen for a husband had also turned out to be a patient, kind, and tolerant father.

But the walls of orchid and green were no more, having been covered in a light, muted taupe—and recently, too, if the acrid smell of fresh paint was any indication. Also gone was the polka-dotted throw rug. In its place, tasteful sisal. White linen curtains hung at the windows and matched the white spread on the bed. Every trace of teenage Amanda had been erased. Carol silently closed the door and went to Jonathan's room. Maybe that had been spared.

No. The red carpet, the blue walls dotted with posters of various lacrosse and soccer teams, the cheap plastic trophies won for Best Improved Player and Most Loyal Team Member, too, had been removed. Cream walls and that sisal again. A nightstand held art books and a wheat sheaf wrapped in maple leaves. Honestly? Had this decorator ever met a healthy, red-blooded American male in his late teens? What a crock.

Finally, she went around the corner to their master suite that, much to her relief, had been left intact. There was their old king-size bed that they bought when Carol started commuting to New York and would come home so stressed that she'd toss and turn and kick Jeff awake. The quilt Lynne had made them for their twentieth wedding anniversary was still folded over the footboard, but that was the only personal touch. Everything else was missing, even the photos of their family that had taken up one whole wall. What she saw there, instead, was herself in a square mirror looking worn and sad, big bags under her eyes.

He's serious, she realized. Somewhere in the back of her mind she'd been half hoping that this was a ploy to win her back, but no. This was no trick. There'd be no one leaping from behind the curtains to shout, "Surprise!"

She had left him and now, at last, he was finally leaving her.

And that was that.

She went out of the bedroom and headed downstairs to deal with the pile of knickknacks.

Afterward, she found an old bottle of rye in the liquor cabinet and one of sweet vermouth. There was an unopened jar of Maraschino cherries in the pantry and even a couple of lemons in the sparse refrigerator. Some bitters, too, so she had everything needed for Manhattan martinis. She poured them over the cherries, took a healthy slug, and called Scott.

"I wondered when I'd hear from you." He wasn't mad, exactly. More like distressed. "I assume you're on the train now. Just tell me when you'll get in and I'll send the car to pick you up."

She bit her lip. "Actually, I'm not on the train."

"You're kidding. When do you think you'll be back?"

"Tomorrow. I'll see you at the office. There's so much work I need to catch up on, so I expect I'll be burning the night oil. I don't know when we'll be able to get together."

Scott went silent. "What's going on, Carol?"

"Nothing's going on. I just . . ." *Be honest. For once in your life say what you want and want what you say.* She put the glass down on the counter. "I don't think it's going to happen for us . . . romantically."

"Ah."

She flexed her fingers, thinking of how he'd dangled the possibility that returning home would change how she felt about him, how she felt about Jeff.

"Is it . . . ?"

"No. Jeff's moving on, selling the house as planned. It's

me. You were right about me hiding in New York. Being back in Marshfield and among my old friends has stirred up a lot of unresolved issues." She took a breath because this was going to be the hardest thing to admit. "You were very kind to find a position for me at the firm, Scott, and be so consoling after I left Jeff. I don't know how I would have kept body and soul together if you hadn't been there for me."

"But . . ."

"I may have made a mistake. Not in rejoining the firm," she added hastily, since losing her job would be devastating. "But in running away."

"Is that what you think you did, ran away?"

Ever the armchair therapist, she thought, smiling. "If I recall, those were someone else's words. Someone much wiser and more mature than I deserve."

"I don't know about that. However," he said, bucking up, "it's good to know you're asking the tough questions."

"Better late than never."

"I have to admit that I wish it were otherwise. We could have had a lot of fun, you and I."

"I know." This was harder than she'd anticipated. He was so nice, so decent.

"I hope you realize my door is open for whenever you need to talk."

"Thanks, Scott," she whispered. "That means so much."

"Then I'll see you tomorrow?"

"Tomorrow it is."

"Take care, Carol."

"I will, Scott. You too."

She hung up and took another sip of her drink. Breaking up in your forties was no easier than breaking up in your twenties, she thought, heading to the living room to make a fire. In fact, in some ways it was harder.

She opened the flue and rolled up the front page of Sunday's *New Haven Register*, setting it on the grate in the fireplace. On top of that, she sprinkled kindling Jeff kept in a corner near the tongs, lit a match, and got a blaze going.

A half hour later, the fire roaring, the front door opened and closed. Footsteps echoed across the pine floorboards and Carol heard the unmistakable thump of Jeff's laptop case on the hall table as he made his way to the living room.

"Hey," he said, unbuttoning his black wool coat. "You're still here. And . . . you made a fire."

"It was a little chilly." She held up her half-empty glass. "I'm drinking Manhattan martinis. Want one?"

He tossed his coat over the couch, and she got up to make him a martini in the kitchen.

"What did you do with all that junk I left in the foyer?" he called over. "When I came in and saw it was cleared out, I assumed you'd packed it up and left."

She brought a new drink and a refreshed one. "I took care of it. Come on. Let's sit by the fire before I head home. It's been a long day."

Jeff went to sit on the couch, but she sat on her spot on the floor, patting the space next to her. "Come on. We don't have to be two old fuddy-duddies on the couch."

"So, what did you do with the china?" he said, joining her, crossing his legs Indian-style. "There's no way you can carry that on the train. There's too much." Absently, he took the martini from her outstretched hand.

She clinked her glass against his and took a sip.

Decorum required he follow suit. "Hmm." He admired

the drink, taking a second gander to make sure he was right. "That *is* good."

"Isn't it? It's an old recipe of DeeDee Patterson's."

"The assemblyman's wife? She's dead now, right?" He took another sip.

"Long gone. I got it from her cookbook." She thought of DeeDee's note: *Makes a man feel like a man.*

He leaned his back against the bottom of the couch, grinning that Vince Van Patten grin. Amid the crow's-feet and occasional gray hairs, the handsome young stud who'd bounded off the courts of the New York Racquet Club and into her heart remained. "How'd the trip go?"

"Exhausting. And illuminating. I'll tell you about it someday."

He took another sip and looked around the room, confused. "Carol?" He put down his drink. "Why are our family photos on the mantelpiece?"

"Because that's where they belong." She picked out the cherry and popped it in her mouth.

"But . . ." He stared at the china back in the cabinet. "They were part of the pile I left in the foyer. You were supposed to take them home."

"I am home."

"What are you saying? Your home is in New York."

"My current place of residence, yes." She wasn't sure how he was going to take what she had to say next. "My heart, however, is here."

Jeff shook his head. "Come again?"

"Look, when I left you two years ago, I was not in my right mind. I was stressed and frustrated and I had this feeling that if I didn't take action, if I didn't follow my dream and become a hotshot lawyer, soon it would be too late." She winced. "I guess you could call it a midlife crisis."

"And Lynne's cancer had nothing to do with your sudden breakdown?"

"It probably had a lot to do with it, more than I'd like to admit. Seems awfully selfish to turn someone else's tragedy into your own, though."

"We're only human, Carol. Lynne was sick for eight years and there were plenty of times when it looked like she might not make it."

"But she always did."

They sat for a while, poking at the fire and thinking about Lynne.

Carol got up and hung the poker on its hook. "The thing was, I had it all backward. I took Lynne's terminal illness as a cue that I needed to go out and live my own life when it was the opposite. After this trip, it dawned on me that Lynne's death meant I had to value my life. *Our* life. Our children. Our home. Our family. And, yes, my career. Because you never know when it's going to end."

Jeff frowned and nodded. "That is the lesson, isn't it?"

"Love is all that matters. Lynne said it over and over, and she was right."

He studied the fire. "So where does that leave us?"

"That leaves *me* asking for a second chance."

Jeff opened his mouth to say something, but Carol jumped in before he could object. "I'm not talking about you changing your plans or welcoming me back with open arms. I know you have goals too, Jeff, and you should go for them. Geesh, I fled to a boutique Fifth Avenue firm. You're going to Haiti to save lives. There's no comparison."

He smiled.

"What I am asking is that you let me stay here while you're gone. Let me rebuild my home and my relationship with Amanda. And, if you're open to the possibility, my relationship with you. Because, that's the other thing I learned on this trip." She gripped the mantel. "I'm still in love with you."

Jeff didn't say anything for an excruciatingly long time. Carol stood by the fireplace, trying to gauge his thoughts. Had she gone too far? Insulted him? Put him in a tough spot?

At last, he downed the rest of his drink and held out his hand. "Come here." He sat next to her on the couch and tucked her hair behind her ears. "You know, I busted my butt painting those rooms this weekend."

"To get the house ready to show this week. I know. I'm sorry."

"No, you don't understand." He grinned. "I knew that if you saw the house stripped bare, you'd freak out—at least if you had any feelings left for our home. For me."

She was taken aback. "You mean, you knew all along?"

"Not exactly. But I had to find out, Carol, what you really wanted. You left so abruptly, in the middle of a conversation, as a matter of fact. One day you were here, my wife. The next day you were gone, my ex. My head was spinning."

"I would never do that now." She couldn't quite pinpoint what had changed exactly. All she knew was that she wasn't the same person. "You might say I've grown up."

"I'm glad." He kissed her lightly on the lips. "And for the record, I never stopped loving you, too."

She flung her arms around his neck and kissed his cheek several times over. "That's the best."

He hugged her gently and also with caution. "However, I think we need to take it slowly," he said, letting her go. "Step by step, day by day. We've got to get to the bottom of why we were fighting to begin with and work up from there. It won't be easy."

"Few meaningful adventures in life are."

"But it'll be worth it, and if we're honest with one another for a change, I'm pretty sure we'll get there. Agreed?"

"Agreed." And they shook hands.

It was the best possible deal she could hope for.

Drake's car was in the driveway when Mary Kay returned from the grocery store, her arms loaded down with brown shopping bags. Setting the bags on the counter, she removed the black velvet box and placed it on the kitchen table next to the sugar bowl and salt and pepper shakers, as if it were an ordinary, yet essential, spice of life.

She resisted the temptation to slip the ring on her finger and continue the merry charade. They could pop open a bottle of champagne and celebrate tonight, call their friends and spread the news. The nurses on her floor would ooh and ahh and declare themselves green with envy since Drake was the last of the stand-up guys.

There'd be a whirl of engagement parties and extravagant planning, a fabulous wedding filled with kisses and good cheers, followed by a romantic honeymoon, just Drake and her on a beach. It had taken years to accept that she would always be the bridesmaid, never the bride.

Yet, by some fluke of providence, she'd been handed all

that had been missing in her life and now, due to her own insecurities, she was throwing it away.

Drake strolled into the kitchen as she unpacked the groceries. He'd gone for a run in the dark and his blue T-shirt sported a V of sweat. She took a mental picture of him like this, to save for when she was old and alone.

"You're back!" He grabbed her and kissed her, not caring that he was sweaty and hot. "You are a sight for sore eyes, my MK." Then he reached down and took her left hand. "Where is it?"

She waved toward the table.

Drake glanced at the box, then at her, then at the box again, his eyes questioning, confused. "I thought we were OK?"

She couldn't stand to see him like this. Stepping away, she sat in the kitchen chair and said, "We have a problem."

"Whatever it is, MK, we can work it out." He took the seat opposite her, his fingers splayed on the table, ready for action.

"Maybe. Or maybe not." She focused on the sugar bowl, running her finger around the rim. "Drake, I can't get pregnant. I'm infertile."

There was a pause and then he let out a short bark of laughter. "Is that it? Is that all? Shit, Mary Kay. Like I told you yesterday, I'm not marrying your uterus. I'm marrying *you*."

She could stop right there and laugh, too. She'd let Drake call her silly and make hopeful promises about moving heaven and earth to have a baby someday. She could marry him knowing that she had performed due diligence, executed full disclosure, but she could not go to bed with him every night and look him in the eye every morning knowing that she had withheld the whole truth.

"There's more. I've known this for quite a while."

Drake quit grinning. "How long?"

"Remember when you found my birth-control pills?"

"A couple of days ago?"

She knew he'd say that. "Two years ago, when we first started sleeping together. You seemed so surprised that I needed to take them."

"You knew then?"

"Years before that. When Tiffany was nine or so, I came down with a pelvic infection, my second one. Lynne had to rush me to the ER and . . ."

"But Tiff's twenty-three now."

"I know." She twisted the sugar bowl lid. "Later that year, I had a laparoscopy and it was confirmed that both my fallopian tubes were scarred tight."

He sat back, running his hands through his hair, trying to absorb this. "You mean, for fourteen years you've known that . . . Then what were the birth-control pills for?"

"So I wouldn't get pregnant."

"But . . ."

"If you get pregnant when your fallopian tubes are scarred, the embryo won't make it to the uterus. It'll be an ectopic pregnancy and, if not caught soon enough, it'll end in bleeding, most likely surgery and, in extreme cases, death.

"That said, I quit taking the Pill when I turned forty for health reasons, figuring the odds of not getting pregnant were in my favor. And they were. We've been having unpro-tected sex for two years, so"—she rapped her knuckles on the table—"knock on wood."

"You haven't quit taking them, though. You take them every day." He said this with such sincerity, Mary Kay wanted to duck under the table.

"No." She lifted her gaze from the sugar bowl. "You thought I was taking them. I wanted you to think I was taking them. So you'd keep on believing I could get pregnant."

He rested his elbows on the table, squeezing his head like a vise. "This doesn't make any sense. I find the pills. You don't say a word. Then what did you do with them?"

"Washed them down the drain." She winced. "I'm sorry, Drake. It started on a whim. I just should have told you in the beginning."

"I agree." He was breathing deeply now. "Is there anything else you've been keeping from me? A past criminal conviction? An ex-husband?"

"Geesh, Drake. No. There's nothing else."

"How do I know?" He slapped the table. Never had she seen him so angry. "You go through all the trouble of buying birth-control pills and washing them down the drain for two years and I'm supposed to believe that you're an honest person, that you're not the slightest bit manipulative?"

She closed her eyes. "Please. It was wrong. I know it was wrong. I knew it was wrong from the get-go."

"Then why would you do it, MK? Why would you intentionally deceive me?"

"Because I loved you." She summoned the courage to face him straight-on. "And I was afraid you'd leave me."

"If I thought you couldn't get pregnant."

"Right." God. It sounded so ridiculous now. Something out of a bygone era.

"That's pathetic, Mary Kay. That makes you seem like a shrew and like I'm some sexist pig who views women as breeders."

"I know." She rested her head on the table. "You don't have to tell me. I know."

He pushed back his chair, the legs scraping the wooden floor. "You're right," he said, snatching the velvet box off the table. "We can't get married now." He headed to the door and stopped. "You know, I was already in love with you before I came across those damn pills. And by the way, I don't know what was going on in your head, but I didn't think twice about them."

Just as she'd feared.

"I thought we were building a foundation for the future. But whatever we built was on nothing, Mary Kay. Nothing but lies. And that's no way to start a life together."

Forcing herself not to cry, she listened to his footsteps march upstairs, then jog downstairs. He'd gotten a few things, she suspected, as he grabbed his keys with a jangle and closed the front door with a slam.

For a while, all she could do was rest her head against the cool wooden table and let the tears flow. She didn't bother turning on the lights aside from the ones in the kitchen. There was no point.

Finally, she went back to the groceries and dug her hand into the bottom of the bag until her fingers landed on the oblong box. She read the directions and carried it into the bathroom, ripping open the foil wrapper with her teeth.

The last time she'd taken a pregnancy test had been before she came down with the pelvic infection, in the 1980s when you had to wait until the morning (in addition to several weeks) after your last period.

Mary Kay couldn't remember when she last had her period. She'd stopped keeping track of that sort of thing long ago. Out of sight, out of mind was her philosophy—until this weekend when the typical symptoms of pregnancy began to haunt her and she couldn't put it out of mind anymore. What if her lackadaisical attitude toward birth control and her cavalier assumption that the chances of conceiving were nil had been a mistake?

What if the nausea and fatigue and cramping weren't simply stress, but signs that she might be suffering from an ectopic pregnancy?

Anxiously, she set the plastic dipstick on the sink as she washed her hands, her blood going cold as the pink line turned from a minus sign into a plus.

Chapter Eighteen

J eff and Carol were drinking their coffee in the sunroom, lingering until the absolute last minute when they had to take showers and get to work. Carol sat in her familiar rocking chair by the window overlooking the lake while Jeff, as usual, sat on the floor, various sections of the *New York Times* spread out in a fan.

Quiet moments like this used to bore her stiff. Jeff hardly spoke, except when he read an occasional snippet, and those were hardly breaking news. Did she know that squirrels could turn their ankles in a 180-degree angle? Or that, according to Paul Krugman, they actually were in a depression? She used to grit her teeth and count the minutes until she could hop the train.

This morning, however, each tidbit was a treasure to her ears. She sipped her coffee and rocked as Jeff moved from the front page to the financial section and finally op-ed. This was what Lynne meant when she spoke about finding the joy in little things, the hummingbird at the feeder, the yellowtail butterfly on the lilac. Krugman prophesying the economic doom of humanity.

With the sun rising over the lake, Carol couldn't remember when she'd last felt so at peace.

Jeff had just gotten up to take a shower when her cell rang. According to her last message, Amanda was supposed to call twenty minutes from the station to say if she was on her way. But it wasn't Amanda. It was Mary Kay.

"Beth's dad had a heart attack," she said breathlessly.

Carol put down her cup, alarmed in light of Chat's questionable test results. "Is he OK?"

"Apparently, he's fine. Marc came over to the house yesterday to drop off some movies and, smart guy that he is, noticed Chat's color was off. They called nine-one-one and, sure enough, he was in the beginning stages of a mild heart attack. I guess they did some emergency open-heart surgery at Grace and, for now, all systems go."

Carol clasped a hand to her chest, relieved. Beth had fretted all weekend about leaving her father. If something awful had happened in her absence, she'd probably never survive the guilt. "Thank God."

"I know. I'm headed to the hospital now. After I'm done, I'll check in at ICU and see how they're doing."

"I thought you didn't have to work today," Carol said, wondering if she should stop by too before taking the train to New York.

"I don't." Mary Kay sighed. "I took a test last night, Carol. Remember all those stomach issues I had on the trip? Turns out it wasn't car sickness. I'm pregnant."

Carol let out a squeal. "That's fantastic! After all that hand-wringing about not being able to . . ."

"It's not fantastic. It's bad," she said tightly. "It's why I should have stayed on the Pill. It's ectopic, and that's why I'm at Grace, for an ultrasound. I just hope it's not too late and they can treat it with drugs."

Ectopic pregnancy was dangerous, Carol knew. It was the leading cause of death among women in their first trimester. "Is Drake with you?"

"That's another thing. Drake and I broke up when I came clean last night, before I took the test." Mary Kay paused and Carol tried to figure out if she was crying.

"I left a couple of messages on his cell, but he's not answering," she said, sounding shaky.

Carol was already running upstairs to get dressed as fast as she could. "I'll be right there."

"You can't be right here. You're in New York."

"Not yet. Jeff will drive me over. Just hang on until I get to the hospital, OK?"

"Thanks," Mary Kay whispered. "Right now, I could use all the support I can find."

There were some advantages to being a doctor's wife, Carol thought as Jeff took her by the hand past security, through the ER to ultrasound without anyone insisting they sign in for a pass.

Carol finally found Mary Kay in a women's waiting room in the radiology unit, already in a white johnny. "I can't believe it's flurrying outside," she said brightly, unwrapping a scarf she'd found in a trunk of winter clothes. "How are you doing, kiddo?"

Aside from her red-rimmed eyes and her slight paleness, Mary Kay seemed reasonably collected. "Can't say it's the happiest day of my life."

Carol sat next to her and patted her thigh. "Don't you worry. Everything's going to work out just fine."

"Yeah, right. Lose the guy. Lose the baby. Maybe a hysterectomy along the way. Good times." Mary Kay glanced away. "But enough about me. How are *you* doing? How come you're not in New York?"

"How about I tell you later." This wasn't exactly the right time or the right place, in Carol's opinion.

"How about you give me a clue now?"

"OK. I'll tell you this much. We had a long talk last night and we're going to try to give it another go." Carol shot a glance at a nurse appearing in blue scrubs with a clipboard.

"Mary Kay?" the nurse said.

"Hey, Barbara." Mary Kay got up and Carol grabbed her purse, following behind.

"So, you think you might be preggers, huh?" Barbara asked.

"Not in a good way, unfortunately."

"Well, let's check it out and see." Barbara pushed open the door to a darkened room occupied by a table and stirrups. An ultrasound machine was on and beeping, ready to go.

"Is Simon here?" Mary Kay asked. Simon Friedman was her ob-gyn.

"He's upstairs, checking on a patient," she said as Mary Kay lay on the table and Barbara spread a sheet over her abdomen. "I'm your escort for the morning to make sure Dr. Friedman doesn't engage in any hanky-panky."

"Lawyers." Mary Kay winked at Carol.

Barbara went over to the machine, punching various buttons. "I know. He's delivered like a zillion babies, he's seen places in women's bodies most men don't know exist, but when it comes to ultrasounds with female patients, the hospital insists on a female nurse being in the room."

"I heard that." Dr. Friedman, a short man with a salt-and-pepper mustache, breezed in and gave Mary Kay a squeeze on the shoulder. "How're we doing this morning?"

"Not that great." Mary Kay described what had happened, Dr. Friedman nodding and taking notes on his laptop. Carol remained silent on a stool by the head of Mary Kay's bed, wishing for all the world that Drake could be there. He should be there. It was his baby.

Dr. Friedman was taking Mary Kay's temperature and blood pressure when Carol's phone buzzed. She stepped out of the room to take the call.

"Where are you?" It was Beth, sounding frantic. "Is Mary Kay all right? Jeff came by to see how I was doing and told me she was pregnant. I can't believe it. That's so great!"

Carol remembered, then, that Beth was unaware of Mary Kay's history. "We're in ultrasound checking . . . things. How's your dad?"

"Out of the woods. For now. I'm right down the hall in ICU, sitting around, waiting for a meeting with his cardiologist that's supposed to be any minute. I'm glad you're with her. Where's Drake?"

"I don't know," she said, which was true.

"He must be going bonkers." There was a commotion in the background and Beth's voice lowered. "The doctor's here. Gotta go. Tell Mary Kay I'm really happy for her, OK?"

"OK." Carol clicked off and went back into the room.

Almost all the lights were off and Dr. Friedman was sitting between Mary Kay's bent knees, his eyes on the screen as he moved the probe this way and that. Mary Kay grabbed Carol's hand and squashed her fingers. "Haven't found anything yet," she whispered.

Carol put her arm around Mary Kay and squinted at the screen. How anyone made heads or tails out of that mess of black-and-white images was beyond her.

"Here's the left ovary," Friedman said. "Normal." Then, shifting the probe, he said, "Here's the right, and we can tell from its condition that there's been an ovulation." He pressed the button for a picture as Barbara took notes.

Where's Drake? Carol thought, wondering if there was some way to reach him. *He should be here for this.*

"OK, so now we're going to wiggle this around and see if we can get a clear shot of the fallopian tubes."

Mary Kay grimaced. Carol hugged her close. "It's going to be OK, MK. I just know."

"Hmmm," Dr. Friedman said.

"Hmmm?" Mary Kay repeated. "I don't like hmmms."

"You might like this one. I'm not seeing anything." He twisted and turned. Mary Kay's fingers clenched.

"Now we hunt for the uterus. You do know, Mary Kay, that it's often impossible to see anything before five weeks," he said, adjusting a few dials. "Barbara, what do you think?"

Barbara peered at the screen and smiled at Mary Kay. "Congratulations, Mom."

Mary Kay struggled to look closer. "You mean . . . ?"

"There's a mass right there," Dr. Friedman said. "Not a very big one. In fact, I'd put it at five weeks on the dot."

"So, I'm . . ."

"Going to have a baby, yes." Dr. Friedman pushed a button to take another photo. "By my rough estimates, I'd say sometime in the middle of next June you'll be a mommy."

Mary Kay burst into tears. Carol, too. For a while, all they could do was cry and hug and blubber like idiots. Mary Kay mumbled something about martinis and Carol told her not to give it another thought, that it was so early in the game no damage had been done.

"How did this happen?" Mary Kay sat up, tears rolling down her cheeks. "I don't understand."

"And you're a nurse," Dr. Friedman chuckled. "Tsk, tsk, Mary Kay. I thought they taught you the birds and the bees in school."

She said, "You don't understand. I was told . . . There was the laparoscopy. . . . It proved . . ."

"It proved that we medical professionals don't always know everything." Dr. Friedman rolled away his stool and snapped off his gloves. "How about you stop by my office after you get dressed to do some blood work and pick up a prescription for prenatal vitamins. Then we'll get you on the schedule and you'll be on your way."

Barbara and Dr. Friedman left the room and Carol sat next to Mary Kay on the bed, bursting with happiness for her friend. Mary Kay, stunned, dangled her legs over the edge, blinking. "I'm going to be a mother." She rubbed her hand over her belly. "I'm going to have a baby. It's a miracle."

The door opened. Beth came in and rushed over to Mary Kay. "So, is it confirmed?"

"Five weeks. I was saying to Carol that it's a miracle."

Mary Kay wiped her eyes. "I never thought I could get pregnant. I'm forty-two and . . ."

There was the sound of the door opening, and the three of them looked up to find Drake standing there, jaw open. "I just got your message. Are you . . . OK?"

"More than OK." Mary Kay started crying again. "I'm pregnant, Drake. Due in June."

Drake swallowed. "*Really* pregnant."

"You either are or you aren't," Beth said. "That's usually the way it works."

"Come on, Beth." Carol nodded to the door. Beth slid off the bed as Drake took her place, enfolding Mary Kay in his arms and bending his head toward hers. They left them like that in their own little world. Drake. Mary Kay. And their baby-to-be.

"You know what this is?" Beth said as they headed down the hall. "This is Lynne working behind the scenes."

Carol smiled. "Mary Kay's five weeks pregnant, which means she was pregnant before Lynne died."

Beth shrugged and twirled her purse. "Details, Carol. You heard what Mary Kay said. This is a miracle. I knew Lynne would pull one sooner or later. I just never expected there'd be three."

"Three, huh?"

"She saved my father from dying, and from what Jeff tells me, she saved your marriage. And now Mary Kay's pregnant. All within a twenty-four-hour period. If you don't think that's heavenly intervention, then I don't know what is."

Epilogue

Mary Kay and Drake's baby girl was born on a beautiful June morning when the roses came into full bloom. They named her Audrey Lynne, Audrey being the name of Drake's mother. She came into the world with Mary Kay's black hair and Drake's brown eyes.

Mary Kay had never been so filled with joy as the moment when Drake laid that howling baby in her arms.

The week after the ultrasound, she and Drake made it official in a short and sweet City Hall ceremony. But they saved the real celebration for when Audrey was four months old and Mary Kay could fit into a reasonably flattering wedding dress.

That they were married in Mary Kay's backyard on the anniversary of Lynne's death was not by happenstance. Sean had suggested it, and they agreed. It was important to send the message that life goes on, and blessedly so.

Fortunately, it turned out to be another classic New

England autumn day with bright blue skies and geese flying overhead, a nip in the air to justify the long sleeves of Beth's dress. Tiffany wore a plum-colored gown and served as Mary Kay's maid of honor, with Beth and Carol serving as unofficial "matrons of dishonor."

Mary Kay was resplendent in a pale cream gown that just brushed the tops of her slippers and, in her hair, tea roses from Lynne's garden. Carol and Beth patted their eyes as Drake took Mary Kay's hand in hers and pledged his undying love. Holding baby Audrey, Mary Kay promised in return to love and trust him until death did they part, and just when the justice of the peace pronounced them husband and wife, Beth looked up and saw the last of the robins sitting on a branch overhead. It tweeted approval and flew off to join its flock headed south.

Bye-bye, Lynne, she thought to herself.

A bluegrass band struck up the Louis Armstrong classic "What a Wonderful World" as Mary Kay, beaming with abundant happiness, and Drake held up Audrey to thunderous applause.

Elsie kissed Chat, and Marc wrapped Beth in a hug. The next day they were leaving for a six-month world tour, from Scotland to the South of France, to Russia and India and, naturally, Amalfi. A wonderful world, indeed.

Carol hugged Amanda, who'd landed a job in New York, working a mere cab ride away from her mother's office. Occasionally, when Amanda needed to escape the city, together they'd ride the train back to Marshfield. Jeff, who'd thrown himself into setting up a new clinic in Haiti, would be home for Christmas if all went well. Carol planned to go all out. Best. Christmas. Ever.

Later, after a reception of champagne, foie gras, caviar, Alaskan salmon, roasted autumn vegetables, and a spice wedding cake, the original members of the Ladies Society for the Conservation of Martinis slipped off as the guests danced to "The Devil Went Down to Georgia" and the Stanley Brothers' classic "I Just Came from Your Wedding." They had the limo take them down to the Old Town Cemetery, martini shaker in tow.

Carol and Beth invented the Absolutely Fabulous Martini together: champagne, Cointreau, a touch of lime juice, and fresh raspberries. It was sufficiently festive to honor Mary Kay's wedding, though they'd been working with the ingredients since their road trip. Bubbly. Rich. Tart. Sweet. That essentially described each of the four friends, Lynne being the bubbly champagne.

They proceeded through the graveyard to Lynne's grave by one of the big firs. Grass had overgrown the summer before and now there were fallen leaves. Beth spread a blanket and they sat in a semicircle around Lynne's headstone, which was only fitting as she was the guest of honor.

Carol poured out three martinis, dropping two fresh raspberries in each.

"This will be the first martini I've had since the trip," said Mary Kay, still in her wedding dress, her bare shoulders protected by a faux mink stole. "I don't know if I should. I *am* nursing."

"My mother had a drink every night when she was nursing, and look how I turned out," Carol said, replacing the shaker in their basket.

"One or two sips," Beth said. "This better not be the end of Mary Kay's fun days."

"To the Society, then." Mary Kay held up her glass. "Who knew that a PTA meeting so long ago would end like this?" They each kissed her on the cheek.

"To Lynne," Beth said. "I don't know about you guys, but I feel like she's here, with us."

"Well, she is." Carol patted the grave. "At least in spirit."

They toasted Lynne in silence, their glasses frozen to their lips as a ghostly figure emerged from the woods, her hair cut short, a vibrant copper. She was hesitant, shy about coming closer, which was understandable, as they must have made quite a scene—the bride and her two matrons of dishonor.

"It's OK," Beth said, assuming the woman was lost. "You need help?"

She didn't say anything, just stood there expectantly.

Mary Kay gave Carol a look. "Can we help you?"

The woman pointed. "Is that Lynne Swann's grave?"

The name. Lynne Swann. No one in Marshfield knew Lynne's maiden name. Then there was the matter of her hair—red—though shorter than the photos in Don Miller's house.

Carol reached for Mary Kay's hand. "Alice," she whispered. "It's Alice."

Beth went white. "By any chance, are you . . . Alice Miller?"

Julia.

Mary Kay, completely forgetting that she was in her wedding dress, got up and tripped on her hem. "Oh, my God!" She slapped her cheeks. "It really is you."

It took some explaining about the wedding and their martinis, but eventually Alice caught on. "Do you like martinis?" Beth asked, stupidly, because at the moment it was the only question that came to mind.

Alice laughed, her eyes flashing like Lynne's used to. "Are you kidding?"

Of course she did. She was Lynne's daughter, after all.

Carol led Alice back to Lynne's grave, where they poured her a glass of her own. Then they sat her between Mary Kay and Beth, who couldn't stop staring, assessing the similarities and differences. She was Lynne, but she also wasn't. Alice was a graphic designer in Boston with two kids of her own (Lynne's grandchildren!), a daughter named Cynthia and a boy named Henry.

There was a picture on her phone. Two curly-headed five-year-olds climbing up a yellow slide, redheads like their mother, their freckled cheeks red from the cold. They were fraternal twins.

"Twins run in the family," Beth explained, telling her about Kevin and Kyle, Alice's half brothers.

"So why did you decide to finally come here?" Carol asked out of the blue. "Obviously, you got Lynne's letter."

"I did." Alice reached into her bag and pulled out the white sheet of paper that had been read and reread so often, one of the folds was ripped. "My father gave it to me last Thanksgiving. He was worried it would upset me, since my mother had just passed away, and it did, in a way. Losing Mom was very hard, and I didn't want to hear from a woman who gave me up for adoption and then didn't bother to write me until she was terminally ill. So I put it aside and didn't read it until spring."

"I'm so glad you did," Mary Kay said. "We went through a lot of effort to find you."

"That's what Dad told me, said you were downright pests." She smiled. "Anyway, I looked up her obituary online and, kind of on a whim, decided to drive down here and pay my respects since she died a year ago today."

What a dutiful daughter, Carol thought. "Do you mind if we read it?"

Alice handed it to her. "That's one of the reasons I came here, hoping I might bump into one of you. If there was any time you'd be here, I figured it would be today."

Carol read out loud:

Dear Julia . . .

That's how I will always think of you, as my Julia, though I'm sure your parents gave you a beautiful name and a beautiful life. I am eternally grateful to them for loving you so much that they welcomed you into their home and made you their daughter. Because, of course, you are their daughter.

Mine, too.

I never stopped loving you from the moment I found out I was pregnant until the night when they took you away. It's an unpleasant story, and not worth repeating. The important thing is that you're loved. And love, I've learned, is all that matters in this world.

Now, there's so much I have to say and so little time left for me to say it. I'm very tired and very ill. My heart is weak but my spirit is strong. Therefore, I will leave the duty of our story to the women who brought you this letter— Mary Kay, Carol, and my dear sweet friend, Beth.

If you have not met them in person, I hope you will

seek them out. They have been my closest friends and my confidantes. They are strong and wise women who will readily assume the mantle of motherhood, the flower of friendship to guide you down any path you seek. I hope you will turn to them as I have, in joy and sorrow. There are none better and they have quite a tale to tell.

So you see, Julia, you have not two mothers, but five.

Until we meet in a better place, all my love and blessings for your happiness . . .

Your mother,
Lynne

Beth blinked away tears while Carol refreshed their martinis. "Well, ladies," Mary Kay said. "Who wants to start?"

"I will," Beth said. "It began with a PTA meeting one fall evening years ago. Today, actually. Your mother and I were new to the PTA and there'd been this stressful discussion that had me totally flipped out, so we decided to make martinis."

"Don't forget the cookbook," Carol added. "We owe a lot to the Ladies Society for the Conservation of Marshfield."

"Martinis," Mary Kay said. "We changed it to the Ladies Society for the Conservation of Martinis."

"That was later," Carol said. "We should start with the original society, DeeDee Patterson's group."

"That's old news, darling." Mary Kay waved her away. "We're gonna bore this child to bits if we go back, what, forty years?"

Beth said, "Oh, for heaven's sake, you two, that's not important. Can we get off the title? It's the friendship that counts."

"Not the drinking?" Carol teased.

"Please. Knock it off!" Beth shouted. "What must Alice think?"

Alice sat back and let them hash it out. How in the world did three so very different women remain friends for so long?

While they argued about how to start the tale, Alice sipped her martini and let her gaze meander past her mother's grave to the woods beyond where she could have sworn she heard, in the waving pine boughs, a woman singing. Yes, dancing and singing a lilting, happy song.

Something about girls just wanting to have fun.

Acknowledgments

This book owes its appearance to three magical gifts: inspirational friends, a supportive family, and my fabulous editor at Dutton, Erika Imranyi, who expertly kept me on track and pushed me to produce my best possible work. Thank you, Erika, for your detailed critiques in an era when books are rushed to production. You are a rare gem.

Mostly, I am indebted to my neighbor and friend Trish McVeigh, who for years has not only valiantly battled cancer, but has done so with remarkable cheer and often sidesplitting humor—though that is where the similarities between her and Lynne Flannery end. I hope.

Trish is more than an inspiration for this story. She is also an inspiration for how to stare down fear with courage and a healthy shrug. I, like all who know her, am simply in awe.

Thanks, too, to Gail Sullivan, for her medical knowledge, Sara Travis, Caroline Scribner, Sarah Semler, Sarah Barrett, Amy Herrick, Kathy Sweeney, Nancy Martin, Harley Jane Kozak, Hank Ryan, Elaine Viets, Patty McCormick, and, of course, Lisa Sweterlitsch, for being my muses.

Heather Schroder at ICM, my agent for ten years, continues to be a wonder of strength and insight. I am forever grateful to Brian Tart at Dutton for his continued faith.

Finally, thank you to my husband, Charlie; son, Sam; and daughter, Anna, who tolerated my long days and nights behind closed doors rewriting again and again and again.

Sarah Strohmeyer is the bestselling author of ten previous novels, including *The Cinderella Pact* and the popular Bubbles series. She lives with her family outside Montpelier, Vermont.

CONNECT ONLINE

www.sarahstrohmeyer.com